Idiot!

Praise for Christopher Klim:

"Mr. Klim has, quite simply, done it again... He returns to his home turf of New Jersey to put together an oddly poignant tale of wealth and emptiness, an extended parable about the nature of money in the United States and how it shapes and reshapes our interpersonal connections more than we might wish to guess or acknowledge. This novel is a song sung to the accompaniment of the Invisible Hand playing upon the harp of the heart.... and due to Mr. Klim's eminent skills of depiction (I like to think of him as a Hogarth of the word kingdom for the twenty-first century), we get to look at it from all angles and hear it in high-impact surround sound. There's even a little O.Henry-style twist further along the storyline, but I will not for the life of me reveal it—it knocked me on my ass with laughter and dismay. Not too many books do that to me, these days. *The Winners Circle* is eminent social commentary by a man who sees what he looks at. Keep 'em coming, Mr. Klim, keep 'em coming!"
     –Jason Price Everett, *The Circle Magazine*

"Clearly establishes Klim as an author of considerable storytelling talent, *The Winners Circle* is perfect reading for those who enjoy the irony of satire."
     –The Midwest Book Review

"While *Jesus Lives in Trenton* and *Everything Burns* sparked the desire for more, *The Winners Circle* is sure to cinch Klim's place among the top humor novelists of the day. He skillfully cuts the difficult task of blending humor and pathos, while telling a lively tale peopled with a variety of enjoyable characters."
     –The Book Reporter

"Klim delivers clever and funny scenes, complemented by solid portraits of [the main characters] and an entertaining array of oddball secondary characters."
     –Publishers Weekly

"Is there no genre this man can't write in? The answer is no. ... Klim shines again in this funny, poignant tale... He has what it takes to make it onto *The New York Times* Bestseller List."
     –The Word Museum

More Praise for Christopher Klim:

"Christopher Klim is that rare talent who brings characters and stories that resonate with the working class and excite the sensibilities of literary connoisseurs. Maybe he's the New Jersey reincarnation of John Steinbeck. More likely he's destined to become someone quite unique in the pantheon of American novelists."
–Robert Gover, author of
One Hundred Dollar Misunderstanding

"Understated humor and lack of pretension lend this wry urban fable undeniable charm... Klim's lighthearted entertainment possesses genuine heart."
–Booklist

"Klim has a colorful past, and it comes to life in the pages of ***Jesus Lives in Trenton***, which has an ear for realistic dialogue and an eye for city grit that would make Dashiell Hammett proud."
–Philadelphia Weekly

"***Jesus Lives in Trenton*** is indeed riotously funny. However, it also works on a deeper level as an allegory about man's thirst for grace in a chaotic world."
–Time Off

"***Jesus Lives in Trenton*** is laden with laughs, insight and an overflowing abundance of literary skill. Amen."
–The Boox Review

"Anybody out there looking for a good read? Here's one for you: a down-to-earth What-if tale of a good marriage and what money—both the lack and surfeit of—can do to it. With credible, sympathetic characters and a well-wrought story well told, it starts like the shock of snakebite and reads on like a breeze. Like Christopher Klim's previous two novels, it's hard to put down till you're done. Christopher Klim's *The Winner's Circle* is a book that will offer good company for a long lonely journey or a lazy weekend on the beach, or anywhere!"
–Thomas E. Kennedy, International Editor, *StoryQuarterly;* author of *The Copenhagen Quartet*

Books by Christopher Klim

Novels
Idiot!
The Winners Circle
Everything Burns
Jesus Lives in Trenton

Nonfiction
Write to Publish:
Essentials for the Modern Fiction & Memoir Market

Juvenile
Firecracker Jones is on the Case

Discover the latest author information at
www.ChristopherKlim.com

Idiot!

Christopher Klim

Hopewell Publications

Published by Hopewell
Publications, LLC
PO Box 11, Titusville, NJ
08560-0011 (609) 818-1049

info@HopePubs.com
www.HopePubs.com

International Standard Book Number: 9781933435237

Library of Congress Control Number: 2007922134

First Edition

Printed in the United States of America

For Karin, always.

Special thanks to Robert Gover,
also Duff, Jeanette, Matt, & Tom.

*Our sense of power is more vivid when we
break a man's spirit than when we win his heart.*
– Eric Hoffer

Chapter One

A Pines Lynching

When they came for Thomas King, he was asleep, locked in a fantastic dream. He was scoring the winning touchdown at Cranfield Lakes High. He'd taken the handoff, tucked the pigskin tight to his ribs, and swept to the open field. Tom knew that his long arms and legs were better suited for wide receiver than running back, but Cranlakers rose in the bleachers and cheered his glorious progress along the gridiron. It was festival season, a time etched in most memories. Beyond the goalposts, bulging ripe cranberries floated atop the bogs awaiting harvest—before the virulent fungus arrived, before the state burned the cranberry vines on a blustery October day.

Tom awoke to fists pounding upon his cabin door. He sat up in the ink black darkness, suddenly aware that he'd never played football, hardly stuck in high school long enough to qualify. He was thirty-two years old and alone, a different sort of Pine Barrens legend. He was a magnet for pranks and nasty rumors. Dozens of "Tom Tales" circulated over beers in The Lazy Eye or coffee in Nat's Cafe. People claimed he was so dumb that he wrote his name on his sleeve to remember it. Others joked that he probably couldn't dig a ditch unless they showed him how. All of his life, he'd been the butt of their lowbrow humor and scape-goating. He'd retreated into the pines just to escape it.

The voices outside his cabin grew impatient. He slid from bed and crept across the plank floor in his bare feet. He considered his twelve-gauge shotgun beside the bookshelf, but the kerosene lamps were dry and he'd need to grope for the buckshot shells in the dark. Besides, the last spot you'd stir up trouble was deep in the New Jersey Pine Barrens. It was a world apart from the cliché Jersey images of filthy smokestacks and mobsters swindling cash. The Barrens was a million-acre wilderness that challenged both the body and the soul. Its dizzying array of evergreens and cedar swamps, even in daylight, made stalwart men doubt their abilities to proceed.

"Thomas King!"

Tom recognized Drew's voice. Drew Spatt was the Cranfield Lakes Chief of Police. He'd been glaring at Tom for weeks, although Tom didn't know why. Tom wasn't the type to encroach upon another man's privacy.

"Come out here," Drew said.

Tom waited, metering his breaths. Would Drew leave without a reply?

Other voices quickly gathered, as more than one set of shoes shifted in the sandy, root-twisted soil beyond Tom's front door. He thought of his shotgun again but decided against a confrontation. He threw the iron latch and faced the night.

Several men from Cranfield Lakes shouldered in the narrow clearing. Tom knew them by sight—Larry, Kevin, Nat, and the others. Drew propped a rifle on his hip. Deputy Rick blared a spotlight in Tom's face. Moths fluttered in the beam, little wings flapping silver and black like coins tumbling through water.

Tom shaded his eyes from the intense light and sniffed the air. Wildfire was a good reason to rouse a man from bed. Cranlakers would be clamoring to battle the flames.

"There's our boy," Drew said.

Tom listened for the firehouse siren—an ominous groan from miles away. He heard only the gentle rustle of the Pitch Pines in the breeze. The men weren't in a hurry. The fire that burned seemed closer to the core of where they stood.

"Drag him out." Larry Mullins spoke from the edge of the pack. He had been a mechanic at the bogs but now scratched out a living by repairing gardening equipment—the weekend toys of white-collar businessmen in neighboring counties. His pudgy-cheeked, playful appearance had transformed into a glower.

Tom spotted a rifle in Larry's hands as well. Most everyone carried a weapon. Nat tucked a pistol in his belt. Kevin Stower clutched a length of wood. No, it was a Louisville Slugger with a taped handle. Three more men fidgeted in the background, less anxious than the others, yet waiting for Tom's next move just the same.

"Come on." Drew was a big man with a head too small for his shoulders. He'd been the real football star in high school. He looked great in a helmet. "It's time to go."

Tom lingered in the doorway. Perhaps they wanted him to join some sort of posse, although he hadn't heard of one forming in these parts and never imagined the townsfolk including him. "What is this?"

Drew pumped a round into the chamber. He enjoyed the big moments, like when he placed a speed trap on highway 623 and lined up the cars for hours to hand out tickets. Harassing speeders and teenagers were among his favorite pastimes. Picking on Tom was another.

11

Tom stepped forward, braced by the chill. Dry pine needles stabbed at his bare feet. He didn't mind this as much as the cold. He hiked the trails more than any piney, from Batsto to Friendship in a single afternoon. He criss-crossed the local Wharton tract often without shoes. The soles of his feet were callused thick, yet read the attitude of the trail by instinct.

"Keep moving," Drew said.

"Filthy son-of-a-bitch," Larry added.

Tom walked past the rusting car frames and assorted refuse he collected outside. There were abandoned shopping carts full of machine parts and milk crates stuffed with what people commonly called trash. He stumbled into a stack of used car tires, almost tipping it over. He was a hard sleeper and just gaining his wits. Tree frogs were emerging from hibernation, singing their three-note tune. Early pine growth curled on the stem in dark fiddleheads, which shone olive green by daylight. The world was in order, except for Cranlakers marching through the woods at midnight, toting weapons and rotten attitudes, spitting and cussing his name. They had come for him.

"Let's take care of this once and for all." Kevin Stower ran the grocery store, including a backroom poker game each Saturday night.

Tom wondered why they weren't there now. He used to imagine himself seated at the table in the back of Kevin's store, just one of the guys, but the cards themselves created a problem. It was more than a matter of memorizing the pictures. Every deck looked different, like a new set of hieroglyphics to decode each time.

"I say we burn that shit shack where he lives," Kevin said.

Tom caught a whiff of Kevin's strong cologne. It was bay rum, like his father used to wear. Unnatural smells, especially when they crowded him, gave Tom a headache. He preferred long stretches of solitude and open space. Indian lore referred to it as a blessing, one that Tom wished he had right now. "If this is about the money?"

"Be quiet," Kevin muttered.

"You'll get the hundred I owe you. Just like every year."

"Shut up."

"You gave me until June."

"How stupid are you, King? Didn't you think we'd find out?"

Tom tried to grasp this strange question, but like words on paper, they didn't make much sense unless somebody drew him a picture—added color in a way that letters and numbers never could for him. "Why aren't you calling me Tom?"

Kevin's brow cut hard angles, the look of a man grappling with two conversations at once.

"Everyone here must owe you money from wintertime," Tom said. "Is that any reason to call the ledger in the middle..."

"This ain't about the money, and you know it."

"Then what's it about?"

"I told you he'd play dumb." Drew fisted his long gun like a billy club, slapping the barrel into his palm. "They all do. They're sneaky that way. A man who lives alone in the woods—that should've tipped us off."

"He thinks he's got us duped. Can you believe that?" Larry rattled down the slope behind the others. In deer season, Tom heard those jingling keys a mile away. With the racket he put up, it was a miracle if Larry cornered as much as a collection of worms.

"Keep moving." Drew cracked Tom in the ribs with the butt of his rifle.

To Tom, it felt like an old scar being tweaked. Drew acted out the stale roles from childhood—a sneaky elbow when passing in school, a quick smack in the back of the head. The whole town seemed caught in the past, but tonight was an uglier version to suit the image Cranfield Lakes had assumed since the economy drained like the stagnant bogs that had fed them for over one hundred years. There were moments when Tom believed he spotted evidence of a renewal, saw the future in the blooming wild crocuses or the nesting birds above, but these were only signs of the woods' natural cycle. The pines had thrived before the Indians and colonials trampled the peat forest. It would outlast the machinations of a generation going bankrupt.

They followed the trail down to the plains. Rick aimed the light at their feet, marking their steps. His name was Victor Richey, Rick for short. He was the only other member of the Cranfield Lakes police force still on the payroll.

Tom's toes grabbed the mossy stones along the slope. He might run and disappear into the swamps. He could lose these men inside thickets they'd never travel, hide among the dormant huckleberry until sunrise, but he thought of no reason to flee. He focused on the darkness ahead, comforted by its black shroud, waiting for one of the quieter men in the back to step forward and calm the others.

But serenity had grown scarce in these parts. Last week, Tom caught Sam DiMeggo boarding up his hardware store off the main drag. Sam swung his hammer like he was trying to bring down the turn-of-the-century bricks and mortar. If he hadn't already left town, he might have been here, too, leading the pack.

When they reached the lowlands, their heads rose above the dwarf cedars and scrub oaks. Brown bats darted across the face of the moon. Tom wondered how he'd brought the town's ire upon him. He had no stake in the dissolution of Cranfield Lakes, saw no real profit in it, unlike the banks that secured doomed loans and then seized the properties in a little over a year. Tom wasn't a man of dollars and cents. The banks likely didn't know his name. Only last year, he planked over the dirt floor in his cabin. Maybe he was caught up in a crazy dream, but he heard Drew lurking in the background and watched Rick's lamp zigzagging the trail. Kevin spit tobacco at the coarse base of a cedar, gripping the Louisville Slugger that he kept behind the store counter, waiting to knock a homerun across the bridge of someone's nose. Tom shuddered. The men's plodding pro-gress, their air of determination, was too visceral to be anything but real.

"What are we doing?" Kevin asked. "Should we toss 'em out with the rest of his junk?"

"My granddaddy would have tarred and feathered him," Larry said.

"That's not a half bad idea."

Tom glanced over his shoulder. No doubt, this was Drew's little get-together. It would have been okay if only Drew pitched mean-spirited remarks. Tom expected as much, but Drew's quiet unnerved him. And the others typi-cally paid him no mind. This was the reverse of the world he'd known before he'd gone to bed.

The gang stopped at a pair of sandy tire ruts that ran along an abandoned cranberry bog. Tom thought he smelled fuel from when the state agriculture agency torched the vines, although it was long gone with the killer fungus it had intended to destroy. After more than two years, blotches of scorched earth persisted—patches of creeping weeds and fruitless vines, as if anyone needed a reminder of the day when nature turned against the course of history.

The chill soaked into Tom's arms and legs. He wore only sweatpants and an open neck thermal. They'd walked the trail for almost ten minutes, and he searched their faces for a smirk or snicker, a hint that this was a country prank gone awry. The moonlight painted their expressions pale and dour.

"At some point," Tom said, "you must explain your intentions."

"Listen to the fancy talk, will you?" Larry said.

Tom believed the right words might break the ice and summon their laughter, but now he fought against his wobbly knees.

"You scared?" Kevin choked up on the bat.

"I'm not wearing shoes. It's cold."

"How 'bout them kids?"

"What kids?"

Larry pulled a yellow sheet of paper from his pocket and read the names. "Johnny Reed? Debbie Jones?"

"Never heard of them."

"Oh no?" Kevin's words were slow and wet. It wasn't bay rum that he wore, just rum. Larry looked tipsy too, rattling his keys more than usual. Whatever this was, it had started over late night drinks in the back of Kevin's store.

Drew reserved comment. The skin at the back of his head folded like a bulldog, a hairy pattern of ridges and dimples, a harsh landscape of its own.

Rick stood guard, never adding more than "yes sir" or "no sir." The others stared Tom down. He was used to being invisible in a crowd, but here, beside the decommissioned bogs, their eyes finally found him. They crafted images of him, filled with contempt and loathing. Even the men in the rear who didn't sound fully committed to their disdain seemed prepared to go along with whatever was about to unfold. This was the worst kind of joke, one without a punch line—a jokeless joke, the kind Drew might invent on his own.

"Take a gander at this." Larry stuffed the yellow paper in Tom's gut.

Tom scanned a document that bore the state law enforcement seal. The spotlight picked up the sheen of the page, making the letters look fuzzy. The smear of the photocopy machine didn't help either. He tended to glaze over simpler paperwork.

"Read it," Drew said.

Tom studied the first line. Despite the cold, his face flushed.

"Out loud," Drew ordered.

Tom stalled, dropping small words from the sentences, like *a*, *the*, and *and*. "Following notice from State N-New Jersey is hereby di-dispatched..." As far back as he could remember, he resisted reading aloud. He knew the words, but he needed to concentrate so hard on pronouncing each one that they became islands with no relationship to one another, magically shifting order on the page, sabotaging any hope of fluid speech. Reading was music and he didn't know the chords.

"The dummy can't even read," Drew said. "And you guys were afraid of him."

Tom fought to pull the sentences together, just to spite the men, but his acute vision flooded his brain with details. The dirty ink floated above the grain of the paper, like shadows on rippled sand. At this point, it'd be easier for him to draw the page, but if he were alone beneath his kerosene lamp, he'd nail every word. It wasn't fair. "G-General..."

"What's it mean?"

Tom fumbled through the legal jargon on convictions for child molestation, reciting case numbers that he'd never be able to repeat in the same sequence, and then he recalled his name on top of the sheet. "M-M-Moderate level of r-risk."

"You've heard of Megan's Law," Drew said.

"I know about it."

"Now we know about you."

Tom stood taller than the others, but his shoulders hunched until he felt lesser in stature. He hardly spoke to children, much less laid a hand on them. "This isn't funny."

"Who said it was?"

"This r-really isn't." Tom hated his stutter. He listened to it as if observing another person. He owned as much control over it.

"F-F-Freak!" someone mocked.

"Get out of town," said another.

The men huddled by an oak stump, conferring like hunters awaiting the release of the dogs. The spotlight caught them from below, and dark rings limned their eyes. Tom felt an overwhelming detachment from Cranlakers, from humanity in general. It was not a revelation. Events only brought it to bear.

"We can go back and burn the cabin." Larry glanced at the others for approval.

"I've got a spare gas can in my car," Kevin said.

"We don't have to get all fire and brimstone." Nat cast his strange eye in Tom's direction. He owned the Lazy Eye bar and the café that bore his name. He was used to effusive men gathering over drinks and heaps of country cooking. He knew how to distill their emotions into a workable plan. "Just have him fill his bags, and we'll drop him at the county line."

Drew rubbed his chin, savoring the gems that precipitated from the discussion.

Tom listened to the short form of his future. They couldn't be serious. He'd spent his whole life in the Wharton Forest. There was no other place for him. He stared at the moon, fighting to reorient his position on the planet. It was like that sometimes, ever since he was a kid. He'd concentrate too hard and become scattered, grasping for his bearings. That didn't happen to other people, not that he saw.

A heavy hand fell on his shoulder. Drew faced him up close. The big fingers squeezed, until the tension shot across Tom's collarbone, cramping the muscles in his neck. Drew was baiting him into a physical confrontation. Tom recognized Drew's lust for violence and a need to control the tangents of the situation by grabbing hold and wrestling it down. Was Tom supposed to wriggle free or take a cheap shot? That might be all the excuse Drew needed to lay into Tom and settle things the way he knew best.

"Do you understand us?" Drew finally asked.

Understand? Tom couldn't form the words to shield himself against Drew's patronizing. Even worse, the situation appeared as if Drew aimed to destroy him in one night. It wasn't the truth of the charge, only the severity of the accusation that mattered. The damage was done. Rumors of child molestation would spread through the barrens like grease on water—difficult to gather, impossible to soak up entirely. He'd be blackballed. Crime was infrequent among pineys, because everyone knew everyone else, down to their shoe size almost. They'd know if he bought a roll of toilet paper south of Trenton. They'd be waiting to run him out of every acre of the woods.

"You can leave quietly on your own," Drew said. "I wouldn't mind that."

Tom tried not to flinch, like when the kids used to jump him in the schoolyard. "Let's get King," they'd shout, and he'd lie on his face and play dead until they gave up the attack. They needed to force him through the wringer first, satisfy their urges.

A pair of headlights appeared on the bog road, bobbing and weaving in the potholes. The men turned toward the sight of it.

"Who the hell is... ?" Drew released Tom.

A white Chevy Impala raced along the southern edge, a dangerous prospect if the bogs were flooded. Even dry, you could roll your car into a ditch and snap your neck. The Impala locked its brakes, kicking sand at their feet. The men had taken a few steps backward, and if Rick hadn't kept the spotlight burning, the car might have mowed them down.

Claire Whethers leapt from behind the wheel. The hem of her white work dress flapped above the knees. The dismount looked reminiscent of her cheerleading days, the surefooted approach of the former Cranberry Festival Queen. But that was more than a decade ago, and by the way she clenched her jaw to the side, she seemed all business as she bore down on the police chief.

Tom studied her, as no doubt the others did. She was as beautiful as ever. Her long black hair sculpted the shape of her head, and her large spread back, ready to unleash the rich sound of her voice. She was a blend of her mother and father but unusual and alluring so that you couldn't help but gaze, try to figure her out, and then look away still uncertain. Every man in town harbored a crush on her at one time or another.

She ripped her motel cleaning apron from her hips, as if she'd just noticed the straps pulling at her waist. Her ponytail was fastened with a cheap hair tie. She preferred not to dress up or wear makeup, which added to her raw appeal. "What are you doing?"

The men aimed their rifles at the ground. Those with split barrels, creased them and draped them over their arms. Rick cut the spot beam. The blazing car headlights illuminated the late night lynch mob.

"Drew, say something." Claire was borderline accusative.

He waited for her to come near. He looked unsure, his plans being reshaped by a woman on the warpath. "What brings you here?"

"I'd ask you that, but I already know."

"How did you find us?

"You didn't keep your escapade much of a secret. I heard others talking in town. I saw the notice."

"What notice?" Drew often embodied ignorance, and it was a surprise to see that he couldn't fake it, not even gather a convincing tone.

She fished inside her apron pocket and produced a crumpled ball of yellow paper as if it had been stuffed inside with anger and haste. She held it up. "This one."

"Excuse me, lady." Larry nodded toward Tom. "He's a child molester, plain and simple. This is men's business."

"Men's business?" Claire tugged the paper in both hands, stretching the wrinkles flat. "Perhaps one of the *men* noticed the dates on this piece of fiction."

"I'm sorry. What's that, Claire?"

"Was Tom in jail three years ago? Perhaps you recall seeing him around?"

"Oh."

"Have you once seen Tom in jail? Or even heard of it?"

"That was awhile back." Larry nervously rubbed his pants leg, rattling his keys like a sack of metal washers. "I don't keep track of him every minute. He roams the woods, you know."

"That's his job! He watches the forest."

"Okay, but the fool could've been in jail too."

"Listen to yourself. You don't make sense. He repaired your fence three years ago. Was he doing it in a striped suit?"

"I don't think prisoners wear striped suits anymore."

"You're a real genius, Larry." She leveled equal measures of scorn and sarcasm on anyone who challenged her. Surrounded by weapons, she needed no more than her tongue.

Her turned her sights on Kevin Stower. "He fixed your roof before that."

"Has it been that long?"

"He's never been in jail, knucklehead!" She balled up the notice again and tossed it at Kevin's feet.

"Are you certain? It says..."

Claire released an exasperated sigh, echoing the breeze that presently whipped over the bogs and turned aside the dry overgrowth.

The men stopped speaking. They suspected she could rebut them all night, and no one wanted an earful of that. Their mission had unraveled. Claire found the first loose thread and yanked it until the entire ill-conceived junket was exposed. They knew how she was lately, how she latched onto an issue pit bull style. No one blamed her either. She was missing something dear, like an animal that keeps searching for her babies and never finds them. Claire thrashed the earth, stamping the dirt, kicking a few rocks. Tom noticed the men shuffling in the back. They prepared to disappear before she turned on them too.

"Can we break up this charade and go back to minding the shops?" she asked without really asking.

Kevin spat on the sandy ground, just missing the discarded notice. "Slow down, Claire."

Claire faced Drew again. Her cheeks flushed the color of bleeding cranberries. "This was your idea. Wasn't it?"

"Don't rush to conclusions, honey."

"A notice like this has to come from the authorities."

Drew's expression went blank. A response tumbled through his frontal lobe that no one was ever going to hear.

"How dare you put Tommy though this," she said.

"Hey, I didn't post it, honey."

"I'm not sure anyone's allowed to post it."

"Rick found it."

Drew's attempt to blame his subordinate hung in the night air, limp and impotent. A Great Horned Owl called in the distance.

"I guess," Drew said. "I should run this thing through again. I still don't trust the bastard."

"Stop it," she said. "Don't prolong this."

The men began taking to the trail, clutching their pride and their weapons. In the grand reasoning of the pines, no one questioned a minor assault on the loner Thomas King. He wasn't hurt; no loss of property. This was local law—simpler than and immune from the complicated state codes. This was a town where folklore was history. The edicts of Trenton's political witch doctors meant little when problems were easily solved with shovels and shotguns. On this night, the people of the dead bogs headed into the pines, tired yet satisfied they'd made their best effort to defend the homefront.

Kevin passed Tom. "We've got an eye on you."

Tom kept several yards behind the retreating party, leaving Drew and Claire at the bog's edge. As he folded into the woods, Tom felt Drew's hot glare on his back. Drew had never gone this far before. Tom hoped this was the end of it, but people seemed to feel better for the night's venture, as if they had the right to kick him harder, owned the paperwork for it, phony or otherwise.

Within Claire's earshot, the Cranlakers were temporarily mindful of their behavior. The men leading the trail were principals from town—the druggist, Nat from the cafe, Kevin Stower. These were sturdy people with a long bloodline, trying to protect their families—those who hadn't fled the state in search of jobs. Now that Claire had defused the situation, Tom didn't blame them for overreacting, although he'd have this nonsense hanging over him for months, years perhaps. It was another Tom Tale, the meanest yet.

Tom heard Drew arguing with Claire back at the bogs. Drew was an ex-jock with a police badge. Life for him was a contact sport, a play in motion, but Tom knew this much about sports: He must rise from the playing field and keep moving as if not the least bit injured. The radio announcers called these undaunted men "gamers." Tom decided a long time ago that he was a gamer in life. He would've never gotten this far without gaming it on occasion.

"Are you all right?" Claire called up the path. "Tom?"

Tom paused among the dwarf pines at the edge of the plains. He no longer saw her face, which was fine for the occasion. He didn't much like taking the brunt of humiliation in front of her. "I'm good."

"Are you sure?"

"Yeah."

Her voice rose in the opposite direction, impugning Drew with renewed acidity. It seemed to scorch Drew's ego even at a distance.

Tom felt his fear and shame melt away. These weren't emotions that he held onto or put to good use. If he forgave the flaws of the others, it was a whole lot easier to forgive his own, and there were plenty he could name for you, just like any man if he was honest. Instead, he put his mind to the wreckage all around him. He was a salvager of other people's trash. He made use of the things they left behind.

The Chevy door slammed shut, and the car sped off in the fashion in which it had arrived. Sand and gravel churned toward the highway. Claire was a nasty cat when she got going. Maybe it didn't happen that often, but it was a sight for sure.

Tom treaded barefoot toward his cabin. His bones ached, yet above him, the stars shone like crystal specks in the icy sky, mapping out the ancient constellations. This clear view, like nowhere else in Jersey, restored his hope for the future, made him realize that time passes and nothing outlasts the heavens. It was good to see Claire again, witness the vigor in her words and the urgency in her steps. Everyone was waiting for the town to bottom out, and maybe tonight was it—the breach from the past, the liberating disconnect that propelled them into a rebirth. It was long overdue.

Chapter Two

Sour Mix

The Impala cooled beside the house. Claire Wethers smelled the transmission burning all the way to the front door. She'd been thinking about what a tyrant Drew was and how she cursed him out because the men were standing around like a private army. But as she reached the craggy bricks on her front stoop, she felt safely away from that nonsense, the madness that occasionally boiled inside men's hearts.

She slipped inside the foyer and out of her cleaning uniform, leaving the dingy motel dress in the hallway. Sweat percolated down her neck. She needed a tonic and went for the bottle beneath the kitchen sink.

Claire preferred whiskey. Her ex-husband liked to uncork a bottle of wine after a bad day. Elliot was big on red wine and the English language. He used to peruse the dictionary, posting exotic words on the refrigerator door for them to discuss and apply to made-up sentences over a bottle of cabernet or zinfandel. The more complex the wine, the denser the language, but alone and left to her own terms, Claire's vocabulary gathered phrases like Rob Roy and Whiskey Sour. She forgot when she made the jump from varietal wines to hard booze, from the poets' vernacular to the bartenders' lingo.

Ice cracked and popped in a glass tumbler on the kitchen counter. She poured in the golden brown liquid and cut it with water. She squeezed lemon over the top and scooped in sugar. It couldn't get easier than that, except for straight whiskey, but she swore she'd never go that far.

Claire stood in the dark, gulping her first mouthful. She hardly tasted it, waiting for the numbness to overtake her.

The mail fanned out on the table. It reflected the moonlight, which draped the table like a sheer silver cloth. She spotted letters addressed to both Claire Wethers and Claire Bogdon. Her married name seemed like a transplant that never took, and after ten years of better intentions, Bogdon acquiesced, mopping up time in its wake. She took another sip from her glass, trying to apply the brakes.

Among the scattered mail, she saw a letter for her nine-year-old daughter, Faye. Claire tore into the colorful envelope. It was crazy to expect a clue. How would the sender know Faye's location? It was absurd, but Claire did it anyway. She sifted through the glossy advertisements for unneeded books and videos, invitations for magazines and clubs for kids. They had no answers. They only hoped, like Claire did each passing hour, that her children still lived at home. That Elliot hadn't carted them off to God only knows where.

Claire's glass was dry. The rattle of the cubes summoned a refill. *Bad girl, the ice not even melted yet.* She mixed her second Whiskey Sour and wandered into the living room in her underwear. She pressed the cool glass to her temple, appeasing the ramble of thoughts and prayers that filled her head.

The house overlooked Main Street, and the gate in the white picket fence swung loosely in the breeze. Claire hadn't wanted to paint the fence white, but Elliot had insisted. He had insisted on many things that summer after high school. He decided to skip college and stay at the bogs and learn the old trade. He was determined to override his mother's wishes for a life in academics. He convinced Claire to keep the baby and marry him.

Claire insisted on keeping the gate open. When Elliot disappeared with Faye and little Ronald, they'd left the gate ajar as if they'd only gone for a short walk. Kevin Stower, who noticed everything from his grocery on the corner, said Elliot took the kids early for the weekend. It was a warm Thursday afternoon, a day ahead of Elliot's schedule, just hours before she arrived home from work. "No matter," Kevin told the police. "Claire must have arranged it," and they'd lost the critical first twenty-four hours, as Elliot slipped into the unknown with the kids.

In the small hours of the morning, Claire tried to clear her head of these piercing memories. She curled up in the bay window, but the front gate glowed in the moonlight, conjuring its magic. She imagined her sweet children—the kids that she smelled in every corner of the house—rushing up the flagstone path and into her arms. She heard the gate creak, bracing for the first steps inside the foyer. She waited for Ronald's uproarious laughter and the unmanageable curl of hair beside his ear. She pictured Faye's bitten down lip, a private token of the troubles that her daughter refused to share. Had Faye somehow colluded in her departure? Had she known and kept the secret for days? Had Elliot prepped them, hinted at their escape, depicted it like an exotic adventure?

These questions stretched the limits of Claire's patience for sanity, although patience wasn't her first inclination. For months, she'd questioned cranberry farmers from Wisconsin to Massachusetts by phone. She called the State Police and the FBI. She dropped her last dime on a private investigator in Philadelphia. She stood guard at the front bay window, and the gate remained ajar. A whole year turned like the watering wheel at the bogs—no beginning or end, no progress, no use for it either.

Claire saw car headlights rounding the corner. They hit the living room with a white flash, like an x-ray passing through her skin and bones. She looked up the street and noticed the trestle silhouette above the squad car roof. Drew was coming.

Drew Spatt parked the squad car in the driveway behind her Impala. She hated that, and her temper discovered another piece of fuel.

She saw him marching up the flagstones. His big feet trampled the hyacinths that lined the path. In high school, she'd turned him away on a half dozen occasions. People wanted to see the football star with the Cranbury Queen, but she resisted. How had he imposed himself so confidently? He even blocked her driveway at will.

As Drew pushed through the unlocked door, she retreated to the kitchen and topped off her drink. She rushed to throw her garden smock over her bra and panties. She wasn't in the mood for a midnight rendezvous and loathed the suggestion of tempting him.

She fastened all but the top button. The cotton smock was old, and the cup of her bra poked through a ragged tear. She yanked the material away from her chest. "Drew?"

The sound of his clunky boots ceased on the steps leading upstairs. "Yup."

Her instinct was to lower her voice and keep the house quiet, but there was no purpose to that. "You don't knock anymore?"

"I didn't want to wake you." He came back downstairs.

"I'm wide awake."

They met in the narrow hallway that joined the dining room with the kitchen. Pictures of Faye and Ronald lined the walls. She was vaguely aware of the protruding nails that once held her husband's photos. For a while, she'd kept his pictures hanging for the sake of the kids. Erasing their father from their minds was never her intention. Apparently Elliot—and certainly his mother—harbored other ideas.

Drew propped his hands on his waist. His index finger played with the handle of his revolver. "You did a bad thing tonight."

"I hear that's been going around lately."

He flashed the boyish grin that some women loved, although it made Claire feel like he held something over her.

Drew somehow sensed this and grinned even more. "I didn't appreciate your intrusion at the bogs. Don't ever do that to me again."

She hoped he might read her mind and leave. How had their clumsy tango begun? The start seemed foggy. One night, she looked up from her drink in the Lazy Eye, and he was seated across the bar. Or was she trying to fist her keys into the Impala's ignition, and he was leaning inside the car window, offering to make things less complicated? She recalled when she dropped a sack of potatoes and it split open on Main Street. Drew appeared out of nowhere, that big guy with large hands and shoulders, an ever-present shadow. He snatched three potatoes with one swipe. He might lift her up with a single index finger. She'd never stumble again.

"What do you want?" she asked, wishing she'd phrased it differently.

"That's getting to the point."

"I'm tired, just ignore me." Claire checked her patience, what was left of it. Drew was the antithesis of Elliot, neither facile nor bookish. He was a great immovable object blocking her path to bed.

"I want to sleep," she offered.

"You can sleep, afterward."

Afterward? After nothing. She tried to push past.

He clutched her arm. "Can't we kiss and make up?"

"Let go." She sprinkled honey on her reply, but it didn't sound sincere even to her ears. She wondered if he got the point.

"Don't you love me anymore?"

She was grateful for the dark, for not having to face him cleanly. She was half naked and alone with the Chief of Police, her sometimes lover. That was enough trouble, without his tiresome cute expressions and decidedly sexy manhandling. "Not tonight, Drew."

"Why not?"

"I have work in the morning."

"Get off it. Nobody stays in that motel."

"I still get paid for cleaning up." She took a long swig of Whiskey Sour. This was Drew's method of foreplay, belittling her job. *A real charmer.* She was never big on the propaganda of her fame, but she'd rather scrub the toilets in the Lakeside Motel than spend another night with him.

He shook her once. "Is that how you want to spend your days?"

"I can get real work."

"Real work?"

"The work I'm qualified for." She hated when he pretended to forget. Cleaning the Lakeside was not a coveted career move. She used to run the accounting office at the cranberry cooperative. Three people called her boss. "There's plenty of work in Philly."

"Yeah, right."

"What are you saying?"

"You're not going anywhere."

She saw the front gate shift in the corner of her eye, and then she ripped her arm free. "Did you check with the missing persons unit? I mean, the state can do more..."

"How many times do you want me to call them?"

"Did you check?"

"I wish I had better news."

"Nothing?"

Drew didn't reply.

Her face felt warm. The booze was kicking in, thank God. "Elliot didn't work for the CIA. He can't disappear with two kids."

"That's what he's probably done."

She despised his half answers. With Drew, she saw infinity extending toward nowhere, and nowhere was a place that she could no longer find. "Isn't there anything we can do?"

"We're doing it."

"Can't we do more?"

"If a lead pops up, I'll follow it. You never know when leads develop."

She looked at Drew, the self-imposed cornerstone of her life. Like the effort to locate her kids, she failed to puzzle out a solution. Every attempt, every path she selected, Drew crossed her, changed her direction, stopped her cold. Was she too loud? Did she give off a scent? In the mornings, she scrubbed her skin raw, scouring his smell from her body, her own smell even, yet he found her. He sniffed her out in the grocery and at the Lakeside Motel. Sometimes as she hiked through the woods, he tracked her down. That was how the trouble with Thomas King started. They'd only been talking. Tom was harmless.

She drained her glass, dribbling a small amount on her cheek and then wiping it with the back of her hand.

"Don't you think you've had enough?" Drew said.

That was an interesting question. All she imagined was refilling her glass, just a little whiskey cut with water this time. She tried to pass him again, but he held her to the spot like an unruly child.

"Lose the drink and come to bed," he ordered.

"I'm going to bed, just not with you."

"Be nice."

"Aren't you tired after tonight's escapade?" She didn't care if she bruised his ego. It felt good. Her venom might be the antidote to his bravado.

"You want to discuss that again?"

"What were you thinking?"

"I'll tell you what I'm real tired of—your questions."

"You should be ashamed."

"I asked you to be nice." His grin was a menacing thing, bridging humor and spite. It was that easy for him to make the switch. "It's my job to watch over this town."

"Get real. I read the notice."

"I didn't..."

"Please, I know it was you. Johnny Reed? Debbie Jones? Pretty original names. I'm surprised you didn't use Jane and John Doe."

"That's enough, Claire."

She got in his face, close enough to smell the tobacco on his breath. She was on a roll, and the insults flowed from that dark and nasty well that she tried to keep capped but never seemed fully sealed, never revealed a bottom either.

"All you care about is being Mr. Big Shot. That's what this was about. A feel-good-Drew moment."

"I'm…"

"Mr. Big Shot, with your uniform and your precious police force of one and a half men."

"I'm warning you."

"Warning me?" She laughed so hard that snot sprayed the edges of her nostrils. Her vision was blurry, and Drew looked like a big punching blob.

"You go too far." He gripped her harder.

"Dragging Tom from his house in the middle of the night, I guess that's not going too far."

"Claire."

"You're the stupidest person I've ever met." She searched for the words that would gall him the most. "You're as dumb as Tom."

The back of his hand slashed across her jaw so hard and quick that she never saw it coming, and she'd been a girl who was good on her feet. She slammed against the wall and dropped, as the wind shot from her lungs. The tumbler shattered on the hardwood floor beside her knees. Curves of jagged glass rocked on the oak planks, between small puddles of booze. More puzzle pieces for her to face.

She hunched over, drawing up her limbs, unable to get small enough.

In the predawn silence, she gasped for air, until the worst shock subsided and the white spots disappeared from her vision. She stared at the scuffed tips of Drew's big boots, still speckled with moss from the forest.

Claire cradled her jaw, slowly opening and closing it to see if it worked. She'd bitten her tongue or the inside of her mouth, and the alcohol stung the wound. She refused to look up and let him see the pain welling in her eyes.

"I'm sorry I had to do that," he said.

His words wrought enough irony to form a joke, but she felt too scared to react in any way. She stayed down. Her stomach was queasy. In her time with Elliot, even when he lost his job and the marriage stretched like a rubber band and snapped, she never felt afraid. Why did Drew force these moments? It wasn't even fun for him.

"Get out of my house," she murmured.

"What's that?"

She cleared her throat. "Please leave."

"You can be a real bitch, Claire."

She remained on her knees, listening to those boots march out the door. She shortened her list of safe places. No Lazy Eye. No grocery. Just the motel and home, but Drew was showing up at her house uninvited, letting himself inside. She started to cry, at first fighting off the worst of it, but her tears were so loaded, a cacophony of emotions, that she bled out the misery as comfort. *The only place left is the bottom of the lake.* She'd thought of it before.

As the squad car receded down Main Street, Claire got to her feet and swallowed the blood in her mouth. She wiped away the wetness from her eyes. "No." Faye and Ronald will be back soon. She didn't know how, but she just knew it. Their mother needed to be at home.

Strains of orange light seeped through the bay window. The sun rose over the long eastern horizon, ignorant of the night's craft. It overtook the tops of the pines, turning the slate roofs of Cranfield Lakes metallic silver and blue. It looked pristine and beautiful, a complete fantasy.

Claire poured another whiskey and headed upstairs to check the kids' bedrooms—her ritual to leave their bedroom lights burning all day and all night.

There was still time before work, and as she slugged down the drink, it pooled in her throat. She couldn't swallow fast enough, unable to stand another minute replaying his big paw crashing across her face, wanting to wind back the tape only to erase it, tear it from the wheels and start over. She didn't have to remember. She could skip it. She didn't have to feel anything if she chose not to. She didn't need to think much either. She might not even have to breathe if she shortened her breaths to a whisper. She only needed to be here when her time came back around.

Chapter Three

Old Forge

T om dressed in his park service shirt and a green woolen vest and hiked the Old Forge Trail at dawn. He was a part-time ranger, looking after a diverse stretch of the vast Wharton tract. Mist rose off the big lake, as Mourning Cloak butterflies clung to the damp pine trunks. Tom felt the dew between his toes. His bootlaces were tied together and draped over his shoulder. He relished the tactile experience of walking barefoot in the forest. He'd earned the right. The park service had tried to replace him because he'd twice failed the civil service exam, couldn't negotiate the columns of dots and letters on the standardized test, but the pay for the position was scant and the health insurance was nonexistent. Not even the unemployed bog workers wanted the job. Like many of Tom's endeavors, he succeeded by patience and attrition—the last man standing theory.

The trail swung toward the ridge, crossing Holub Road near the intersection with highway 623. The Mourning Cloaks tailed him, fluttering about his ears. He watched one descend upon a discarded box of Newports. The spots along its wings caught the sunlight, and when it flapped, a line of indigo eyes winked back.

Tom nudged the butterfly free and whisked the spent carton into his satchel. He'd been finding these cigarette boxes for months. He wondered who smoked Newports. Kevin chewed tobacco. Deputy Rick puffed Camels. Tom patted his satchel. *Case #477, the smoker.*

Crossing the road, he rejoined the trail to Old Forge. The image of Claire Wethers came to mind. She was strolling beside him, in brown leather sandals, bluejeans, and a cutoff Philadelphia Flyers T-shirt. He remembered seeing her like that last fall: her belly exposed, the soft almost invisible hair at her navel. She looked underweight but irresistible none-theless. She rambled on about Ronald and Faye and bitched about her motel job and the "sleazebags" who ducked in and out during the afternoon like "criminals." Tom pictured her stories in motion, running circles around him. She was a gypsy dancer of conversation, a gorgeous bundle of nerves, unraveling before his eyes. When she gathered a head of steam, he wondered if she noticed how closely he watched her. It wasn't that she was beautiful, he decided. Maybe people had the wrong impression about her. Maybe it was her energy, like an untapped resource, that summoned him and others to be near her.

As Tom climbed the stony path to the next wooded plain, he thought of Claire again. He envisioned a different meet-ing, where he assumed the lead and spoke without a stutter—that insuppressible pausing and retooling of words. Around Claire, he felt as if he operated a clutch and incessantly ground the gears, but unlike the dreadful me-chanics of speech, his fluid stream of thoughts fastened Claire's attention to his own.

Claire looked rested. Her violet eyes captured the sun, like one of the Mourning Cloak butterflies. He imagined her stopping to cut a wild orchid to press for her dried flower collection.

"That's Arethusa." Tom kept to the facts. For years, he'd amassed enough trivia about the Wharton Forest to write a book. He considered his process of mangling the English language into prose. He could envision a book. He might even dictate a book onto tape if he were sitting alone and had time to revise his sentences, but actually penning one on paper would be akin to painting a masterpiece with your eyes closed.

"I thought it was called dragon's mouth?" Claire asked.

"Arethusa Bulbosa is the official name."

He saw the surprised look on her face. *Yes, I know all the names of the flowers.* He'd tried to create this impression for years—that he wasn't the mindless ranger depicted by others—and now the silly botanical name of a flower had convinced her.

This thought dispersed with the shade, as sunlight overtook the thin tree cover. Tom often fantasized about the world he knew, struggling to balance a realistic image without slipping into a mere reflection of his dreams. But that was the whole point of dreaming, to bridge the gap between reality and desire. While the world within his grasp often baffled him, the world in his mind was organized and tangible, creating sense of the external disorder.

Tom passed through a corridor of low growth. Pockets of crowberry bloom were well underway. The twiggy, anemic-looking shrubs bordered the trail, before the trees resumed and the chatter of nesting birds filled the air.

The path led to the place Cranlakers called Old Forge. It wasn't a destination found on the map. It wasn't even a ghost town, more of a ghost site. The property held a dilapidated colonial house and a weathered iron forge.

Like most Cranlakers, Tom knew the legends that centered on this deceivingly humble spot. The Holubs once distilled grain alcohol here, until they were gunned-down by state police during Prohibition. Before that, a runaway slave practiced voodoo, casting spells on his former master. A libertarian couple from the Midwest performed abortions for a fee. There were a dozen more stories ranging from the mystical to the fantastic, each one harboring a fair amount of tragedy. Tom wondered if any of the accounts were true, if the myth of the place gathered stories like a folksinger gathers elaborate tales about simple country people.

Tom oversaw the property on his regular hikes. In the last half of the decade, the house remained empty, although teenagers visited on weekends to drink, carouse, and neck by campfire. He spotted empty Miller bottles and crumbled Peanut M&M wrappers near an ashen pit in the soil. He guessed it was the mayor's daughter and her friends. He'd learned some of their habits. People discarded trash like carelessly placed notes, and he knew how to read them. Your choice of refuse gave you away. This was why the question of the Newport cartons confounded him. They appeared too often to be from a mere passerby. And another thing: The lids were crushed on the top—a signature action—as if the smoker drove his thumb down inside the cartons before tossing them aside.

Tom gathered the garbage into his satchel. The bottles clinked on the bottom. Once, a man from New York City had tossed a plastic trash bag with a credit card receipt out his car window, and Tom tracked him to an apartment on York Street just to issue a fifty-dollar littering fine. The stunned expression on the man's face was worth the trip. On the other hand, Tom would never think of ticketing the mayor's daughter and her friends. They were Cranlakers, and unless they seriously damaged the woods, he left them to their business.

An adult bald eagle glided overhead. Tom felt graced by the sight of it. He walked to the house and ran his fingers over the bullet-scarred doorframe for good luck. It was his ritual when visiting Old Forge.

The house appeared in more distress with each visit. The roof of the colonial-era structure buckled and swayed where it hadn't fallen through. Only the canopy of pines showed it mercy from the weather. Still, no windows remained. Tom had rounded up the remnants of thick colonial glass and stored them in a plastic pickle barrel at his cabin. He'd rescued the fallen cedar shakes from the ground and stowed these away too, but kids tore others free and tossed them like frisbees. They'd ripped off the outhouse door and burned it in a campfire. Pitted sprays of buckshot decorated the walls, along with occasional graffiti art and teenage love note wrought with a penknife. At a glance, the place verged on collapse, yet it exuded a deep impression from a catalog of unsung American history. The grounds reeked of conflict and illicit activities: ash, old wood, and stale beer. That was why teenagers kept coming, year after year, to leave a mark of their own. Tom valued this place more than any downtown landmark, but he also understood that he'd likely witness the last wall crumbling during his lifetime. Old Forge seemed destined to sink into the sphagnum soil that had consumed the remains of the living ever since the great oceans receded and created the Pine Barrens.

Tom retrieved his notebook from his backpack in order to document the site. He already owned many photographs. Some he took himself, and others he clipped from the news. Most pictures were before the graffiti got crazy. He recorded the orientation of the structures in his near illegible script. He sketched pictures, preserving the pitch of the roof and the soffit details. He surmised how the forge shelter looked, before the Holubs dismantled the roof for their grain still and their wicked batch of hooch that had driven god-fearing men from New Brunswick to Philadelphia near madness.

The forge masonry caught Tom's attention. His favorite legend involved its original builder—a Revolutionary War era blacksmith, known as the Bachelor of the Barrens. Some called him the Wharton Wanderer. The story was that he'd fallen in love with a married woman and, after a difficult romance, retreated into the woods forever.

Since Tom's last visit, a stone had fallen from the base of the forge. He knelt down to return the bachelor's stone to its original position, but the colonial mortar was exhausted, and the hole seemed hardly capable of holding the stone any longer.

Tom began packing mud in the joint as a temporary fix, until he noticed an iron plate imbedded in the masonry. It rode above the hole that Tom intended to seal, but now the hole didn't seem right. He felt for the telltale grit, a hint of the old cement. It was as smooth as the rocks in the creek. The fallen stone, as well as three others that remained in place, were meant to slide free.

By rocking it back and forth, he worked a second stone loose. It was oblong and heavy, but once Tom got both palms around it, the stone fell. He bent to the ground. He needed a flashlight to peer inside the dark cleft. He reached inside, up to his elbow, and touched the rough wood grain and then something else. It was stiff cloth, an odd material for the inside of a blacksmith's forge. He reached again and the object shifted freely.

Tom removed the third and fourth stone and dragged an old wooden box into the sunlight. It was wrapped mostly in sackcloth, which quickly tore away as it slid into daylight. He set the box softly to the ground, trying to preserve the covering, but the withered material disintegrated, and the scent of ancient rag made him sneeze.

The box appeared to be in decent shape. The base was dry rotted, yet spared water damage by the elevation and expert construction of the forge. Insects and vermin hadn't found it either, which was amazing by any measure.

Tom washed his hands from a canteen in his backpack and pried off the box lid with his pocketknife. He saw a book wrapped in yellowed linen.

The legends of Old Forge piqued his thoughts. Was it a ledger for the Holub still or maybe a journal from the abortionists? The box seemed fragile and musty, clearly older than those tales. He thought of a century-old manual of voodoo rights. That would be a showpiece for the museum curators in Trenton.

The linen was almost unwrapped from the book, when Tom heard men approaching. He peered around the forge, listening to twigs break and dry leaves rustle underfoot. The urge to view the book was strong, but the voices grew louder. He thought better and shoved the assembly back inside the hole with as much fast care as he could manage.

It was Drew Spatt and JJ on the trail. Tom gathered their words from the trees. Men spoke differently in the forest. A conversation that might normally be whispered gained expression within nature's deaf ear, but Tom was a listener if he was anything. Women appreciated this skill, even unfamiliar women: lost hikers, mothers in the Medford Acme, the auto parts dealer in Pleasant Mills. They sensed he wouldn't judge their trivial confessions. They often grabbed his sleeve and held him to one spot. Most didn't even know his name.

The men became louder, although JJ was hard to ignore at any distance. His high-pitched voice registered just below the quavering whistle of a screech owl. One might easily assume JJ suffered from a throat condition, but JJ's voice was just another disappointing hand-me-down from his father, like the mayor's job in an insolvent town.

"We need to clear most of this to get access from the road," JJ said. "It'll be a real project."

"We can sell the lumber." Drew operated in his comfort zone—short unchallenging sentences. "Make a good buck of it."

"Selling the trees is one issue. Cutting them down is another."

"Not if the town approves."

"That's another thing. This isn't exactly approved land use. You need state variances before you start chopping in the Wharton Forest."

"That's your job, but if the trees are the only problem…"

"What do you mean?"

"There are ways around everything."

"I don't want to know about it."

"Leave it to me."

"Don't get yourself embroiled in something." JJ appeared on the trail ahead of Drew. The mayor brushed the seed burrs from his pants leg. He strived for a crisp Reagan look: dark suits, darker hair, but his squirrel-caught-in-a-rattrap voice killed the illusion.

"These buildings have to go," Drew said.

"That's unavoidable, I guess. What a pity."

"They've been nothing but a hassle."

Crouched behind the forge, Tom saw JJ's face beyond Drew's wide back. The two men were at the eastern corner of the house, where Tom stacked cedar shakes to put in the recovery bin. The people Tom encountered at the forge typically roamed the abandoned structures, hoping to glean a bit of history by breaking off a piece as a keepsake, but

Drew and JJ impressed Tom like a couple of real estate brokers. They started pacing the area and turning their view. Their words and expressions were connected to a vision apart from the history of Old Forge.

"It's a pity about this place," JJ said.

"Not every old house has history." Drew sounded as if he'd memorized a line from a fortune cookie.

"I don't know. A lot of people need to be persuaded."

"The land is perfect. Look how level it is, and no more than a thousand yards from the highway."

"It's always been a prime spot."

"We can start out small, build a few amusements and a miniature golf course. Refreshments. Souvenirs. There's nothing between here and Medford."

"I see what you're saying."

"Hundreds, no, thousands of people drive through on the weekends for the shore. We can make them stop. Put in outlets for all the big chains."

JJ turned away. "If my father could hear us talking."

"That would be a miracle."

"You know what I mean. We're going to wreck this corner of the woods and then some."

"There's a million, no, billion pines. Who needs this collection of overgrown Christmas trees?" Drew stopped. "Hey, that's an excellent idea. Christmas trees."

"Alright, don't get too far ahead of yourself."

"No, I'm serious. It'll give us working cash."

JJ spoke above a whisper. "If my father heard us talking about mowing down Old Forge, he'd claw out of his grave and kick our asses."

"Your father didn't have a town in hock."

"Don't exaggerate."

"Whatever you say."

"I've got a line on someone for the bank building. Maybe if..."

"No disrespect, but I've heard that for a while." Drew dropped his hands on his gun belt. He reviewed the obvious facts as if preparing to issue a speeding summons. "The bank's empty, right? The gas station's gone, the hardware store now, and so are a dozen other places. This is something we can do."

"Well..."

"Well, what?"

"Well... you know."

"Look, we can leave the house standing if that makes you happy. Paint the house red and call it the Jersey Devil's Den."

Tom cringed at Drew's suggestion. He stood up and stomped from behind the forge, if only to derail the conversation. He pretended to be coming from a routine hike in the woods, but his backpack and boots sat beside the ring of campfire stones across the property. He regretted heading in that direction, because they saw his gear waiting.

Drew glanced at Tom's bare feet. "Forget how to tie your shoes?"

Tom ignored the comment. He picked up his boots and slung them over his shoulder. The trouble from a few nights earlier was fresh in his mind. He wondered which side JJ took. Did the entire town have it out for him?

"What do you want?" Drew asked.

Tom thought of the park service emblem on his shirt pocket. "I was wondering the same about you."

"It's none of your business."

"Good morning, Tom." JJ stepped forward, extending his hand. Everyone received JJ's rigid handshake, regardless of the occasion. "We're just looking around."

"Looking around?"

"For possibilities."

"We need to take care of this place, don't you think?"

"Yes, of course."

Tom plucked another M&M wrapper from the ground. He thought of JJ's daughter hanging out with frisky boys by the campfire. He wasn't going to tell JJ, not yet anyway.

Drew circled the forge. He raised his boot to the foundation and kicked a few stones loose. "In another year, this place will be a pile of rubble, all by itself."

"This is sacred land to Cranlakers." Tom hoped Drew didn't spot the hole with the box inside. He pulled his eyes away from it just in case. "Even that forge has history."

"I know." JJ seemed annoyed by Drew but not enough to stop him.

"Alicia Hardaway told me that the blacksmith made musket balls for The Revolution."

"My grandmother used to say that."

"Give it up." Drew knocked down another stone. It rolled from the forge like a dead soldier. "This place is history."

Tom stared at the onetime pro football wannabe. *That is why you want me out of town.* It had nothing to do with child molestation. Old Forge was the real target. Tom's presence as a part-time ranger meant that the state kept watch over the property. With him gone, Drew and JJ would have free reign. Tom envisioned the ugly chain of events as if they had already occurred: whining kids putting golf balls through plastic replicas of the White House and the Eiffel Tower, souvenir shops peddling statutes and trinkets destined for landfills, and no trees standing from here to the road, just pavement, parked cars, and the smell of exhaust and rancid garbage baking in the sun.

Sunlight hit Cranfield Lake below. Tom saw a sliver of it through the pines. The surface sparkled like crumpled aluminum on fire. This section of the Wharton tract, like thousands of Barrens acreage, formed a chain of debates and legal battles that predated the forge. Sometimes just one man stood between preservation and destruction.

"You know the trees are why this area thrives," Tom said.

"There he goes again about the trees." Drew planted his foot on the fallen stone. "If I want advice, I'll read a book from an expert. Ever do that? Ever read?"

Tom was thinking the same about Drew. At least Tom listened to books on tape. He wondered if Drew understood literature only from prime time television and Walt Disney.

"That's enough," JJ said. "There's no need to get personal."

Tom heard resignation in JJ's voice. How could anyone get away with wrecking the site, tearing down the woods? He stared upward. The tree branches spread out like busted veins. "As long as there are trees, this place will remain."

"We understand," JJ said.

Drew kicked the stone like a soccer ball.

The men were closed in their thoughts, each set against the other, although Tom felt further from the center of consensus. He waited for them to leave.

As Drew and JJ disappeared down the trail, Tom gathered the rest of the trash. Soon, the only sound he heard was the lonely sway of the pine branches and his heart drumming in his chest. The solitude calmed him.

The bald eagle swept overhead, skimming the base of the sun. Tom studied its flight anew. An eagle was supposed to be good luck, but for whom? Eagles needed the trees to survive. Tom placed his trust there.

He shouldered his things and continued on the trail. His encounter with JJ and Drew had rattled him so much that he almost forgot the box in the forge. He padded back to retrieve the mysterious case.

Chapter Four

The Turnley Diary

A t the cabin, Tom spotted several yellow jackets con-
structing a nest above the door. He ignored them,
tossing the trash satchel against the split log siding.
He headed indoors to investigate the booty from Old Forge.

He placed the old box upon the kitchen table and
removed the lid. Stars were etched in the wood, but he
passed them over and eased the linen wrap from the book.
The cover was deep green, with a recessed black border. A
slit ran the length of the spine, and silky threads dangled
from the corners. He hesitated to take the slim volume into
his bare hands.

His first aid kit contained a pair of latex gloves. He ripped
open the package and stretched them over his fingers. He
turned back the cover of the strange book. The spine
cracked like the brittle skin of a mature shagbark hickory
tree.

In the center of the first page, someone had drawn a star
inside a circle. Two blank pages followed. They were yellowed and wavy, smelling like musty burlap. Through the tips
of his latex gloves, they felt dry and fragile. He held his
breath, expecting the pages to disintegrate with each turn.

He came to the first block of writing. It was a stretch of
tight and curvy script. The ink faded in spots, before the

writer refreshed his quill, sometimes blotching the page where the new letters formed. Still, the scribe managed neat paragraphs without benefit of margins or lines.

I am nothing that I seem.
I am a figment of my hopes.
I cannot be trusted.
I avoid suspicion
like the moon hides in day.
People view a solitary man
who earns his wage in the south woods.
I wear this disguise.

Tom understood that he viewed a colonial relic. The passages were written sometime before the 1790s, when the town assumed the official name of South Woods. In 1831, it had been changed to Cranfield Lakes, after the late Colonel Cranfield of the 1812 War.

That first day keeps with me.
You pretended not to know me.
I shoed your mare.
The animal was small for you.

*You said my hands
were not those of a tradesmen.
You were wonderful in the beginning.
I do not resent your choice,
but I cannot bear your departure.
Is it cruel for you?*

Tom rubbed his eyes. His keen vision channeled him into the details, the very fiber of the paper, rather than the whole composition. The ink script blurred his concentration, curling and weaving like French lace. Over the years, he'd learned to focus better on words and sentences, but as a kid, he struggled with everything from schoolbooks to hand-written notes. The mere texture of the page or the colorful borders often distracted him. Money confounded him, too. A fresh dollar bill, with its rough rag paper weave, looked like a printed swatch of corduroy. His prolonged inspections often shortened the patience of people in lines at banks and city offices, and in his darkest moments, he thought that if he were blind all would be forgiven.

In the box, Tom discovered a red velvet pouch. The material appeared as exhausted as the linen wrap, permanently creased into the position it'd held for centuries. He spilled the contents on a paper towel, and five silver buttons tumbled free. Each had a raised and burnished star, now dulled by time. He gathered one into his gloved palm. The area surrounding the star was blackened, as if coated with pitch tar and burned to a finish.

He flipped to the front of the journal. The lead sketch matched the button design. Tom copied the image into his own notes.

I am blamed.
And you are guilty
for knowing me.
Parker brought a lock
from his smokehouse.
There is no other forge for miles.
We barely spoke.
I am blamed.
I do not visit town.
I am blamed.
You are gone.

The legendary Bachelor of the Barrens came alive before Tom's eyes. Tom glanced up at the wooden slats of his cabin roof, considering his next move. Who should know about the journal? JJ was the right man, but he feared the mayor's close association with Drew and their god-awful plans for Old Forge. What did it mean? And what did everyone think of him after Drew's most recent antics? How far had the rumors spread? And what if Drew got his hands on the journal? The brilliant police chief might throw it out because it was old-looking.

You spoke as if
you never knew my first name.
'Good day, Turnley' you said
and broke from me.
This is what remains.
Your teapot sits on my mantel.
I fancy your hands upon its belly,
in your parlor overlooking the river leeway.
I see your finger
with the pearl ring tapping the cup.
We sit by the fire,
sharing tea.
Neither of us appreciate coffee.
I will never drink coffee
and in these times.
Alone we share tea,
and no one knows.

Tom paused to record the name. An hour passed, and his eyes began to tire. The letters looked more like the spiraling scribble of a five-year-old, and when he glanced at the page, the words jumped positions. He strained a last look to record the name, and then copied "Nutley" into his notes.

Tom drove along Main Street to the outer clearing, which was no longer a clearing but a huge library and parking lot. The eight-year-old building stood three stories high. It was the tallest structure in town, eighteen inches above the water tower. Its redbrick veneer and smoked glass windows never sat well with Cranlakers and their quiet lakeshore manner, but the county freeholders wanted a modern center for the entire district. Cranlakers called it "the factory" or "Christie's" after the governor who had insisted on the project.

With the lights on after dark, Tom saw straight through the library annex above the public theatre—the big empty meeting hall for the emptying out town. Alicia Hardaway sat at her desk. He didn't expect to find the reference librarian anywhere else but flanked by her coveted tomes.

He carried his notebook past the checkout desk and the shaded columns of nonfiction books. He saw Alicia turning the pages of the latest *Booklist* magazine. She wore a tartan vest over a white open-neck shirt. At her back was the alcove of reference indexes and the doorway to the medical reference and picture archive.

She tracked his approach. Her eyes rode above her glasses, with a librarian's expectation of a question. The fan beside her desk tousled her sandy brown hair. She had an evolving hairstyle, something between a standard bob and a bridal shag. Tom suspected that she cut it by herself in front of the mirror. At times, he sized up people by their hair. Claire's flowing mane asserted her endurance and a tendency for nature. Drew's short crop mimicked an action figure. Alicia's hedge trimmer job said that she wasn't finished yet.

Tom stopped in front of her. He wondered if Drew's nasty rumors had reached her desk. The checkout clerk had given him a double take when he marched through the front doors. It'd take a long time to squelch the accusation of child molestation, or maybe it'd never pass. He hated just thinking about it.

"I have a question," Tom said.

"I'm sure." Alicia folded her hands over the magazine.

"Who's Nutley?"

"You mean where is Nutley, as in Nutley, New Jersey?"

"I hadn't thought about that, but who is Nutley?"

"It's the man they named Nutley after. Would you like the volume on that?" Her response smacked of a call for research. Even if she knew the answer, he wasn't going to get it without first performing the research. This was why teenagers rarely stood at her desk, unless defeated by slacker alternatives on the Internet. Adolescent Cranlakers sat as far away from Alicia as possible, fearing she'd dispatch some sort of homework assignment or book report.

Tom wasn't afraid of hard work. He feared the Dewey decimal system—that insidious combination of letters and numbers. "Was there ever a famous Nutley in the area?"

"Now or prior?"

"Prior."

"How prior?"

"Colonial, pre-South Lake period."

"Now that's an interesting question." She wrinkled her nose. It was the Hardaway gesture of approval. Step one was to know your question. This was another reason why teenagers loathed Alicia. The malaise of puberty made it impossible to endure a dialogue with the meticulous fact-finder. "May I ask why?"

Tom hadn't fully mapped out his reasons. He only knew he didn't want anyone to know yet about the forge diary. He decided to go with the flow of the conversation and work it out. "I found something in the woods."

"Animal, vegetable, or mineral?"

"It's not a secret. It's a—a horseshoe."

"Congratulations. You're a lucky guy."

"It says Nutley on it."

"And what makes you think it's pre-Revolutionary?"

"It says, 'forged at the south lake' as well."

"The south lake?"

"Yes."

"It says all that on a horseshoe?"

Tom visualized that phrase running the curve of a thin piece of iron. He might as well have said it had the Declaration of Independence stamped on it. Perhaps going with the flow wasn't his best plan. "Amazing, isn't it?"

"It must be a big horseshoe to say all that."

"It's very big. I'm not sure it's for a horse."

"Interesting. I don't think they put shoes on elephants."

"It might be a decorative piece."

"May I view it?"

Tom feigned a search for the imaginary item, before realizing that a big horseshoe couldn't possibly fit in his pants pocket, even baggy pants, even those silly oversized pants that kids wore. "Oh no."

"What's the matter?"

"I left it at the cabin."

Alicia's seal of approval seemed to dissipate into the bookshelves, but she wasn't about to chase Tom away. She'd known Tom since childhood, being a few years ahead of him in school. She'd tried to teach him long division. It was a massive headache for both parties. As far as Tom was concerned, the advent of inexpensive calculators was an act of God.

From beneath her desk, Alicia slid out an artificial leg. She'd lost her right leg below the knee in a car collision with a slow-moving harvester. She needed only one prosthesis, but she kept her best walker for getting around and an easy-on suction cup model for short distances in the library. She called the latter her "slipper leg."

When he saw her reaching for the slipper leg, he knew they weren't going far. He watched her stand. Her skirt dropped below her knees, covering her link to the suction cup device.

She walked to a row of blue and gold binders. Her red sock inched down her lifelike leg. "Here's the historical record of New Jersey. Rachelette put it together in 1973."

"Where do I start?"

"Try the index."

He accepted the volume and went to work. The bold print helped, but he quickly learned that Nutley, New Jersey or any other Nutley drew no resemblance with anything in the county, not to mention the Nutley in his journal. His Nutley remained a virtual unknown.

When he turned, he saw Alicia watching him from her desk. "Nothing in here."

"I didn't think so."

"Is there any other place I can look?"

"Lots, but if it's not at least mentioned in Rachelette, it isn't promising. Where did you find your *ceremonial* horse-shoe?"

Tom wondered what to say. He decided to release his next clue. "It was buried at Old Forge."

"That place?"

"I thought the horseshoe might be connected to one of the legends."

She closed the magazine on her lap and dropped it on her desk. Legends had no place in the reference alcove. "I've never heard a Nutley story."

"Me neither."

"If there is one, I'm sure it's covered in gore."

At first he thought she was referring to one of Gore Vidal's historical novels—he'd listened to *Lincoln* three times on tape—but then realized she meant plain old gore of the blood and guts variety.

"It seems like every bad rumor about the pines comes out of that place," she said. "I'm surprised the Jersey Devil wasn't born there as well."

"Me too."

"Why don't you nail your monster horseshoe above your door and see what walks out of the woods looking for it?"

"Good idea."

Alicia raised an eyebrow. She twisted a finger through her butchered, sandy blonde locks. Her voice changed from hard-lining librarian to interested single woman. "I have a batch of new medical photos, if you care to look."

Tom hadn't expected this turn in the conversation, but he rarely did. When he visited the library to check out an audiotape, she sometimes propositioned him. He'd tried over the last three years to anticipate this by her tone of voice or choice of leg, but Alicia held her feelings close to the vest, unless she was ready to play, then even her vest was coming off.

With the Rachelette volume still in hand, he considered her offer, but not too long. Alicia hid a pretty tight body beneath those loose-fitting clothes, and he wasn't getting it anywhere else. Like every other time, he thought, what the hell, why not.

She returned the reference volume to its slot and led him into the medical reference and picture archive. She wore the key on a chain around her neck, which she used to lock the door behind them. She always seduced Tom in the library and always in the medical archive. This guaranteed a measure of privacy, while obscuring their relationship from the public.

It had been four months since she last pulled this move. He'd been checking out the audio version of *The Iliad*, when she caught his eye near the New Fiction rack. The very first time, Tom was skimming through the drive shaft diagram for his pickup truck, when she discreetly grabbed his ass beside the shelf of *Chilton's* manuals. The reference section had become the kind of deep research that he'd never imagined.

"I'm ovulating." Alicia said this often, but as far as Tom knew, she never got pregnant.

She pressed her mouth to his, probing his tongue with hers. She tugged at his shirttails. He followed her cues. It was time for a different set of instructions.

"Take off your pants," she said.

Tom's mind harkened back to his times with her in the sixth grade. This sure beat trying to divide 438 into 105,637. Just thinking about it made him dizzy.

He undid his belt and stuffed his pants onto one of the shelves. Her skirt was coming down. Her slipper leg already stood next to the center table. He glanced at the dimpled stump where her right calf was supposed to begin. He was careful not to stare.

The bell rang at the reference desk.

"Ignore it." Alicia backed up to the table, donning a wicked smile.

This had happened an earlier time in the archive. Before that, Tom never thought much about an unanswered bell in a shop or post office. Lately, he was aroused by the short crisp tone—a private call to sustenance that beat anything Pavlov had in mind.

He helped her onto the table. Her breasts looked a tad larger. She'd added a couple of pounds. Her flat belly had developed a subtle curve, nothing to complain about. She'd look great in a bikini, but he knew that her leg caused a great deal of embarrassment for her.

She scooped her hands beneath his shirt and buried her nose in his collar. "You're in good shape, Tommy. Why aren't you seeing anyone?"

"I'm just not." *You don't even want to be seen with me.*

"You're not unattractive. You're spending too much time in the woods."

He realized how alike they were. He stuck to his cabin and his trash collection. She hid in the reference alcove with her books. They created their own isolation. It was easier than dealing with the stares and comments. They each heard the noise of disapproval when walking through a crowd. It never entirely filtered out of their ears.

His fingers fell between her legs, making her moist. Everything he knew about sex, he'd learned from Alicia. Long division too, although sex was a whole lot easier to figure. He put himself inside her, as she leaned back on the table. He was bigger than average, longer mostly, but he never worried about Alicia. She was always ready.

He cupped her knee in one hand and the stump in the other. It was the only time that she invited him to touch her stump. The harder he gripped it, the more turned on she became. He imaged the disconnection of veins and nerve

61

endings, phantom sensations perhaps. She pushed so hard that he felt the severed bone in his palm.

Leaning over the table, watching her unfinished hairstyle splay over the dark wood grain, he worked her into a frenzy. The keychain traveled over her shoulder, with short jerking hops.

She moaned as the bell rang again. The blood rushed to his center, taking him to a new level of hardness.

Ding.

Alicia's breathing grew rapid. She mumbled phrases that Tom barely understood. It sounded like Fagle's translation of *The Odyssey*. He loved the Greek classics.

Tom left Alicia's legs and leaned forward. He smelled her now and not the volumes of old books surrounding him. He rose to the balls of his feet, his elbows sliding forward on the table.

Ding. Ding.

The person outside grew impatient.

Tom noticed Alicia reaching her peak. She moaned louder, unable to form complete sentences, a thesaurus of Greek mythology.

Her tongue groped the corner of her mouth. He offered his finger for her to quietly suck.

Ding. Ding. Ding. Ding. Ding.

The steady ringing of the bell was more than Tom could handle. He released just seconds after Alicia, offering the strength he built behind her passion. She reciprocated by squeezing her hips. She vacuumed his index finger in a way that he believed he'd never get it free.

She sucked his finger clean with her lips, then licked it wet just to be cute. "I'm thinking about your horseshoe."

Tom was catching his breath, still smarting from where the table edge bit into his thighs and caused a horizontal dent. One day, they were getting a room at the Lakeside like every one else. No, that wouldn't work. They needed the volumes of ancient lore to protect them.

"What's that?" he said.

"That humongous horseshoe ornament of yours?"

"What about it?"

She hiked up her skirt and dropped her still buttoned shirt over her head. The tartan vest came with it. "Why don't you run it by Stan Zytko?"

"The historian?"

"He lives outside Atlantic City."

"Do you know him?"

"He calls for research now and then. He knows I'll do it right."

Tom didn't argue with that. He couldn't argue with much. He scanned the floor for his underwear. It dangled from the suction cup of her artificial limb. "I have his field manual on the pines, but I never thought…"

"Zytko's the authority, Tommy. I'll give you his number." She eased away from the table and into her slipper leg in one fluid motion, utterly deft at the maneuver.

Tom wondered if Zytko made personal visits to the library. "Do you think he'll take my call?"

"Tell him Alicia Hardaway sent you."

"Okay."

She watched Tom fumble to put his feet through his underwear. She was impatient to unlock the door. "Get your pants off the Merck Manuals, will you?"

Chapter Five

The Last Shooting Star

O utside the Lazy Eye bar, Claire Whethers leaned against the hood of her Impala. Tom spotted her down the street from the library. Her white uniform stockings reflected like downy snow in his truck headlights. Her arms were folded, and her chin was tucked into her chest. She appeared to be taking a standing nap.

In the library, bringing his lust to bear upon Alicia Hardaway, the notion of Claire had crossed his mind, and now he was minutes away from the warm librarian's talent among the books and pulling alongside Claire's frozen form in the street. The two women wove threads through his desires, inseparable by design. A man just knows what he wants, and a woman makes a futile accounting of it.

He leaned over and rolled down the passenger's window. "Claire?"

Claire's knees were locked, and the pleats of her dress shaped the car hood where they touched. Her legs were drawn in a straight line from her hips to the balls of her feet, and the muscles along her legs tensed like a gymnast holding stance.

"Hey." He tapped the horn lightly, and a squeak shot from the engine compartment.

He scanned the desolate street through his rearview mirror. Blue smoke billowed from his tailpipe. A cat walked atop the opposing curb. He returned to the Impala. It looked idle and cold, as iced to the spot as Claire. "Are you OK?"

"That's a loaded question." She spoke without opening her eyes. The orbs of her eyelids appeared thinner, more fragile than most, yet the lush song of her voice emanated from deep in her throat.

"Having car trouble?" He could jump start her car and get her back on the road in no time. He thought about the tools he stored in his truck. "I've got jumper cables."

"It's not the car."

"Need a lift somewhere?"

"I can't drive anymore." She looked at him, suddenly alive again. "I just can't do it."

"You can't?" He wondered how that was possible. It was akin to forgetting how to brush your teeth. Or was she giving up driving by choice?

"The lines are dotted," she said.

This set Tom in another perplexing direction. He pulled back from the car window. He felt slow and loose from his library encounter. Alicia had that affect on him.

"The lines." Claire came to the open truck window. "The lines on the road. They're dotted."

"Aren't they supposed to be?"

"I can't drive on them."

"You're not supposed to. You're supposed to stay to one side."

"You don't get me." She pressed both hands against the door and leaned into the truck. Her sights roamed over the trash upon the front seat. A milk crate brimmed with beverage bottles and cans. The broken lid to a barbecue grill sat on the floor. "What is this stuff?"

"Garbage."

"I can see that."

"I'm working on it."

"You don't work on garbage. You throw it out."

He was familiar with this circuitous path of questioning. It was his fault. He confused people. It was as if he didn't know the rules for regular conversation. Bewilderment reigned over the simplest discussions, such as talk of the phone bill or his credit card statement. He'd make an inquiry to clarify the god-awful sequences of numbers, only to send the other person into a mental logjam of explanation. He just didn't say things the way he meant them, and whatever afflicted his brain seemed to infect other people and then ultimately made them wary. He waited for the signs of intolerance in Claire.

"I'm not really working on the garbage," he said. "It's part of my work. It's an investigation."

She let the question drop, more interested in reacting to his words. "You're working on trash."

"That's what I said." *Good, she understands me.*

"Just what this town needs—a trash scientist."

"Actually, it's called, garbologist."

"You must be kidding."

Tom noticed her clinging to the car to balance herself. He smelled liquor on her breath. It was a distilled hard brew, not the sweet stuff that the kids at the forge drank, such as peach schnapps or fruity wines with bubbles.

Claire reached into the truck cabin and picked up an empty soda can. She examined it with one eye closed. "Is this part of the investigation?"

"Yes."

"I don't see anything special about it."

"It's not the can. It's where I found it that matters."

"Where did you find it?"

"At the truck turn-off, near the highway. I found a hoagie wrapper with it." He glanced at a greasy paper beside the barbecue lid.

She chucked the can back in the pile, harder than she intended. It rattled to the floor. "Oh brother."

Tom didn't mind. Most of the forest in the area was clean because of him. That was enough praise. "See those stripes?"

"What stripes?"

He scooped the deli wrap from the floor. "This hoagie wrapper. The grocery in Middleton uses wrap like that."

"Are you trying to get a merit badge in this or something?"

"I'm going down to Middleton in the morning to ask about the wrapper. They might know who's hoagie it is."

"Tom, how many hoagies do you think they sell?"

He opened the wrapper. "Check this out: lettuce, tomato, and look, a piece of hot pepper. How many people eat hot peppers?"

"I don't know."

"A lot less than those who don't, I suspect."

"Brother, you are a trash-ologist."

"Garbologist."

"You should teach a course."

He saw her expression straddling utter confusion and bursts of sarcasm. Tom noted his uncanny stroke of luck. Tonight, in Claire's booze-laced brain, the playing field was level. She was ripe to be flustered and disoriented, just as she routinely made him.

"So, you need a lift home?" He dropped the wrapper on the floor.

"Anywhere but there."

"Where to?"

"I don't care," she said.

"Do you want to go somewhere?"

"Of course I want to go somewhere."

"Did you forget where?"

She brought up her eyes, a shock of purple in the night. It was a glimmer of the passion that he longed to experience up close. "If you keep taking me literally, I'm going to throw up."

"I get you," he said, yet to understand most of what she said. He thought that the alcohol blew her words out of proportion, but he didn't hold it against her. It'd take a lot more than a bad attitude to yank her from his favor.

She opened the door and slid inside. More soda cans clinked and rattled to the floor. "Take me to the windy place."

"Where?"

"You're the one who seems lost."

"I never heard of the windy place."

"Haven't you lived here all your life?"

"You know that."

"Just drive."

They merged onto 623, near the cranberry processing station, where the cooperative once washed and barreled the harvest. The idle conveyor belts and holding bins loomed in darkness like parts of an alien spacecraft. JJ claimed that someone was converting the property into a personal storage facility, but people discarded those promises, and now Tom did after hearing the candid way Drew discounted JJ's talk. If Cranlakers had reason to stow something for safekeeping, it was into the back of a moving van before leaving town.

"Go left," Claire announced.

Tom veered into the sandy offshoot for a tree farm and stopped abruptly before the steel gate.

Clare braced herself against the dashboard. "Your other left."

Tom reached to feel the tiny mole on the back of his left hand, realizing he'd crossed up the directions. "Sorry."

"I don't need you to start crashing fences." Claire pushed a soda can off her lap and onto the floor. "I can't believe this."

The uncontrollable feeling came upon him, like he'd start stuttering in front of her. He raised his hand to cover his mouth. When people saw him struggle, they seized the words from his lips before he got them out. He smelled Alicia on his fingertips and pulled them away. What an evening this was turning out to be.

He backed the truck onto 623 and turned left at the next crossroad. They drove a mile or so, before Claire pointed her right hand out the window. "Turn, please."

Tom pulled into the entrance of Woodrow Wilson Park. Cranlakers knew to take the towpath around the locked gates at night. It wasn't open or even the season for swimming, but free access to the lake for nighttime skinny dipping was a matter of tradition.

The truck curved through the forest, feeling out the rocks and potholes like braille. Clusters of sassafras glowed yellow and green in the bobbing headlights. Tom saw the sky open up, where the towpath lead to the lake.

He parked in the gravel lot and cut the engine. A streak of moonlight snaked across the placid water. They both gazed at the calming sight. South Lake's ebony shoal waited patiently for summer. It was a promise that no matter how bleak the winter everything was going to work out. He wondered if Cranlakers still remembered that.

Claire braced her feet on the dashboard, bringing her knees to her chin. "Now you know where I mean?"

"I get you. Breezy Point."

"That's what I said."

"Actually, you said..." Tom saw her cheek in the luminescent reflection from the water. Beneath her left eye, her face looked bruised and swollen. "Did you get hurt?"

"Hurt?" She saw him staring and turned away.

"Did you fall?"

"Yeah, that's it. I fell. I fell big-time. I fell right out of the game."

Claire slipped outside and staggered for the lake. She paused to kick off her white sneakers and continued toward the water.

Tom walked after her on the stiff and crusted sand. Her abandoned stockings rode the small impressions left by her feet. She discarded her work apron, and it fell in a lump like a crushed hat.

Claire waded into the lake up to her ankles. He watched her undo her ponytail. Her black hair fell between her shoulders like a tousled rope, unfurling with the breeze. She spread her arms as if to gather the stars to her chest.

He stopped shy of the lake. He hoped she took off all of her clothes, even if she was drunk. He'd respect her. He wouldn't make her feel stupid about it later. The urge to stutter, do the nervous things he did, stirred inside him. He promised to stay cool, talking himself through a slight panic. He considered the possibilities. No matter what she decided to do, he'd act unsurprised, be ready for whatever came.

"Going for a swim?" He saw her teeter and prepared to enter the icy waters after her. "Claire?"

She tilted her face to the sky. Concentric ripples of water expanded from her calves. Her skin reflected everything, like the smooth stones on the beach. She was part of what made the beach glisten at night.

He stepped closer. The toe of his boot patted the water, creating a wave of its own, but he felt that he couldn't break the skin of the surface, as if the water was thicker for him than her. Instead, he grasped for the act that most challenged him—striking up casual conversation. "Hey, have you ever heard of a Nutley?"

"It's a town in north Jersey."

"No, a man named Nutley from long ago."

"A man?"

"Yes."

"Was there a man?"

"It's just something I'm working on."

"More trash?"

"Could be."

A streak of light zipped through the sky. Tom saw it on the lake surface and looked up. Claire did too. He could tell by the way she dropped the thread of the conversation and twitched her head.

Claire still hadn't turned around. "Did you see that?"

"Yes."

"Was it a shooting star?"

"Too fast for a plane. It could be a meteor."

"I just want to know if you saw it."

"I saw it."

"Then I wasn't imagining it."

"No."

"You think it's too late?"

"Too late?"

"To make a wish. Are you supposed to make one right away?"

"You..." He didn't know the rules for wishing upon a star but realized that it didn't matter. He saw the reason why they came—the unexpected. "You need to be the first. That's all."

"Did you make one?"

"Not yet."

"Please don't."

"It's all yours." Goosebumps rose on his arms.

She spread her arms all the way, as if she could fly, as if needing to visit the stars to submit her request. "I wish, I wish I could roll time backward."

"That's a good one."

She sloshed her foot in the shallows. "Oh no, I wasn't supposed to say it out loud."

"It doesn't matter when you're standing in water."

"Are you serious?"

He held control of Claire's wish, channeling life into it. He was getting a wish of his own. When he spoke, she didn't question him or pick on his choice of words. Even his lies made sense. "It's an Indian legend. It goes all the way back."

She showed her face. "That's a nice thought."

"It's the way it works."

"You know, you'd be good with kids."

"Why's that?"

"You'd make them believe anything."

"I don't think..."

"You'd make them want to stay."

Tom pretended he hadn't heard her, not wanting to prolong the subject of children, her missing children, children in general. Lately in public, he pretended children didn't exist. If he ignored them, it might ease people's fears... if they had fears. He didn't need to know the answer to that. He was not sure he wanted to know. He wanted the whole ugly business to go away.

"Kids want to believe in magic," she said. "Ronald still believes in Santa Claus, or he did. I wonder if Elliot ruined that, too."

"Kids aren't my specialty." He'd seen little Ronald on the trail with Claire once and showed him the tree frogs by the creek. Ronald was a lot like Claire. He held a tiny frog softly in his palm, studying it as it breathed quickly. He appreciated things for what they were. That wasn't a talent a lot of people had.

"It's okay," Claire said. "I don't believe a word of what Drew said. I'm just not sure why he did it."

Tom decided to stay mute on that point as well. Living in the woods, he never had much to say to people, but tonight, he harbored enough secrets to fill the night with conversation.

"It's my fault," she said. "I had a suspicion."

"About Drew?"

"No, forget him. I'm talking about Elliot now."

"Oh, him."

"He took the kids, you know."

Everyone knew what had happened. Tom watched the sadness creep back over her face, like a cloud passing before the moon. He couldn't recall many times when he looked at someone and felt sorry for them, especially for a woman who once had everything going for her. For months, Tom observed the breakdown, as if she'd disconnected from the attributes that made her great, pawned them off or simply abandoned from them.

"But I didn't think Elliot would do that," she said. "His mother, Geneva, put him up to it. I just know she was behind it."

He followed her legs up from the water, over her waist and the compact strength in her smallish shoulders and arms. He saw her bruises in more detail. She might have bumped into a door, or she might be tearing apart at the seams. He saw her step backward, deeper into the lake. He worried that he might not get her out of there. "How far do you want to roll back time?"

"To that day. I'd stop him. I'd be there. If he saw my face, he'd never go through with it. He'd never take them."

He edged into the shoal. His socks grew damp, as the icy water seeped through his laces. The cold stabbed at his toes like pins and needles. "Do you think the kids are all right?"

"He wouldn't do anything to them, I don't think. I don't know."

He needed to keep her still, get close enough to keep her from falling in the water. He fought to keep his teeth from chattering. "I know you miss them."

She looked as if she'd melt into the black water.

"Sorry, it was a stupid thing to say," he said.

"No, you're right. Why wouldn't I?"

Tom extended his hand. "Come on out. It's cold in here."

"It's not bad really."

"That's what I'm afraid of."

"What?"

"It's the alcohol."

Her eyes caught his, a hint of embarrassment she'd never shown him. "I guess you can tell I had a couple."

"Everyone does now and then."

"Do you?"

"I have enough trouble writing checks without it."

She laughed. He was pleased that he'd made that happen, though he doubted she'd recall it tomorrow. Her lips looked blue, and her skin was paler than ever. She edged near exposure. She didn't even wear a jacket on a chilly spring night. The self-neglect was evident enough to paint a picture.

When she took his hand, he discovered his courage. He knew exactly what he needed to do, although he couldn't visualize the correct path. It was a lot like traveling in the forest at night. He grasped only a sense of time and direction by the position of the moon and stars. There was a way out somewhere for her, if he was able to quiet his mind long enough and see it. "I wish you could roll back time too, then you'd have your kids and be just like you were."

"You hit the nail on the head," she said without malice. "Whoever says you're an idiot is an idiot."

They left the water. Tom was relieved he'd gotten past that.

He stayed by her side. Sand clung to her wet feet. The night by the lakeside seemed just for them. He saw the tree line. The breeze swung the branches in quick succession, pulsating with the same breath that surged within him. Claire smelled of whiskey and cedar water, all sweet now, up into the open air.

The forest brought them closer, although Tom's sights never left the trees. A light, like a shooting star at first, cut close and low, and then he saw the headlights rounding the corner and the shape of the squad car exploding into white before the high beams blinded their eyes.

Drew Spatt pulled into the parking lot. The police lights started flashing, and he gave the siren a quick whirl.

The door creaked open, and bad vibes covered the beachhead like morning frost. The police chief rose from the car. His face scrunched up like one of the imploded soda cans in Tom's truck, and his big hands cut by his side, grasping for something to throttle. "Did he lay a hand on you?"

Claire hugged her sneakers to her chest and mumbled. "Not again."

Tom squished in his boots, his pants legs sticking to his shins. He watched Drew close the gap and braced for the first insult.

"Did he touch you?" Drew barked. "Just give me the word."

"Drop it," Claire said. "I asked him to bring me here."

"What?"

"Don't look at me like that. You're not my keeper."

Drew turned on Tom. "Why do I have to keep running into you?"

Tom saw the way Drew looked at him, like Tom was an eyesore, a jagged stone to be raked off the sand before the tourists arrived. Even Cranfield Lakes had its hierarchy, and he lay somewhere near the bottom with the weekend drifters and the road kill. Tom didn't mind that people didn't understand him. He'd gotten used to the misconception, but here, in front of Claire, after he'd given her a shooting star and saved her from the lake, the general disdain of Drew and Cranlakers in general stung him like never before. It pierced his thirty-two year old shell, and he felt the old hurts reaching back to his childhood, like there was a heavy anchor shackled to his leg and with one glance Drew had tossed it overboard. The chain trailed underwater faster than he could manage.

"Do you think Claire even wants to spend time with a man like you?" Drew asked.

"I, I..." Tom despised his stutter. He hadn't done it all evening.

"That's probably a stupid question. You like little kids."

"Oh, for god's sake, I'm walking home." Claire peeled away, but Drew snatched her arm in his fist, and her body jerked backward.

"Get in the car," Drew ordered.

Tom no longer needed to wonder about her bruises. Drew's grip alone might leave a mark. Tom's blood quickened. He suddenly had that anchor from the past hauled back into the boat, and he was going to use it on Drew.

"Your problem isn't with her." Tom thumped his hands against Drew's chest. It was solid, but he moved Drew backward.

It caught Drew by surprise. A car crash of words rear-ended in his brain. "Wha, what?"

Tom wanted to take a fistful of Drew's shirt, rip the badge right off and feed it back to the jerk once and for all. This is it. It had to happen. Like his father had said a long time ago, his biggest mistake was not bringing Drew down the first time.

Drew lunged forward, just as Claire wedged between them.

"Stop it!" Claire nearly took a shot to the face as Drew reached for Tom. Wildness flashed in her eyes, the fear that a woman her size couldn't control two men tangling in the woods. She latched onto Drew's right wrist with both hands, like she already knew what he could do once he got started.

Drew tugged it free. His fat fingers fell to his side. He probably used a toenail clipper to cut those things. "You know what I don't like about you, King?"

"That you can't get rid of me?" Tom tasted his anger. It mixed with his nerves and a desire to rush hell-bent into trouble.

"I can get rid of you." Drew balled his fists. "That's for sure."

"Give it your best shot." Tom planted his feet, ready to deflect the first punch. He'd get his shots in before the worst of it. He counted on Drew being strong but predictable in his delivery. Like when Drew played football, he was known for blasting straight up the middle, nothing fancy, no finesse.

"No." Claire forced her head and shoulder against Drew. Tom felt her feet bracing against his own. "Enough."

Drew gripped the knob of Claire's shoulder to swipe her aside.

"I want to go home," Claire said. Her change in tone caught everyone off guard, disarming the men.

Drew looked down. "I can take care of this."

"I know you can, honey." She relaxed her body and stepped off Tom's toes. She tilted her face toward Drew.

"Then let me do it," Drew said.

"Let's go home, please." She no longer sounded afraid, more like a cajoling wife.

Tom couldn't tell if it was for real. He took a step back.

Drew released his fists. "You want to go home?"

She gave a half turn. "That's what I want. I'm not waiting around either."

Tom wanted to tell her that she didn't have to do this, but he recalled his place in the big picture. She was Drew's girlfriend for some inexplicable reason. She might really want to go home with him. In the end, this might be what turned her on. Alicia was full of complicated motivations. Why not Claire? Why couldn't she be just another page in the script that he couldn't decipher?

Claire gathered her sneakers and grabbed Drew's wrist again, tugging him toward the squad car. She didn't look over her shoulder, much less in Tom's direction. Was it on purpose, or had she already forgotten he was there? Tom hoped she'd cast a sign in his direction, but nothing came.

The squad car left the gravel lot with Claire in the front seat. Tom remained on the beach. Like always, he waited for the person who approached—who penetrated his space when they had no right—to leave of his own accord, and then Tom found himself alone with the pines and his lingering thoughts.

The car taillights burned red, disappearing into the trees. Tom felt a void opening up. It was the absence of Claire balancing herself in the water. The scene was imprinted on his memory. He'd allowed her inside a place that he never allowed people, not even Alicia Hardaway. He'd swung the door wide-open, and Claire came in, walked around a bit, and left. This was why Drew had gotten the better of him. He'd let his defenses down. He'd thought of revenge instead of letting things pass like always.

Tom fought to shake it off, grateful that they'd left him alone. He'd known Claire for a lifetime. She existed mostly in his imagination—a dream that would never be his in the flesh. He searched for a glimmer of the squad car trailing away. He and Claire had briefly connected, a shooting star and nothing more. A smart man, he thought, lets the stars just hang in the sky and doesn't try to reach above his head.

Chapter Six

The Lakeside
by the Hour

C laire awoke from a fitful sleep and sat up in bed, breathing hard as if just emerging from water. The stale remnants of booze and cigarettes burned her eyes. She draped her legs over the bed and waited for her head to stop spinning. Photos of Faye and Ronald lined the wall, like windows into her thoughts. The framed images captured the sunlight and became the only lucid image in the room.

The mattress sank behind her. She didn't have to look over her shoulder. The menthol on Drew's breath jogged her memory. She recalled a starry sky, the squad car, and too many Whiskey Sours. Gritty sand still stuck between her toes, and the smell of sex lingered. Her stomach turned on that thought. It was weird not knowing if you'd enjoyed the night before or if it made you sick and curl up on the floor like a discarded shrimp. Maybe she'd done both. She didn't know whether to thank someone or say she was sorry.

She crept into the shower and assembled the tools. Her exhausted arms and legs operated by remote control, even shaky as they were. Steam painted the glass doors, as she scrubbed her feet with a luffa sponge, releasing the last grains of sand. She twice rinsed her hair and lathered her body with a fresh washcloth. She rubbed her skin raw in places, until the filthy evening spiraled down the drain and only water swirled near her feet. She imagined a brush that could exfoliate memory, a bleach capable of passing right through her and cleansing her inside.

The bathmat was soft beneath her feet, and the drain cleared behind her. She was attuned to her surroundings, everything but the world straight ahead. If Drew awoke before she left for work, she decided to become deaf and blind. She'd never lay eyes on him, eclipsing his voice from her ears. She vowed to make it a permanent state of mind.

She wrapped the towel tight around her body. It felt like a rope across her chest. She created almost no reflection in the foggy mirror, yet she recognized herself through the film of steam and water, a smear of the wreck she pretended not to notice. The booze wasn't helping any longer. It always led her back to Drew, until he became so large an object that she saw nothing else. *So much for drinking yourself blind.*

Claire reached the Lakeside Motel before 6:00 A.M. Mist rose off the beige stucco walls, and a patch of dew lingered where the building cast its shadow upon the fractured, weed-creviced blacktop.

The cool air did nothing to ease Claire's hangover. She usually downed a couple of shots for breakfast: one to loosen her joints and another to stoke her resolve. It was a proven remedy. The first shot blanked her mind, and the second numbed her senses. She'd crawl inside herself and concentrate on the menial highlights of her job, but today, she had left her flask on the kitchen counter. She wanted to tow the line. She needed to convince herself that she still could.

Claire found the boss's office unlocked and went inside. She heard Raffi shifting in the bathroom. The smell of curry permeated the small space, and she held her apron over her face to keep from losing whatever lingered in her stomach from the night before. She reminded herself that her days at the Lakeside were numbered. Raffi had bought the motel after the bottom fell out of the local real estate market and the property became an immigrant's bargain. As soon as Raffi's daughters arrived from Kashmir, Claire would be out of work, again scratching for time in the unemployment line two counties away, not a task that any Cranlaker was inclined to undertake.

She pulled the keys from the occupancy board and headed for the door, spotting the mail on the front desk. She tucked the overdue motel electric bill into her apron. If Raffi asked, she planned to act stupid. The letter would be ripped to shreds and scattered over the highway. *I'll deal with the unemployment line. You deal with the lights going out.*

Claire pushed the cleaning cart to room 1B—one of the matinee rooms. It was one of four Lakeside rooms that opened from the back as well as the front, creating discreet exits for occupants that stayed only as long as it took to screw and construct alibis. Raffi rented these rooms by the hour. The rear doors were close to parking and beyond sight of the highway. The Lakeside was forty-five minutes from Camden and an hour from Philly. A long lunch in the country threw a blanket excuse over most visits.

Whenever Claire visited the dismal appointments of 1B, she never knew quite what to expect. Not even dirty sheets and towels were guaranteed. Some people never wrinkled the bed, tossing aside the pillows on the couch instead. She'd gotten used to the loners who masturbated to the porno videos; at least, that's what she assumed they did. A box of rubber bands and a length of chain held her curiosity for a while, but she'd discovered a fetish magazine in the trash and solved the mystery by flipping through the sordid color photography of couples acting out medieval desires, although she doubted that anyone in medieval times had cans of whipped cream and diamond-studded dog collars.

When she used to work at the cranberry co-op, the strangest behavior she noted was a young accountant from Tuckerton, who liked to photocopy his ass in a variety of women's underwear. She'd giggled about that with the other ladies in the coffee room. She had no idea how low people might sink. Lately, she thought there wasn't a bottom to it, only plateaus on the way down.

Claire flicked on the lights in 1B. The place smelled like potpourri and the layers of aerosol she used to mask the smell. She didn't really plan to clean the room. Who would complain? No one ever paid with checks or credit cards. No one dared ask for a refund. She doubted the names on the registry matched their driver's licenses. Women in dark sunglasses surreptitiously darted in and out, apart from their male companions. In their cliché covertness, they broadcast their business to anyone with eyes.

Elliot had done it the right way, Claire thought. He'd snatched the kids in broad daylight, as if doing nothing out of the ordinary. No shame. No admission of guilt. In less time than it took to drape a big scarf over your head or don a trench coat, he'd ripped the kids from her life. She bet that Faye and Ronald hadn't even cried. She bet he'd sold them an amazing story. It tortured her that there might be a story that made children give up on their mother.

The bedcovers at the Lakeside were green with blue geometric patterns outlined in black—the worst of art-deco sensibilities and 1960's color schemes brought together. Claire found the bedcovers piled at the foot of the bed. The sheets were pulled from the lower mattress corners. Two dry and cloudy glasses sat on the TV, and a pair of condom wrappers lay crumpled on the nightstand. *A standard suck, fuck, and duck.* She pulled the sheets straight, gave them a cursory glance, and threw the bedcover over top. The linen needed more mileage. Perhaps the fetish couple would show up later. Last week, they left behind a roll of duct tape and a heap of questionable rags.

The floors looked okay to Claire, but the bathroom deserved attention. She folded up the used towels and hung them on the bar. Raffi appreciated the reuse of linen. Somehow this added up to another nickel saved. She didn't care.

She strapped a sanitary seal around the toilet without cleaning it and sat on the lid. It was her usual time for her third drink of the day. She felt her apron where the flask would be, imagining the oak-cured taste of whiskey coating her tongue. She closed her eyes. Spots gathered in the dark, collecting into a bright white fist that pressured the back of her eyes, but it was really her own fists digging into the sockets. As soon as she realized, she dropped her hands and made for the door.

Alright, that's three drinks I didn't have, three removed from my life's total. She envisioned her soul on the mend. Her body floated toward whatever lay ahead in that big blank nothingness of the future.

Claire locked 1B behind her and pushed the cleaning cart toward the next room. Geneva Bogdan's silver Cadillac zipped past the breezeway between the two main buildings.

Claire considered leaping inside the nearest room. She fumbled for the key, as the car rounded the corner and headed toward her. She turned her back and started her trick of blocking out the world around her, but without the booze to fortify her, the noise and smell of the car encroached upon her flimsy veil of separation.

The Caddy beeped twice, as the power window retracted into the door. Geneva wore a flowery printed dress with a soft blue sweater. A thick gold necklace of Egyptian links draped upon her full chest. She flicked her bangs with one hand. She was on a mission, Claire thought. Geneva always had a purpose. She never browsed or wandered about a room. She made you feel like you were wasting time if you paused to tie your shoe.

"Good day, Ms. Wethers," Geneva chirped. No one wanted Claire to return the Bogdon name faster than Geneva. She achieved a genuine state of euphoria, just saying Claire's maiden name aloud.

"Geneva." Claire yearned for a quick belt of the hard stuff. Mother-in-laws were sticky business, but ex-mother-in-laws like this one made bamboo shoots beneath her toenails seem like a reasonable alternative.

"Are you too tied up to speak?"

Claire smoothed her cleaning apron to her thighs. Her first few days in the uniform were a humiliating symbol of a derailed career and failed marriage, but that was months ago. Now it served as a trite reminder of the facts. "What do you want?"

"How's my house doing?"

"Still standing." Claire rummaged through the bottles of window and toilet bowl cleaners, to keep from acknowledging Geneva's pleasure with the circumstance. When Claire got the kids back, she would regain leverage over the woman. Claire never used the kids against their grandmother. She would never consider it, but just having them at home, kept Geneva in line, made the bitch think twice

"Are you changing the furnace filters?" Geneva asked.

"Just like Elliot did."

"Oh, have you heard from him?"

Claire choked the spray bottle in her grip, and a burst of blue liquid shot across a clean stack of linens. She despised Geneva's pretending not to know Elliot's whereabouts. She imaged secret phone calls and letters. She begged Drew to tap Geneva's phone line and check her mail. Of course, none of that was legal, and it was unlikely Drew possessed the capacity to pull it off. But she needed to know how deep Geneva's collusion ran.

The Caddy idled nearby, like a war tank set to level its target. Claire turned toward Geneva. "Do you think Elliot calls me to chat?"

"No. I don't." The woman seemed unfazed. A hint of her accent still lingered after four decades in the states.

Claire believed it was Geneva's harsh Basque attitude that drove Elliot's father to the grave. "Then you've answered your own question."

"My, my, we're blunt this morning."

Claire did her best to stomach the response. From the very start, Geneva demeaned Claire, treating the Cranberry Festival Queen like she didn't know which end of a pencil to use. Geneva held an unwritten standard, to which only Elliot aspired. Claire was preordained to fall short, and any success she achieved, Geneva assumed she'd obtained by guile. On the night she and Elliot were engaged, Geneva pulled her aside and said, "Congratulations. You've closed the trap." That was when Claire saw everything she had refused to believe.

She rolled the cart a few feet away from the Caddy. "The house is fine. I'm sure that's not why you're here."

"Actually, that's exactly it."

Claire stopped and looked back. She wondered who'd brought up the subject of the house. She thought it was the Basque bitch.

"The house has been a nice investment over the years," Geneva continued. "I think it's worth a nice penny by now."

"I suppose."

"I've been checking the market."

Claire's hands trembled like they had first thing in the morning, and she clutched the edge of the cleaning cart to control them. Geneva owned the house and a few others in town, but this was the house where each of Claire's children was born. She'd delivered Faye in the living room because the girl came too fast. She bore Ronald in the master bedroom with the aide of a midwife, no longer fearing the process. Elliot's father had promised to sign over the deed to his grandchildren that day, but his sudden heart attack scuttled those plans.

"I think," Geneva said, "it's a pretty big place."

"We're comfortable."

"We're?" Geneva teased the fact that the kids were no longer at home. She played it like a burn.

"Ronald and Faye love their rooms."

"Yes, they did."

"They do."

"I don't want to mince words with you, sweetheart." Geneva called people "sweetheart" whenever she meant it least. "You could use a lot less room."

"Do you want boarders? Are you looking for rent?"

"Oh no, nothing like that will be necessary. You have enough to look after with your schedule." Geneva panned Claire from head to foot.

"What is it?"

"Will the end of the month be enough?"

"For what?"

"To pack your things, sweetheart. You have to get out."

The tires were rolling, as Geneva delivered her ultimatum. Claire watched the power window ascend. She grew speechless with the motion and reached toward the Caddy, but the big car seemed to slip through her fingers like everything else.

In the Lazy Eye—the bar connected to Nat's Café—the cigarette smoke and the moan of the jukebox blurred peoples' best and worst ideas, until every one seemed to hum the same foggy tune. Claire assumed the barstool in the dimmest corner, near the beer logo mirrors and the lit display case of collector bourbon decanters that no one ever bothered to view.

Nat took his post behind the bar, from the food counter next door. He was an older black man with salt and pepper hair and recessed cheeks. He worked along the wooden bar top with a hand towel. It must have been after 8:00 P.M. He usually switched over from the bar when the café crowd thinned. "Need another?"

Claire was trying to recall when she started with the hard stuff. In high school, she sipped whatever the boys brought along—beer, peach brandy, wine coolers—never enough to get her into trouble. The boys liked that she drove their cars if they got loaded. She was smart and cool. She wrote her own ticket.

When she'd hooked up with Elliot in their senior year, she turned away from the schoolgirl nonsense: the passed notes, the weekend liaisons, the romances that built up from gossip. She thought she could keep this one. She never saw the possibility of being thrown back into the pool.

"Claire?" Nat stopped wiping the bar. His bony fingers clawed the towel.

"You have any peach brandy?" she asked.

"What's that?"

"Peach brandy."

"I suppose. A shot or a glass?"

It suddenly seemed like a big decision. She lifted up the empty drink in front of her. "How about another of these instead?"

"Whiskey Sour, coming up."

Claire started to sense the sway. She hung to the bar-stool. If she rose too fast, she'd tumble. Okay, not drinking during the day was a good first test. What did her horoscope say? She'd picked the wrong day. Her planets were all wrong. The full moon was taking up residency in a house where it didn't belong. Tomorrow, she'd check her stars again, try to go a little further.

"Here you go, honey." Nat set the glass on a fresh cocktail napkin and slid the bowl of peanuts closer, even though Claire could already reach it. "You want something to eat?"

"I'm watching my weight." Claire just now realized that she said that often.

"You look hungry."

She wondered what hungry looked like. She knew that her clothes hung off her frame more than usual, but she didn't think she looked that bad. On Tuesday, a man from Pennsauken sat next to her and boldly asked her if she'd ever stripped for cash. He claimed she had the right stuff: the body and chest that men liked. "Exotic eyes," he'd said, dropping his card. "Can you dance with a load on like that?"

Claire laughed aloud, just like she did that night. A decade ago, she would have blushed. Two years ago, she would have been insulted. She stared into her drink, knowing that business card still sat on her kitchen table with the unopened mail awaiting a response.

"What's so funny?" Nat asked.

"Nothing."

"How about that food? It's on the house."

"You better scrape it off then."

"Serious, Claire. Whatever you want."

"I want to finish this drink." But Claire wasn't so sure. Her stomach felt full up to her throat. She should have mixed in more water. Now she was wavering.

"I have a nice lasagna and wild blueberry pie."

"Blueberry?"

"Blueberries from Maine. Go figure."

"Somebody's got to grow them."

"So what do you say?"

She drifted off again, aware of her mistake. One drink was okay, but she'd had several, making up for those missing dailies with the gusto of a bog worker on payday. She was glad the beer logo mirrors at her back didn't really catch a decent image. She feared turning around and glimpsing herself. The booze put lines on her face faster than the scratches on Nat's glass wear.

"Claire?"

"I have to go." She slid off the stool. Her foot was asleep, and she limped along the bar, until her circulation returned.

A full Whiskey Sour waited on the bar, but she refused to go after it. She pulled herself slowly toward the exit.

She pressed her palms on the door and hit the outside air. Okay, she'd made it this far, a small accomplishment in a rough day. She stood on Main Street and did the quick numbers. *Alright, that was one less drink, Claire. One less to your life's total.* If she kept skipping drinks like this, she'd fill Nat's shelves with unopened whiskey bottles. That would be something.

Chapter Seven
Rebels in the Woods

Lieutenant MacDowell
approached me in June.
He sought loyalists to the crown.
I laughed.
I am not even loyal to myself.
He seemed prepared to offer rewards.
He promised to elevate my station.
The town will be reorganized
when the rebels are put down.

Tom wrapped the diary in plastic and pointed his pickup toward the Makepeace Wildlife Area. Thanks to Alicia Hardaway, he had a brief phone conversation with Stan Zytko and was invited to discuss his find from Old Forge. He drove beyond the city limits of Cranfield Lakes and brought his truck up to speed. He debated whether or not Zytko should learn about the diary. His discovery at Old Forge was either something amazing or amazingly ordinary. He might take a chance. If anyone understood the history of the Pine Barrens, it was Zytko, who'd written several books on the subject.

The terrain fell low and flat, preparing to accept the interior salt marshes of New Jersey. Tom passed over the Atlantic City Expressway and found the firebreak that bisected the road. The overgrown path felt spongy beneath his tires, and he slowed down to keep his truck from fishtailing into the underbrush.

He switched on his headlights. A wall of Pitch Pines masked his view on either side. He couldn't see farther than twenty yards into the forest. Interpreting someone else's trail directions was a challenge. Thank God, Zytko had offered visual cues as guideposts. He understood those tidbits the best. You could write down a street name or house number for Tom or describe what the pebbles in the street looked like, and he'd find the pebbles first.

The road submerged where the river flooded the plains. Tom saw Zytko's green van parked beside a slanted cedar row. He looked for signs of life at dusk. The tree frogs peeped. The swamp water splashed and gurgled under his wheels.

He took to the trail on foot, hoping to locate Zytko's cabin before dark. The early azaleas bore spiky crowns, which edged toward bloom, and a large garter snake slithered past his boots and disappeared. He worried about rattlesnakes in the damp lowlands, especially at dusk. One bite altered your plans for the entire evening, maybe the whole month.

The trail descended a gentle slope. Tom avoided the thickening mud by hopping from stone to stone. He looked up and spotted a long metal structure reflecting the fading sun. It definitely wasn't supposed to be there. It might be a junked car. The pines were full of them. People drove them as deep as possible and then walked away. And that wasn't the worst of it. Everyone from the mob to serial killers eventually found the pines as the perfect junkyard for corpses.

"Hello." Tom poised on the rock, studying the odd yellow and blue sight. It looked like a school bus that was raised from the ground on a trestle of treated lumber, but the roof held a series of metallic rectangles resembling black mirrors. A deck ran around one side, which connected to a modest greenhouse covered in clear plastic. Black compost barrels lined the southern wall, and the scent of lime, peat moss, and decomposing vegetables wafted uphill.

"Hello?" His voice echoed through the swamp. He stepped toward the makeshift shelter, until a distinct sound seized his attention and caused him to freeze.

It was a shotgun being loaded in the background. He recognized it cold: the sliding of a shell into the chamber, a brass cap poised behind the firing pin. He'd heard that sound dozens of times during the hunting season and from great distances too. He hunkered down, waiting for the first blast of lead pellets to cut the air.

"State your business," a man called in the background.

Tom stood again and raised his hands, teetering on an uneven stone. He slowly turned to view a man stepping from the shrubs. "Mr. Zytko?"

Several yards away, Stan Zytko aimed a shotgun at Tom's throat. He resembled the photo in the back of his field manual: bald, stocky, a natural double chin. He dressed in mostly black, including a pair of dark green field boots. It fit with his camouflage gunstock.

Zytko cocked back from his weapon, firing his question instead. "State your business."

Tom clutched for a reply. He was pleased to meet the famous naturalist but annoyed to be staring down the business end of a shotgun for the second time in one week.

Did he really look dangerous? He was taller than most, but he felt that he had gangly arms and legs. Was that threatening? Perhaps threatening like a big spider.

"We spoke on the phone," Tom said.

"Yes." Zytko sounded unsure. He kept the gun raised.

"Alicia Hardaway sent me. I'm Thomas King."

"Right." Zytko lowered his weapon. His toned softened, but he didn't appear apologetic. "You can't be too careful."

"I was following your directions."

"That's good of you."

Black gnats nibbled at Tom's neck. He wanted to slap them away but feared any sudden movement until introductions were firm and Zytko had the shell out of the chamber. "Don't tell me you get trouble out here?"

"This is where trouble begins and ends."

Tom glanced around and then up to the trees. Several sparrows took flight. "It seems pretty tranquil to me."

"Wait 'till the bulldozers arrive. There'll be plenty of noise then."

"Bulldozers?"

"Yup, the Terrapins are coming."

An image of harmless turtles marching on the pines came to Tom's mind. "Why are terrapins a problem?"

"Not terrapins, The Terrapins."

Tom kept to his stone, already regretting his next question. The conversation felt like opening a book in the middle. "What's the difference?"

"I'm talking about the Terrapin Brothers."

Tom now pictured a group of roughnecks, like what he saw in the movies. He'd heard of renegade truckers who dumped toxic waste in the Barrens. The list of secrets got pretty unusual out here, and ugly too. "Should I ask who the Terrapin Brothers are?"

"Come up to the house, and I'll enlighten you."

Tom followed Zytko to the school bus and climbed the stairs to the deck. The closer he came to the place, the more practical it appeared. In front was a regular hinged door, and many windows were covered with sheet metal that was welded in place. A satellite dish angled for the sky, and an array of solar panels lined the roof. Tom heard water trickling through the panels.

"I like the set up," Tom said.

"It's not mine, except for the electronics. I'm borrowing the place."

"I was thinking about putting in solar panels myself."

"Can't help you with that. They were here when I arrived."

When Zytko opened the bus, an Asian woman in a Philadelphia Sixers T-shirt and chinos blocked the door. She wore rubber gloves, clutching a scouring sponge. A few soap bubbles stuck to her dark bangs. "Shoes off. No shoes on carpet."

"This is Mary." Stan slipped out of his rubber boots and placed them beside the door.

Tom figured he'd better do the same. He dropped his boots on the deck. "I'm sorry. I didn't get your name."

"Maly," Mary said. "You want drink?"

"A glass of water is fine."

"Sit down," she ordered.

The seats were stripped from the bus, and the forward section was separated into a working kitchen and sitting room. An add-on trailer turned away from the back, perhaps housing bedrooms. Stacks of books and papers covered the corner desk, and newspaper articles and charts lined the walls. Tom heard a police scanner going. Zytko had a beeper and cell phone strapped to his waist. He didn't miss much in the woods. He was more tuned in than the cops.

"The Terrapin Brothers suck." Zytko summoned Tom to the couch.

Tom sat down with his glass of water. "Who are they?"

"A commercial construction outfit in A.C."

"Why would an Atlantic City firm bother you here?"

Zytko swept his arm in a horizontal arc. "Think of this place as a row of condominiums and a waste-of-space golf course."

Tom was impressed with the transfiguration of the school bus. It put his cabin to shame, but a row of condominiums was hard to imagine in the swamps. "I don't get it."

"They want to backfill the land and pave the goddamned thing over."

"This is public land. It's a reserve."

"Not all of it. If they destroy what's next door, they'll ruin the preserve, too. Do you have any idea how important an estuary is?"

Tom hesitated to flaunt his knowledge in front of Zytko. "I understand it's important."

"I'll sum it up. It's damned important. It cleans the goddamned soil and water."

"I know that."

"Then why didn't you say so?"

Zytko's cell phone rang, and he pressed it to his ear. "Yes? ... I understand. ... Sons a bitches. ... Call me when you know for sure."

Although Zytko hung up, he still seemed distracted by the call. His eyes moved rapidly, his mind fluttering with activity. He glanced at the piles of paperwork on the desk, as if he needed to move toward it.

Mary banged pots and pans in the kitchen sink.

"I can't believe they'll get away with it," Tom said.

"Mister, you know nothing about the gears of the universe. I can't blame you. They want it that way. They don't want you to know until it's over."

"Who's they?"

"Big brother. He's running the bank. He's filling you up at the gas station. He owns the supermarkets and malls. He owns your job. You used to get credit from the local store and barter with the doctor. Now HMOs, GE—all of them—and their goddamned lawyers broker the system. For them, taking this land is a small conquest. The eminent domain laws weren't written for the benefit of the community. That never was their intention."

Tom almost joked that his town had very few of the features that Zytko mentioned and even less every day, but he got Zytko's point. Housing developments and shopping centers had been chewing up the Barrens at an accelerated rate for half a century. These were outside interests with giant machinery, who didn't seem to understand the sacredness of the land, only demarcation lines, sewer tunnels, and telephone poles. Every week Tom eyed another Cranfield Lakes foreclosure, and so it wasn't difficult to plot the future. There wouldn't be any argument when someone bought up the whole place at a discount.

"I'm talking about the World Bank, mister, the whole money gang," Zytko said. "They make people like the Terrapin Brothers possible. They're friggin' hitmen on the economy, on civilization."

A small monkey descended from one of the bookshelves and perched on Zytko's shoulder. Tom recognized the species from *National Geographic* but forgot the name. It had a pink face with a wide crinkly nose. It looked like a little, fuzzy human being with a functional tail. It gave Tom the creeps.

The monkey picked through the hair on the back of Stan's neck, plucking and pulling along the groove of Stan's spine. Its tail furled and unfurled during the activity.

Zytko reached back and patted its head. "Monkey thinks we're related. I found her orphaned in the Congo, and she bonded with me."

"How'd you get her through customs?"

Zytko's eyebrows—the lone hair on his face—knitted together. "So why are you here?"

Mary burst into the room. "Shoo, monkley. Shoo!"

Monkey leapt to the shelf and picked up an orange.

"Stay off." Mary waved her hands in the air, miming her request to the nervous primate.

Monkey scowled and hurled down an orange peel.

Mary scooped up the scrap from the couch, as another fell from the shelf and plunked her head.

Monkey screamed like a shrunken down three year old, and Tom felt the hair on his own neck rise. He hoped Monkey didn't have any designs on grooming him.

"Bad monkley." Mary clenched the peel in her fist, but the animal only grinned and squealed.

"Don't get her upset," Zytko said.

Tom wondered to whom Zytko referred. He wasn't about to guess, although he clearly fell on Mary's side of the dispute, aligning himself with the higher level primate.

"Dirty animal." Mary scurried to the kitchen. "I hate monkleys."

The encounter left Tom curious about how Zytko got Mary past customs as well. The entire set up—the interior trailer, the monkey, Mary—seemed like a collection of things he'd gathered during his famous expeditions.

"I found something interesting," Tom said.

"Let me see."

"I left it back in the truck."

Zytko dipped his chin, dissatisfied. "What is it?"

"It's a colonial artifact."

"What kind of artifact?"

Tom tossed aside the notion of a giant horseshoe, digging for a better story this time. "It's a tankard."

"What's it made of?"

"Bog iron, I think."

"How do you know?"

"I cleaned it."

"Man, be careful with it."

"It's okay. It had writing on it."

"What does it say?"

"Forged at the south lake, by Nutley."

"Nutley, New Jersey?"

"No, I'm pretty sure it's a man named Nutley. Have you ever heard of a Nutley in the pines?"

"What's the research say?"

"Alicia and I couldn't find anything."

Zytko's beeper sounded, and he unclipped it to read the tiny screen. "Bingo. Gotta' go." He leapt off the couch and swiped a zippered leather case from the kitchen counter.

Tom searched for a place to set down his water glass. "Mr. Zytko?"

"Sorry, ahhh, what did you say your name was again?" Zytko slipped into his rubber boots by the door.

"Thomas King."

"Sorry, Tom. I've got an emergency." He threw on a black nylon vest with baggy pockets and strutted for the deck.

Mary shut off the water and turned from the sink.

"Code red," Zytko said.

"Take hat, Stanny." She yanked a suede safari hat from the hook and tossed it through the door.

Zytko was already stamping down the stairs. He reached up and snatched the hat from the air, slapping it on his head. They'd been through this drill before.

Tom tried to match his steps in the dark. Zytko was surprisingly swift afoot. He skipped over the stones on the incline. He was halfway up the slope by the time Tom put on his boots.

Zytko moved even faster on level ground. Tom hit the muddy trail, running. When they reached the cars, he was huffing for air. "I was hoping to discuss my find some more."

"Follow me." Zytko jumped in the van, which was aimed in the direction of the nearest clearing. He revved the engine.

The van started moving. Tom managed to pull himself into the seat and shut the door without spilling onto the forest floor.

They drove as fast as the wet trail allowed, perhaps a little faster. Two white-tailed deer leapt clear of the head-lights, and the tires skidded in the mud. Tom reached for the seatbelt and pulled it tight.

"Let me see that tankard," Zytko said.

Tom offered a blank expression.

"You left it in the truck?" Zytko's eyebrows did their trick again.

"I didn't exactly have time to..."

"Well, describe it to me."

Tom hadn't expected that. He thought of a pewter tankard that his dad won in a Knights of Columbus raffle. It was supposed to be an authentic replica. "It looks like a genuine mug from the south lake period. It's smooth. It has a handle. You can drink out of it."

"Sounds somewhat ordinary. You should run it by the state curator."

"I was hoping Nutley turned out to be important."

"It doesn't ring a bell. I'll check my notes. Write that name down for me."

"I was hoping it might bring things at Old Forge to a halt."

"Old Forge? What's happening there?"

"It's where I found the t-tankard." Tom stuttered because he'd almost said horseshoe.

Zytko used the maintenance access road to enter the Atlantic City Expressway. It was an illegal move, bypassing the tollbooths, but Tom wasn't surprised. It seemed that rules existed for other people than Stan Zytko. Tom clutched his seat, as Zytko pressed the gas pedal and invented a new speed limit.

"Man, Old Forge." Zytko said. "There's a lot of unproven history there. It's one of my favorite ghost towns."

Road signs flew past Tom's windows. "It's like your Terrapin trouble."

"What about those pricks?"

"Not them. I've got my own Terrapins. A couple guys in Cranfield Lakes want to mow down Old Forge."

"What do they want with it?"

"They want to build a miniature golf course and an ice cream stand—stuff like that."

Zytko shook his head. "It constantly amazes me how limited people's imaginations can be."

Terrapin Brothers Construction Incorporated sat between two mega oceanfront casinos that they'd helped to build. That was all anyone needed to know, and by the time Zytko's van reached Atlantic Avenue, Tom had already guessed their destination.

"It's a public hearing, if that's what you call it." Zytko searched the crowded avenue for an open parking space. "It's more like a public farce."

"Can the Terrapin Brothers hold a public hearing in their own building?" Tom asked.

"Doesn't that tell you something? They're trying the bum's rush approval of the whole project. It's 800 friggin' units."

"That's like a shopping mall."

"They're planning one of those too. These guys won't be happy until every last piece of nature is covered in synthetic and toxic materials."

Zytko slid beside a fire hydrant and got out. He took his leather case but left the keys in the van.

Tom found himself playing catch-up again. He jumped out of the van, slamming the door shut. "Just because they want a huge complex in the pines, doesn't mean it's going through."

"That's the attitude." Zytko smiled for the first time that evening. Some of his teeth were crooked, and silver caps replaced others. He possessed the jagged expression of a broken zipper.

Tom watched Zytko dart in a new direction. Nothing seemed capable of pinning Zytko down. Tom considered revealing the secret about the forge. It was either Zytko's bravado or all the hovering casinos that summoned the notion to take a risk. "You know, I don't really have a tankard."

Zytko glanced over his shoulder. "What are you talking about?"

"I have an old diary."

"How old?"

"Colonial. Pre-south lake. I found it hidden inside the stone foundation at Old Forge."

"Are you kidding me?"

Tom dug into his pocket and removed the star buttons. "I found these with it. I think the forge operator made them."

Zytko took one and rolled it over his open palm. His eyes went wide. "Man, this is good stuff."

"Is it enough to save Old Forge?"

"You can create a state park with material like this."

"Do you think so?"

"I can write a book about it, if I can prove its value."

Tom savored the notion of grasping his dream. He might harvest his own bit of magic, saving Cranfield Lakes by cunning and luck. What would Cranlakers do with him then? It was too strange to imagine, too askew from the past to fathom. He pitched the fantasy aside to stay focused.

The sky looked black and lifeless against the garish veneers of the giant boardwalk casinos. A dozen people marched up the sidewalk, gripping signs, talking furiously among themselves.

"There's my connection," Zytko said. "I want to discuss this later. I want to see that diary."

"You've got it."

Zytko joined the marchers and pointed toward a turn-of-the-century building that had somehow escaped the wrecking ball. In the last three decades, the slums of Atlantic City had been refashioned into a thriving enterprise and political heresy rolled into one—a virtual money machine and the broken promise of salvation for the poor. The old building that Zytko's group approached no longer made sense in the modern resort town, until Tom read the polished bronze header above the door: TERRAPIN ASSOCIATES.

Tom called to Zytko. "Should I wait here?"

"Come along," Zytko said. "Watch and learn."

They penetrated the front foyer. It was polished granite with brass inlays. Scalloped sconces fanned the walls, splaying fingers of light toward the vaulted ceiling. The building was a showpiece. It reminded Tom of a rich man who wore antique golf clothes or drove a classic car. He did it because he could afford the luxury and for no other reason than you couldn't—three-dimensional arrogance.

Zytko's crew quickly located the basement meeting room. A hearing was in progress, and a pack of city officials and business partners ran the agenda from the dais. Zytko whispered a few names in Tom's ear: the mayor, the freeholder, Terrapin brother Sal, Terrapin brother Frank—the leaders of the Terrapin patriarchy. The heavy hitters up front outnumbered the people in the audience.

That was until Zytko's crew began filling up the seats. They openly spoke among themselves, and the screech of metal chairs on the floor upset the calm. Some held signs with catchy slogans above their heads.

DON'T MAKE PIECES OF
THE MAKEPEACE RESERVE.

SAVE THE TREES. SAVE THE CHILDREN.
SAVE THE FUTURE!

Tom took a seat to the side, keeping his distance from the others.

A young woman, dressed in black like Zytko, stood up once and shouted. "Stop the construction now! Don't make pieces of the Makepeace Reservation."

The mayor simply ignored the comment and pressed on, passing the microphone to the next speaker.

Zytko folded his arms across his chest, his hat tilting forward. He showed a bit of his teeth. He looked like the man at a poker game who held a tentative hand.

A television camera from the local news appeared on the stairs. Tom recognized the bullet logo on the side of the shoulder video camera. He glanced at Zytko. The renowned author and naturalist released his arms from his chest and prepared to go on with the camera lights.

"This is an illegal proceeding!" Zytko shouted, aiming his fingers at the designer-suited Terrapins.

A man at the podium was discussing a slide presentation on the Makepeace construction proposal. Two colorful pie charts with sketchy numbers displayed side by side. He tried to ignore the disruption but lost his corridor of thought. He put down his pointer and combed his bangs aside with a swipe of his hand. "Excuse me."

Zytko took to his feet, the camera fixing on him. "You can't hold a public hearing on private property and without due notice."

The man shuffled through his notes. "As I was saying…"

"This is an illegal proceeding!"

The speaker had a reserved voice, perfect for board-rooms and status quo accounting. He couldn't match Zytko's intensity even with the microphone cranked up. "This is only a discussion of the environmental impact report."

"And who executed this report?"

"There will be time for Q & A when…"

"Terrapin Incorporated. That's who funded it." Zytko turned toward the camera. "I find that more than a simple conflict of interest. Don't you?"

The man shuffled through his papers again, as if he'd prepared answers ahead of time and searched for the right response. He spanned the crowd. "That's not entirely…"

"I have my own impact study." Zytko produced a heavy document from his leather case. "I'd like to make it a matter of record."

"Alright now. You can't just waltz in here and…"

"You're saying I'm not invited to this public hearing."

"I'm not saying that. I'm…"

"This hearing is a sham."

"Mr. Whoever you are, there's no need to…"

A police officer had been seated at the back of the stage. He was already on his feet. He started to the podium but decided to cut a path for Zytko.

"I don't think I need to introduce myself," Zytko said.

He didn't. Several men on stage were already frowning. They started mumbling among themselves. The man at the podium looked like he wanted to wrap up his part and leave.

"This stinks!" Zytko produced two large glass vials from his vest and hurled them forward. They smashed, leaving with subtle yellow streaks on the dais.

People leapt from their seats. They paused for an anxious moment, waiting for something big to happen—a burst of flame or puff of toxic gas, but the substance appeared harmless, if not a shade pleasing, like the happy sunglow dashes from Matisse's paintbrush.

Then the smell hit them.

At first it resembled rotten eggs, until it changed into the most awful odor that Tom had ever encountered. Three years ago, he'd discovered a dead bear near Gold Ridge, and that was a pleasure next to this. This was a vapor of hideous proportions, a gaseous release from the bowels of hell, a stink bomb coup de grace.

People clutched their faces and scrambled for the door. A woman held a file folder to her nose. The man behind her yanked the toupee from his head and covered his mouth. No one beside Zytko had seen this coming. His crew joined the exodus, shoveling chairs aside, gasping for fresh air. They jammed the basement exits, gagging and coughing.

Six police officers parted the fleeing crowd, forcing their way down against the rush. It was as if Zytko scripted their entrance along with the television cameras—too coincidental for Tom. He guessed that no one watching the evening news might suspect that the big gears of the universe, as Zytko called them, included the gears that Zytko set in motion.

Tom clasped a handkerchief over his nose and mouth, fighting nausea and an overwhelming urge to sprint for fresh air. Elbows and knees jostled ahead of him, but he refused to feed into the panic that sometimes swept over perfectly sane people. Their eyes grew wider, even their facial pores seemed larger—expressions of burgeoning madness. Their hands reached for open space. Their heads now burrowing in the backs of others. Tom retained control by a hair of reason. Tears streamed down his cheeks. He let others pass.

The police had entered with confidence and muscle but reeled in disgust as the smell overwhelmed them. They hunched over and grit their teeth. One spit on the floor. If Tom hadn't felt so much like throwing up, he'd have found humor in the humbling transformation. One cop muttered, "Screw this," and joined the retreat.

The crowd pushed, each man for himself. The better part of humanity—the organized exodus you saw in Red Cross commercials—didn't exist here. Tom waited for the stairwell fiasco to thin, before traipsing upstairs with the cops.

Several police occupied the sidewalk, managing the basement refugees. The oldest required oxygen from the back of an ambulance. The rest were relieved to inhale the salt air and car exhaust wafting across the avenue.

Tom took solace in the open space. People gathered to watch. A reporter snapped pictures. A brown dog dragged a leash, dodging feet and ankles at every step. Tom tried to stamp on the trailing leash and snag the pup but missed.

Zytko was an easier catch. Two city officials pointed him out as he lectured his entourage near a mailbox. The cops immediately moved in for the arrest.

The master of mayhem turned his back and offered his wrists, like he'd done this before, another photo op. Tom wasn't sure if Zytko had even bristled at the sight of the handcuffs.

Two more squad cars arrived, and anxious cops hit the curb. Tom shuffled backward. He had his fill of this place— the noise, flashing lights, the monster casinos looming over- head. He didn't need a mini-riot to convince him that the countryside was the right place for him. He wanted to get home and clear his head. Beyond that, he had to start all over again with his colonial diary. Perhaps, Alicia would have another suggestion.

The cops led the protesters past Tom. Zytko walked with the first batch, spotting Tom by a row of parking meters. "What's your name again?"

"Thomas King."

"Right. Take my van back to Mary, will you?"

"Sure." It seemed like a fair swap to Tom.

"Tell her what happened. She'll know what to do." Zytko ducked inside the squad car, and the door shut tight. His larger than life profile disappeared behind tinted glass.

Tom lingered on the sidewalk but only for a second. He didn't want to be dragged into this mess. Thomas King— loner, part-time ranger, infamous Cranlaker—adeptly slipped into the assembling crowd.

The curb bustled with gawkers and gamblers searching for action, but Tom turned sideways and let the oncoming throng cut past. They seemed unaware of his presence, like the swift waters of Oyster Creek, barely creating a wake as they trailed around him. He'd spent a lifetime practicing the maneuver, being wherever people weren't. A long time ago, he used to search a crowd for people of a similar mind, but no more. Now he appreciated the solitude.

Tom saw an opening up ahead and Zytko's van with the keys in the ignition. With the nightlife of Atlantic City assembling for the impromptu street theater, Tom moved beyond their stares and huddled shoulders. He vanished altogether, his escape act perfected long ago.

Chapter Eight

Grateful

J ust after daybreak, mist pooled inside the disused production bogs, and lavender wisps of smoke burned off in the sunlight. Claire walked the unkempt trails, stifling her need to block the past with a morning nip of whiskey. It seemed as if nature was doing a pretty good job of erasing history on its own. The cranberry vines were gone and patches of wild grass assumed the flats. Spears of goldenrod grew beside bright orange postings from the State: CONDEMNED, SAMPLE SITE 3274-B. Those signs looked like headstones to Claire.

She used to explore the bogs during her lunch break, while the growers waited for the cranberries to assume peak color. She'd catch her father in his bluejean overalls, thumbing through the immature vines. He was one of the grateful ones. He'd accepted early retirement and bought a beachfront condo on the Delmarva Peninsula. Claire was grateful too, grateful that her father didn't have to witness the deterioration up close.

Her thoughts wandered into the mist. Should she leave Cranfield Lakes? Could she? If she accepted her father's invitation to relocate to the south, her children might never see their mother again. Moving away would make it that much harder for them to reconnect. She'd always been practical, but the notion of abandoning her post held a blade to her last thread of hope.

And it wasn't just her fears that edged her toward her most dreaded choice. When she closed her eyes at night, no matter how much whiskey filled her belly, she felt Geneva Bogdon pushing her away from town, sealing the deal like only Geneva knew how. Geneva wasn't a common gambler or even a bully. She stacked the odds against you. She'd built an army of resources and surrounded Claire, applying the pressure, slow yet certain.

When the sun hit the rim of the bogs, the Lady's Slipper orchids glistened like Tiffany glass. Claire pinched off the perfect flower heads and eased them into the sagging pocket of her old gardening smock. The last of the damp air eased her mind. The bogs were as much a part of her as her children. She examined the remaining petals for brown spots, even though she knew the killer fungus wouldn't take the violets. Still, it had taken everything else.

Gas-powered engines revved in the distant woods. Claire turned her head and followed the sound uphill. At first, she fancied the activity to be a promise of industry, but soon the noise resembled the hum of a mini-bike, and then it gave way to the crackle and swoosh of a falling tree.

She located the ridgeline that led to Old Forge. She pushed through the low weeds. Dried burrs clung to her bluejeans, and as she rose from the bogs to the historic place, the sound grew intense. Chainsaws whirled, biting and spitting fresh pulp. The tip of a tall cedar shook and disappeared below the tree line, snapping branches on its path to the ground. The crash vibrated beneath her feet.

Years back, Tom said something that had always stuck with her: "If someone was lucky enough to visit from another planet, they'd remember the unique trees wherever they went. It might be the only reason they'd return."

Fifty yards shy of the colonial ruins, Claire ducked behind a mature hickory. The scent of sawdust filled the air. It nearly made her sneeze. *They're cutting the trees at Old Forge.* It was almost make-believe, something that would never happen in real life. She was too shocked to shudder.

A series of low stumps surrounded the colonial ruins, like eyes peering up from the earth. Two men cleaned and sectioned the fallen trunks, while others loaded the back of a yellow dump truck. She didn't recognize their faces, except for Drew. He glanced in her direction while smoking a Newport.

Claire hurried into the woods. She left the trail and descended the ridge, with bounding steps. She stumbled on a boulder and rolled, regaining her feet without looking back. *He can't see my face.* She felt pale and exposed, like those tree cuts behind her.

The ridge ran to a short wooded cliff. She'd lost her bearing but knew she needed to reach the bottom to locate her car. The racket of Drew's heavy boots swelled in the background. He clumsily snapped the twigs and rustled the leaves. *It's him.* She almost smelled the menthol on his breath, that ghastly scent of close proximity.

She recalled the human pyramid from the high school squad. It'd stood three-girls tall on the hard parquet floor of the basketball court. She'd been the smallest and most athletic on the cheerleading squad. More than once, she leapt from the top.

Drew's blue satin police jacket flashed staccato views through the trunks, like a movie film run off its track. She pictured his stupid grin emerging into the clear.

Claire rushed the cliff and jumped. Her body sailed several feet across the open space, cold and weightless. For a second, she felt ghost-like, invulnerable. She spread her arms, lunging for the trees, but she'd jumped too hard and missed the first, slamming sideways into a mature oak.

Her face and shoulder scraped the bark. She almost bounced clear, before throwing her arm around the trunk, wrenching her shoulder socket. She started to drop but held fast. She gained control, metering her fall.

When her sneakers touched firmly on the ground, she still wasn't certain how she'd done it. Part of her didn't want to land so well. Part of her wanted to smash like a melon. Part of her wanted to choose how she paid for her mistakes, but brush burns covered the inside of her wrists, and she felt her thighs burning beneath her jeans. She glanced back at her descent. It looked higher from the bottom. An involuntary shiver snaked through her spine.

Drew appeared on the cliff. "Claire?"

Claire raced into the underbrush, allowing the briefest glimpse. Drew peered down and scanned the forest.

The huckleberry was fresh and easily bent aside for her. Blood tinged her mouth. She must have split her lip on the jump. She licked it clean, stomaching the salty taste. It was the taste of fear, something she knew well. Drew had introduced her to the finer points. Not even leaping off a cliff wrought the sensation so acute as when his temper alit her space.

Her breathing grew rapid, and she paused to fight the stabbing pain in her side. She leaned over, bracing her hands against her knees, regaining her strength.

Footsteps wove through the trees. She crawled into the deepest part of the shrubs. Drew approached faster than before, perhaps gaining her scent. She wasn't certain. He could track her almost anywhere.

She buried herself in the leaves and dried winter over-growth, but the crinkling noise alarmed her, and she stopped moving.

The footsteps came nearer. She laid still, low to the earth. Her heartbeat reflected off the ground.

Drew passed through her sights, taking the trail to the lowlands. Chainsaws buzzed on the ridge. They weren't supposed to be cutting trees, and she pleaded for Drew not to find her. She'd lie about it later, invent a story about how she saw nothing, thought nothing too. After a couple of drinks, she'd spin a tale his mother would believe.

The shrubs hung so low that only his boots showed. She lost him for a while, before spotting his scuffed boot tips near the outer huckleberry canes. It was pathetic to her that she'd become so intimate with the details of his shoes.

Claire prayed. She'd stopped praying awhile back but prayed for him to never find her. She prayed because she'd stopped believing God listened and needed to prove it over and over.

Chainsaws ripped through trees at Old Forge. She waited for him to continue downhill. Was he going to stand there all day and sniff the air? A cigarette butt dropped to the trail, and the boots moved from sight.

Minutes passed as she held her breath. Leaves shifted in the background. She whipped around and looked. Nothing. She eyed the low ground for his boots, hearing him snort in the background. *God, I'm done.*

Drew's big hands locked around her ankles. He dragged her, like a bag of bones, out of her makeshift lair and into the dappled sunlight. She dug her fingernails into the soft peat, grasping at the roots of a sassafras tree. Two shallow ruts trailed behind.

He flipped her over, like a felled deer. That's when she saw his face, his repulsive pleasure with his catch. Her feet dangled in the air. Her back wasn't even touching—only her head, chin folded to chest. Crushed flower petals tumbled from her smock and over her cheeks.

"Look what I found in the woods." Drew stood in his socks, his boots tied together and slung over his shoulder. His size thirteen feet stuck out like short white skis. "I learned something from that idiot friend of yours. You can't hear a man coming without shoes."

Claire still couldn't speak. She licked the blood from her lip. Her breath felt hot on her tongue. She tried swallowing, but her throat knotted shut.

"How'd you get down here so fast?" His right shoulder blocked the sun, forming a blinding halo, as if set aflame.

She squinted her eyes.

"What?" Drew shook her legs, like a man controlling a leash, expecting the animal to heel, but there was no fight left in her. If he wanted, he could rip her in two. "What did you see up there?"

"Nothing." Her voice sounded thin between gasps for air. Her chest heaved, as her neck and shoulders pressured the ground. A sharp stone bit into the back of her head.

"Are you following me?"

"No, I swear."

"This is none of your business. Do you hear me?"

He released her. Her tailbone punched the ground, and then her legs and heels, sending a shock wave throughout her body.

"I don't need you ruining my plans," he said. "Do you hear me?"

She was certain he'd deal his open palm across her face. There was no stopping him. It was so like Drew to bring the point home with everything he had. He argued that way. He fucked that way too. And to think she once believed his stamina worked in her favor.

"It's for the good of everyone. You'll see." He bent down and took a fistful of her smock and raised her up. The largest hole in the material tore even more.

Her chin fit in the palm of his other hand like a small stone. She wasn't sure if it was adrenaline coursing through her brain, but they'd both gone crazy for a diverse set of reasons, unable to control the least measure of themselves. She might ramble like a madwoman if he forced her to speak again.

"You know," he said. "You're the only one I ever let laugh at me."

Her eyes darted wildly, searching for the placement of his hands, the one he'd strike her with. She deserved it. *Dumb animals got punished.*

She flinched, as he reached to wipe away her tears. The rough tip of his finger gently limned the corner of her eye, and she flinched again.

"Don't worry your pretty face about the details," he said. "You'll appreciate this when it's all over. You'll see."

Chapter Nine

Missing Persons

This spring the catkins bloomed
before the snow entirely thawed.
I wonder if there is snow
on the Chesapeake.
I should never travel there.
I should never feel
your warm embrace again.

"I think I might be pregnant," Alicia said.

"What?" Tom replied.

"You know, when two people get together and make a child."

Alicia Hardaway had tracked Tom down in the nonfiction aisle. He was pondering a romantic passage from the colonial diary, when he looked up and saw Alicia coming around the stacks. He thought she wanted another go-around in the reference alcove, but as she closed in, he detected a lopsided look on her face, and her complexion was green, like she'd eaten a bad piece of cheese and needed to lie down.

"I might be expecting," she said.

Tom knew as much about pregnancy as any man who'd been suddenly thrust into the paternal arena. "How sure are you?"

"I'm a week late."

"Is that unusual?"

"You mean, statistically?"

"Should someone be picking out names?" He hadn't meant to be obtuse, but the word "we" seemed like a forward assumption. Was it his baby? Probably. What was he supposed to do? Alicia probably knew an answer or at least a good reference volume to recommend for him.

She touched his arm, a bold gesture this side of the medical archive door. "Don't worry."

A pair of teenaged girls squeezed past. They pinned their arms to their sides, nudging the bookshelves. Malone's volumes on Thomas Jefferson slid to the left, until the entire row collapsed like dominoes.

Alicia cleared her throat and glared at the kids.

They ducked their heads, and in a flurry of giggles and jangling jewelry, they disappeared behind the stacks.

She returned to Tom. "It'll be fine."

"Fine?" How will this be fine? A flat tire will be fine. A slightly burnt can of tomato soup will be fine, but a baby with a woman that he'd periodically screwed in the back of the library didn't fit neatly into the category of fine.

"I mean it," she said.

He held a thin volume on colonial customs. He slid it back on the shelf, careful to relocate its original slot.

Alicia withdrew her fingers. "Still trying to ID your mysterious horseshoe?"

Tom seized upon the change of subject. "I—I still believe Old Forge holds the answer."

"What do you know so far?"

"Everything there is to know about the place, which isn't much."

"What about the horseshoe? Have you shown it to Zytko?"

"That's another story."

"I've got the time."

Tom saw her probing gaze. She was still talking about the baby. The undercurrent ran clear. Everything was going to be different, but he refused to give in. She didn't even look pregnant.

"I thought I'd start by researching the colonial trades." His hand still clung to the bookshelf.

"There are better books in the children's section."

There she goes, he thought. She'd worked children back into the discussion. He glanced at her midsection, wondering what was going on in there. It was unreal.

"I don't expect an answer right away," she said. "A baby's a big deal."

"Yes."

"I wasn't going to tell you so soon, but I saw you coming through the door."

"I need a minute to digest this." He needed a week or two, perhaps a year.

"It had to happen one day."

"It did?" He watched her fidget beside the shelves. She wrung her hands, and her stump pivoted in the suction cup of her artificial leg. Up until tonight, a colonnade of books appeared the most comfortable place for her to stand.

"Maybe I should have asked you first," she said.

"About what?"

"I just assumed you didn't care."

This was a veiled question, but he couldn't resist asking one of his own. "Why did you think that?"

"I don't know." She twirled a finger through her hair. It looked spikier than usual but crushed on top, like a worn toothbrush. She saw him staring. "Do you like my hairdo?"

"What about it?"

"I did it myself."

"You've been busy, haven't you?"

Tom left the library, promising to phone Alicia to "chat," although they'd never established a time or reason why, planning instead a vague notion of a future appointment. He felt their spontaneity solidifying into predictable detail. The aspects that he cherished the most—her guarded privacy and reckless passion—had realigned into fearsome certainty on a nine-month schedule. He only hoped the baby didn't have her wild hair.

He drove through town, searching the lit windows and closed down shops. He of all people wanted a friendly face. Perhaps he'd spot Claire and force a chance encounter. He needed to spill his guts and let her crack her sharp wit over his problems. She'd make easy work of his situation. He had seen the way she handled Drew Spatt that night by the bogs and yet again by the lake. He overheard her with others in town—direct, plain talk in a time when no one wanted to deal with what was happening all around them.

At a quarter past ten, Tom spotted Claire's white Impala outside The Lazy Eye Bar. He got out by the curb. The neon beer signs flashed in the smoked-glass windows, and the faces at the bar reflected the gray light of the television.

He'd forgotten the last time he set foot in The Lazy. Should he stroll to the bar and pretend to see Claire across the way? And what kind of drink should he order? Claire sipped the hard spirits. He'd smelled it on her. That was too much for him to handle. Maybe The Lazy wasn't the best place.

The Richey twins barreled through the door, laughing, knocking elbows. Victor Richey, the cop everyone called Rick, shared an identical face with his brother Craig. They were difficult to tell apart, until one of them opened his mouth.

Craig was an unemployed bog worker, like many Cranlakers. He moved as if trudging through a flooded marsh, as if he carried a load in his pants and regretted shifting his legs.

"Geez, look at this, will ya?" Craig eyed Tom by the curb.

Rick wore bluejeans and his police uniform shirt. His unclipped badge bulged inside his breast pocket.

Craig stepped toward Tom.

"Alright, bro." Rick placed a hand on his brother's shoulder.

Craig shrugged it off. "If it ain't the child fucker."

Tom leaned back against his truck and folded his arms across his chest. He wondered what Craig might say about Alicia Hardaway. A child molester wouldn't have the courage to touch a woman like her. Alicia might take a dull man like Craig and crush him with sarcasm.

"You're not going to find what you need here." Craig was wet-breathed, proud of his witlessness.

Tom followed the cracks in the sidewalk. The twins owned little in common beyond their looks. Rick hung back, wiping his nose with a handkerchief. He let his brother run off at the mouth. Even as kids, he let Craig go loose before coming to his rescue. Rick was quiet and sensible. He followed orders. Craig was loud and hard to control. He sounded drunk, even when he wasn't.

"Schools out 'til Monday." Craig looked as if he might stick his thumbs in his ears and wiggle his fingers.

Tom waited for Craig to waddle off. This was the new level of noise that greeted Tom in town. He'd done his best to avoid it, but now he thought about Alicia's baby. No one must ever know the truth. The child couldn't bear the weight of the abuse, because of a father accused of the most hideous of crimes.

"Waitin' for the little girls to come by?" Craig asked. "Or is it little boys that you like?"

"Let's take a walk, bro," Rick said.

"Got your eyes on someone special?" Craig asked.

Tom pulled himself away from the side of his truck, until his back was straight and his boots firmly touched the sidewalk. He looked Craig dead in the eye, something Cranlakers weren't used to seeing. "Are you tired?"

"Huh?" Craig wobbled to the left.

"Are you tired?"

"Say what?"

"Are you tired of being so stupid?"

Once Craig got over being stunned, which was longer than it took to scramble an egg, he was insulted, and then considered being angry. The changes rolled through his eyes, like the wheels of a slot machine, odd notions searching for a match. Tom could have turned Craig's jacket inside out, waiting for Craig to decide how to react.

Rick returned his hand to Craig's shoulder. "Bro?"

"Wait." Craig looked Tom over, like a hard to figure piece of art.

"Let's get in the car," Rick said.

"Hmmm."

Tom had taken away Craig's words—a pleasure in its own right—but he reveled in the notion of defending the future honor of Alicia's baby, even though he prayed the child didn't really exist.

Tom's truck engine was warm. He heard the old metal contracting beneath the hood. The beer signs cast an orange glow over everything. He watched the twins amble away, before he got back into his truck.

He drove through town. Main Street appeared the most defeated at the south end. A For Sale sign at the gas station flapped on its post, and old weeds strangled the shrubs outside the abandoned bank building. The flower shop was shutdown, and newspaper covered the glass front. He hadn't heard about that one going under. Hardly anything remained on the south end, as if the killer fungus from the bogs had crept out and ate the town from the edges.

The forest outside of town appeared black beneath the new moon, and the road ahead vanished into the trees. Tom flicked on his high beams, and a glimmer of white flashed inside the bus stop alcove.

Claire lay on the metal bench. Her stocking foot jutted from behind the plexiglass alcove. A pair of sneakers scattered on the walk.

He pulled beside the alcove and got out. Claire was balled up in the corner like a sleeping cat, oblivious to the cool night and her own discomfort. No bus was due until 7:00 A.M. Anyway, it didn't look like she was taking a trip, other than into the recesses of her mind.

"Claire." He shook her arm a couple of times. She felt warm. Her pulse was steady. She exhaled warmly into the palm of his hands.

"Claire!" He shook harder and nudged her cheek with a finger. He couldn't leave her. It was getting chilly, and she didn't look dressed for the cooler evening ahead. Her arms were bare. Her sweater was off and bunched up between her legs.

She rolled over and faced the inner wall. "Go away."

"Don't sleep here." Tom saw headlights coming up from behind. He took off his woolen vest and tossed it over Claire's body, covering her head.

Rick paused his blue Toyota alongside his truck and called out the window. He spoke in elementary terms, as if Tom needed to be reminded. "You're blocking the bus stop."

Craig sat in the passenger's seat. The radio was tuned to a classic rock station in Philly, and Neil Young thrashed the night with discordant waves of guitar feedback. Craig's head bobbed back and forth.

"I'm okay." Tom said.

"You can't idle here all night."

"I'm sorry." Tom realized that they didn't see Claire over his truck. He stopped himself short of saying so.

"What are you doing?"

"Picking up garbage."

It was the only fact people knew about Tom for certain. Rick nodded. Craig shook his head and started drumming the dashboard with his hands.

Tom scooped Claire's sneakers from the ground. "I found these."

"Are you sure it's garbage?" Rick asked.

"Who leaves shoes at a bus stop? They probably chucked them out a car window."

"I guess. Why don't you dump them at JJ's?" Rick was referring to town hall. Everyone called it JJ's place, like they did for JJ's father and grandfather when they were stewards of better times.

"That's a good idea." Tom tossed them through the open window of his truck. He heard them crash into the peach basket full of empty cans and bottles.

"Keep up the good work," Rick said and drove off.

Tom slid his arms beneath Claire's back and legs and lifted her from the bench. Her hair and clothes smelled like smoke from The Lazy. She felt hot, yet very light. He expected an adult to weigh more.

She fit easily into the space beside the peach basket. He buckled the seatbelt across her waist, watching her tilt against the door. Her body was limp, as if the alcohol leached the rigidity from her bones.

"I'm taking you home, Claire."

"No!" She didn't open her eyes, tossing her head once to the side. "Let me sleep here, Drew."

"I'm Tom, Thomas King."

She stared at him, half dead to the world, no bearing on time or space. "What are you doing in Drew's car?"

"This isn't Drew's car. I'm taking you home."

"No, not there."

"Where to then?"

"Anywhere but there."

He feared he'd had this conversation before. He waited for a reply, but she passed out. He felt her pulse. Her breathing was sound and regular. She was bombed. He never imagined seeing her this far gone.

"You've got a problem," he whispered, knowing she didn't hear. He started driving, turning back into town. "You shouldn't be doing this to yourself."

When he approached Claire's house, it was almost 11:00 P.M. There was a lamp on in the hallway, and he cut his headlights and idled, waiting for signs of life. Should he leave her on the porch? Would anyone see him? He had enough trouble, without becoming a party to more questionable acts.

"Claire." He shook her arm. It felt like the limb of a fir tree. It was connected to the main trunk but easy to bend in any desired direction.

He let go and watched it flop onto the vinyl bench seat. "Come on, Claire. Wake up."

He listened to her snore. She wasn't very loud. It'd be funny any other time. "I guess I could drive you around until morning. What do you say?"

Her chest rose and fell. Her top two uniform buttons were undone, and he saw where her breasts disappeared into her bra. Her skirt was twisted around, and her thighs were well-shaped. She was untouchably beautiful, even as juiced up as someone's rotten uncle on a bender.

He fell into a spell, familiar to any man bewitched by a woman. He longed to harvest rewards for her and lay beside her. *What do you need to make things better? What treasure? What risk do I have to take?*

"Claire." He began talking freely, no stutter, no flush of embarrassment. "Do you want to sleep it off at my place?"

Claire swallowed. Her neck undulated with the motion.

"Okay Claire, if you want."

He drove outside town and into the woods. His cabin was fifteen minutes away, tucked in the Pitch Pines and ancient cedars. The last stretch was a dirt path, filled with rocks and sand. He took it slow, so she didn't knock against the truck door.

"Do you want a cup of coffee?" he asked. "Some toast or something?"

Claire's head rolled toward him as the truck pitched in a rut.

"What do you want?" He saw the shape of her eyelids, those fragile spheres from the night at the lake. "I know what you want. You've already told me. You want that wish of yours to come true."

Claire slept. Her hands drifted, palm-up across the seat.

"I'll make a deal with you," he said. "You stop drinking, and I'll help find your kids."

The truck climbed the ridge leading to his place. He watched his headlights bob in the trees. He slowed to a crawl.

"Pull over." Claire's voice emerged from the dead.

Tom was stunned. How long had she been listening? He immediately took inventory of what he'd said. He'd talked a mean streak all the way back from town.

"Pull over," Claire said, more insistent this time.

Tom hit the brakes, and the headlights ceased jumping.

She opened the door and braced against it, leaning outside the truck. Her body wrenched forward, her head disappearing between her shoulders. She sucked air between convulsions.

He heard her spit. The second time, Tom came across the seat, reached out, and rubbed her on the back. "It's okay."

After awhile, he withdrew his hand.

Her head came back into the truck. She breathed fast for a spell, before getting control of herself. "Sorry about that."

He pretended he hadn't heard her. He looked into the trees, which were awash in white light.

"Sorry," she said.

Before she could wipe her mouth with the back of her hand, he handed her a tissue. "I hardly noticed."

"How could you miss that, Tommy?"

He felt comfortable with her agitation. It put everything back in place, safe even.

She closed the door. "Where are we?"

"About a hundred yards from my cabin."

"Why?"

"It was going to be awhile before the bus arrived."

"What are you talking about?" A funny look came over her, like perhaps she knew.

"I thought you'd like sleeping in a warmer spot. We went to your house, but you weren't in the mood for that."

She covered her mouth with a hand.

Tom didn't know if she was nauseous or ashamed, but he understood the essence of being disoriented and the humiliating process of piecing together a recent event in hindsight, analyzing it until it made you soul sick. "I thought you'd like sleeping on a bench in my house instead."

"Oh God," she mumbled. "I'm so embarrassed."

"Why?"

"Don't be nice to me."

"You kind of agreed. We we're having a perfectly wonderful conversation."

"Stop it." Claire snorted, as laughter escaped beneath her fingers. "I'm so embarrassed."

"Don't worry. Nobody ever talks to me."

"It's the second time you've dragged me off the street."

"That's my job, cleaning up."

"Stop joking." She put both hands across her stomach. "I can imagine what you're thinking."

It felt sharply peculiar to Tom that anyone worried a lick about his opinion. "I was hoping that I didn't have to do this too often."

"Don't do it again," she said. "Just leave me next time."

"I won't do that. A friend wouldn't."

Claire straightened her uniform around her hips. Just moving her hands over her legs seemed like the greatest effort. She pulled her collar straight and brushed her hair to the side. "Where are we going?"

"My place."

"Yes, right."

"I didn't know what else to do. I was going to toss you into bed until you pulled it together."

"Your bed?"

"I—I was going to sleep on the couch."

She stared ahead, as if she hadn't heard his reply.

Tom listened to the engine idle. The eyes of an opossum reflected silver in the headlights, before it retreated into the brush. The grimy smell of truck exhaust mixed with the pines bleeding sap in springtime.

"Let's do it," she said. "But I'll take the couch. I'm not putting you out."

Tom slapped the truck into gear and granted her request.

Chapter Ten

Human Nature up Close

They spent an hour talking on Tom's couch, perhaps longer. Time passed faster than he realized. Claire complained a ton about Geneva Bogdan, and Tom fed Claire water and Saltines, watching the color return to her face, hearing the richness seep back into her voice. No lights were lit, except for the twisting flames inside his stone fireplace. Perhaps the fire wasn't necessary, but Claire looked like she needed warming up. The mortar joints in the log walls caught the reflection, and silver dashes twinkled about them, as if suspended in air.

Claire's eyes drew to slits. She leaned across the couch and set her hand upon his knee. "I'm keeping you up. Go to bed, Tommy."

It was the second time she'd called him by that name, the nickname his mother had used. The mere mention of it in this place—the cabin retreat his parents had built after the war—reached back toward memories that Tom reserved only for private moments. His mother had been his advocate, his protector and savior. She begged the principals in school to pass him from grade to grade. She pulled the older kids off of his back in the street. She taught him to smile, because "smiling people get helped first." She was forty-five when he was born, and he was beginning to believe that her early century ideals had died along with her.

Tom glanced up to the mantelpiece. In a gold-flaked picture frame, she watched over the main room. He sometimes thought of her, whenever he sloughed off a harsh remark or pulled himself up from defeat. She'd taught him to move past those indignities with a certain amount of grace, although he never felt particularly graceful or magnanimous. He felt bitterness residing in his darkest heart, but he never let it get the best of him. And he always had the cabin and the woods. He'd been offering his confessions to the pines since childhood. He couldn't ask for too much more out of life.

Tom pulled his mother's hand-sewn afghan from the chair and tossed it on one end of the couch. "Good night, Claire."

She pulled it over her legs and gathered up her limbs like she did in the bus stop alcove.

Tom lay in bed, reviewing bits and pieces of the evening. It was odd that Claire had made him think of his mother. They couldn't have been more different, but Claire was a mother herself. Perhaps all mothers shared a common thread of dignity and a hope for survival. When tragedy struck, they shielded their children, made the sacrifice look effortless.

But where was Claire's common ground with her mother-in-law? Claire swore that Geneva Bogdan knew the whereabouts of her kids. She told Tom about the time Geneva had snuck into the house, snatched the kids' favorite toys, and denied it later. What compelled one mother to operate against another? Claire had also told Tom about the incident with Geneva at the motel and a few other times when Geneva delivered veiled threats. Tom had never witnessed Geneva being this cunning or callous, but Claire choked up every time she uttered the woman's name. Tom couldn't tell if Claire was angry or sad.

The firelight played fingers of light on the ceiling. No, Tom thought, Claire had to be telling the truth. His tolerance for misdeeds was diminishing with the flames in the next room. He thought he'd taken enough from the locals, but Claire's stories of Geneva scraped the depth of his patience, finally found a bottom to it. There was a limit to what one person could bear, and Claire—feisty, unflappable Claire—was losing her teeth to fight back.

Tom sunk into an uneasy sleep, his mind roving over the mottled piles of trash in his front yard. He pieced together visual clues, concocting plans no one else had the inclination or time to conceive. He kept returning to Geneva Bodgan, the woman who caused such pain for Claire. Intolerance was a new emotion for Tom to experience at full force, and he tried to pocket it away, but it kept surfacing, finding fault and reason to exist. In regard to his own affairs, he had always kept a positive attitude and waited for unexpected fires to burn themselves out, but Claire was curled up on his couch, damaged, bleeding from wounds he didn't fully understand. Tom plotted a course toward Geneva Bogdan, determined to unearth whatever she knew.

Rays of sunlight reached across Tom's bedroom, waking him from sleep like a warm breeze brushing his face. The cracks in the old paint on the windowpane resembled the patches of dried mud beside Cedar Creek in August. He was still in his jeans and shirt. He lay on his back, hands folded across his chest like a corpse positioned for viewing.

He rose, washed up, and walked into the main room.

Claire slept on one side of the couch, beneath the afghan. The earthy yarn colors bunched at her waist.

A single log spit and crackled in the fireplace. He added two more from the wood box.

He set one plate and a knife at the table. He put out a loaf of rye bread, peanut butter, an orange, a banana, a box of raisins, cornflakes, a bowl, spoon, and glass. He had no idea if she ate breakfast or what she liked. He wasn't hungry this early. She looked like she didn't eat much. The shirt clung to her upper body, and as she slept and breathed, her ribs resembled the delicate spines of a wicker cage.

He glanced at the arrangement of food and then back toward Claire. The sun crested the ridge, first pink, red, and finally bright orange. He grabbed his woolen vest and drove toward Cranfield Lakes.

The window vent was open, and clean air sifted into the truck cabin. To dislike the Pine Barrens on Sunday morning was to be so hateful that you abhorred even yourself. In snow, sleet, driving rain, the humid grasp of August, or the crisp slap of a February wind, the pines offered brilliant scenery. Every color was alive, arranged in a private view. The wildlife roamed without fear. If he lay in the road, another soul might not cross his path for hours. If he wanted to stretch his legs or remember the things he'd forgotten, Sunday morning was perfect.

Tom owned a Sunday ritual. He hiked to Old Forge and scoured the site for damage, but this morning he sized up a different sort of recovery mission. He parked outside the church on Decatur Street and waited for the service to end.

St. John's was a white clapboard church, delineated with the pithiness of a Norman Rockwell. An iron fence bound the ragged headstones of titled colonials. The fence was tired and twisted but bathed in black paint every few years to look new. Across the street, as a chorus of voices rattled the old church windows, Geneva Bogdan's Cadillac sat by the curb.

Tom had done work for Geneva, painting the rooms in her apartment building and cleaning the screens in spring. He used to paint her house on Sunday mornings while she visited church and the ladies' auxiliary club. She paid a fair price yet squeezed out extra favors after the deal was set, like cleaning the fireplace or hauling a load of wood. He didn't mind. A day's work was a day's work, even if the job went long. The money only changed hands from her to Kevin Stower, settling his grocery account.

On the radio, Patti Smith moaned 'Strange Messenger' on the weak cross-state signal, digging deep for a bit of history and a taste of something she'd never done. Tom followed her odd poetry.

When St. John's broke service, Geneva Bogdan appeared on the church steps with the last of the assembly. She wore an iris-colored topcoat with a large brass pin on the lapel that shone like armored plating. Black lace draped over her hair. She grabbed the handrail and peered straight ahead. Her steps were brisk and steady for a large woman, like someone who knew her place in the world.

Tom left his truck. The shadow from St. John's steeple painted a dark stripe in the street. He stepped through it and intercepted Geneva at her car. "Good morning, Mrs. Bogdan."

"Thomas?" The sun hit her fleshy cheeks. "Fancy meeting you here."

He glanced back at the church. People dropped into their cars or strolled the sidewalks. A short line formed inside the bakery down on Main Street. "I have business."

"So early? On Sunday?"

"I saw your car." He was no pro at orchestrating chance meetings. He'd tried it a couple of times recently and wound up with chance results. "I was looking for you."

"For me? I don't have work. And Sunday's no time…"

"It's not about work."

"What's the matter, Thomas? You don't look right."

He felt the wrinkle in his brow, a cramped muscle he couldn't relax. "I'm worried about Claire."

"She's a big girl." Geneva brought her keys to the door, slotting the lock as if needing to escape his presence.

"I've noticed a change," he said.

Her halo faded. She'd just left church, full of whatever it was they did in there, and with the mention of Claire, it drained into the gutters. "I hardly see her anymore."

"She's not well."

Geneva looked up at Tom. "I didn't know that you two spoke."

"I think she's in trouble." Tom shoved his hands in his pockets. "I think you can help."

"What are you trying to say?" She pulled the lace from her head and bunched it in her fingers.

"Claire needs to see her kids."

"What can I do?"

"Have you heard anything?"

"Why would I?"

"Can you reach Elliot?"

The crow's-feet beside her eyes clenched into fists. JJ's navy blue Chrysler cruised past, and the priest disappeared into St. John's arched doors.

"Claire needs your help," Tom said.

Geneva's mouth curled, like she'd finally gotten a joke from the day prior. She yanked open the car door. "Oh Thomas."

He looked away from her strange reaction and glanced across the driver's seat, where a greasy paper bag rested on the car floor. An empty pasta box and some torn plastic wrapping poked from the top. He'd recognize a bag of trash anywhere.

"Is this the best that she can do?" Geneva asked. "Sending you?"

He hunched his shoulders. "I didn't mean to offend you."

"Offend me? You couldn't do that."

"Can you help?"

She dropped inside the Caddy. The springs sank and creaked. She threw her legs beneath the column and gathered her hands into her lap. Her knees bulged beneath her coat.

Tom waited, glancing at the sky. Cumulous clouds drifted overhead like clumps of foam in the creek when the water ran low. He wondered if he should leave.

"What do you want from me?" Geneva asked.

"What do I want?"

"Yes, you." Her voice sounded as if it came from behind a locked door—no more airs, all blunt denial. "What do you want?"

"I want answers."

"Do you really?"

It seemed easy to Tom. Geneva either knew something or she didn't. People complicated situations by lying or simply not admitting what they knew. It happened all the time. As he traveled about town, he often heard people making up stories. He was the invisible man, privy to the sordid discontents of Cranlakers. He didn't try to listen, but why was it so hard to tell the truth or show a little compassion? It made him appreciate living alone in the woods, away from the woeful deceptions that passed for everyday conversation.

"I'm going to help you," Geneva said.

"Excuse me?"

"You want answers?"

"Definitely." He imagined Claire's expression when he delivered the goods. "I'd be appreciative."

"309 Main Street."

"309?"

"Go there." She shut the car door and turned over the engine.

He knocked on the car window, waiting for her to roll it down. "Is that all you can tell me?"

"Yes."

"What's at 309?"

"Everything you need to know."

Tom tried to picture the address. Town Hall was at 100 Main Street. He recalled the gold-stenciled letters in the glass above the door. The barbershop was at 210. But 309? It was near the shutdown flower shop. "Should I ask for someone in particular?"

She looked at him above the tinted glass window. Her eyes resembled the brass inlays in the foyer of Terrapin Associates, set and unyielding. "Why don't you ask a friend," she said with a smirk.

Her car moved away then and he mulled over her words. Who would he find at 309 Main? What might this person know about Claire's kids? For certain, there were secrets involved in this riddle.

St. John's stood on the corner of Decatur and Main. The placement had always struck Tom as odd, as if it shied away from town. The morning chill exited, as the sun warmed the clapboards. Tom took off his vest and tossed it through the open window of his truck.

He began walking the main drag. The Lazy Eye Bar wasn't far from the church. In fact, the steeple probably shaded the bar's flat asphalt roof at dawn. The bar's beer lights were dimmed, and the diamond-shaped windows in the front door were dark. Around the corner, the church organist practiced hymns. It occurred to Tom that these establishments alternated hours. If you timed it right, you might shift from one to the other without waiting for the doors to open.

As he passed the bakery, several people turned their heads. A girl with jelly smeared across her left cheek sucked the powdered sugar from her fingers. She stepped closer to the window, following Tom's progress. He smiled and moved past.

The clock tower rang nine times at town hall, scattering the turkey vultures perched nearby. The big birds circled and alit the green copper roofline again, thudding aloft like sacks of potatoes. Several gathered in a row. Their gnarly heads twitched and crooked, pondering the death of an animal unseen.

Kevin Stower swept the walk outside his grocery. Tom listened to the brush of the broom against the rough cement. Specks of glass glimmered upon a small crest of dirt at Kevin's feet.

"Morning." Kevin paused, anticipating his first business of the day. He watched Tom pass, surprised the loner wasn't stepping through for a sleeve of bread or wicks for his kerosene lamps. "Tom?"

"Morning," Tom replied.

"Where you off to?"

Tom glanced over his shoulder. "Business at 309 Main."

Kevin thought about it and propped his hands over the tip of the broom handle. "309?"

Tom nodded, waiting for a hint of his destination.

"What business?"

"Claire's kids."

"You sure you got the right address?"

"That's the address."

"Jesus."

Kevin returned to his broom, shaking his head.

Tom pressed onward. Kevin didn't know his mission.

Four boys played Indian ball where the road dipped in front of Volunteer Fire Company No. 1. The high curb and lack of parked cars supplied the perfect arena for a game where whacking a baseball was essential. Their voices echoed off the idle storefronts and homes, which lined the street like the stocked shelves in Stower's Grocery.

At first, the boys didn't notice Tom. He spotted the Garner boys and two friends. Jeff, about to roll the ball, stopped halfway through his delivery. Paul stood on a man-hole cover with a baseball bat. He'd been teasing Jeff but saw Tom and stopped talking.

The boys stared at Tom. He kept walking. He heard one of their mothers calling them off the street. He knew why and kept moving. He was supposed to be dangerous. Their fear didn't disturb him. He wasn't even aggressive enough to argue his own defense.

For most of his life, he expected nasty rumors to vanish by themselves. He'd seen a few come and go, by laying low and doing his best to not play into them, but now he felt he needed to create a change, pull himself up, and wrestle free of their taunts. He thanked Drew for lowering his station even more. He had nothing to lose now. He remembered Claire asleep on his couch. How fantastic was that? There was something to gain. He refused to put a name on it yet.

Tom reached 311 Main Street. It was the first in a trio of row homes thrown up during the last cranberry boom. He scanned the house numbers: 311, 313, 315, and then he realized that he'd walked past his destination.

He looked for 309 Main and saw the vacant lot where the movie theatre had been. He remembered when the place caught fire. The smoke rose to the ceiling of the sky, flattening and bending to the east. You could see it for twenty miles or more. Volunteer No. 1 fought the flames into the night. The papers claimed that some kids broke in and burned it by accident, although the arson was never proven. That was at least two years ago.

Geneva's sarcasm finally took hold of him. She had sent him on a wild goose chase. The empty lot at 309 resembled the cranberry bogs: scorched and overgrown. She couldn't have planned the desolation any better. He peered down the main drag. The boys were gone. Kevin disappeared into his store. A car drove past, but the passengers seemed unconcerned with Tom lingering beside a vacant lot. It fit his image—the punch line to a town-wide joke. No one really needed to hear the joke repeated. They'd heard it too many times, like a book that had been passed around town and finally returned with everyone's fingerprints decorating the cover.

Tom scanned the windows of the homes across the street, searching for a face, a grimace, a fearful glance away from the town cretin, but not even a dog drew witness. The turkey vultures flew off in search of a meatier feast. They already knew. It was as if all Cranlakers watched him from hiding places.

His shame rose with his anger, two embers of emotion igniting at once. Countless times, he'd shirked public mockery and resumed his day—a mere stubbed toe, quick to heal. But this morning, he held onto the hateful feeling, imagining the taunts of Cranlakers in private. They all ridiculed him. Every house added their twist to it. Kids who couldn't even tie their own shoelaces teased him, not even understanding why, just taking up the chant.

He stomped back to his truck. Their poison words bounced around his head, a wicked combination of insults that people had once whispered in passing or were likely thinking now. He heard them all, filling the blanks with the worst noise. It choked his hearing, crowded everything else from his mind. He wanted to spit back the insults at them. It's no doubt what people expected—to see his humiliation, to confirm their power over him. He latched onto the feeling, tasted it fully, really owned it this time. What was its name? It'd always been a part of him. Disapproval? Disrespect? No, it was utter disregard, like he'd never much mattered to anyone. He was a crumbled wrapper tossed on the roadside, not warranting attention, not worthy of the energy it took to bend over to pick it up. It lacked spirit, and you can't love what possessed no soul. You can't truly offend what was too dumb to comprehend your contempt.

The horizon lay dead ahead. In his picture-perfect imagination, he envisioned Cranfield Lakes catching fire. It fanned out from the vacant theater lot on Main Street, burning in all directions at once, until hope and fear no longer bore discussion and the facts were rendered simple.

Total loss made the most sense.

Move on. Remake yourself.

Chapter Eleven

New Tom Tales

C laire smelled smoke and opened her eyes. She stared at the wood beam ceiling, caught in the strange half-life of not knowing her orientation in the world. She shifted her body on the couch and the coarse weave of the afghan slid over her arms and onto the floor. In the stone fireplace, the last log smoldered, and fat fingers of smoke rose to the blackened chimney.

The drive to the cabin touched her memory like a hazy recollection of a more distant past. She had been sick. The acid aftertaste lingered in her throat. Her head throbbed and limbs ached. She dragged herself off the cushions in search of a glass of water and some aspirin.

She noticed the bedroom door ajar and spotted the foot of his bed. She crept toward it, seeing the blanket pulled tight over the mattress, a military dress-down in the sparsely appointed room. Only a blue chest of drawers scaled the corner.

No sound emanated from any part of the cabin. She was alone. She spotted a sweater on the doorknob and pulled it over her head. It hung loosely on her shoulders. The scent of the fire nestled in the heavy Irish weave. She gathered a bunch and pushed it to her nose.

Sunlight painted the main room in a vein-like pattern, which was wrought by the trees that sheltered the cabin. She scanned the interior. Two coats hung on pegs by the door: a puffy green down coat and a yellow rain slicker with a frayed edge. A shotgun leaned on the fireplace near the woodpile. Milk crates lined the walls with empty bottles, cans, and assorted wrappers. One crate held a suitcase bound with duct tape. Another gathered the parts to a radio and what appeared like a shattered television screen. Each crate showed a bright orange label with a simple identification number and writing scrawled in black marker. From a distance, the handwriting promised to be illegible.

She moved to the shelf, thumbing through racks of books on audiotape. Some were store bought; others home recorded. The same difficult handwriting climbed the edges of the cassettes. She pulled them down and deciphered titles like *The Iliad*, *Grapes of Wrath*, and *After the War*, and the poetry of Dickenson, Frost, and St. Millay.

Elliot owned many of these in hardcover. They'd lined the walls of the old house on Main Street but were ripped from the shelves on a humid August night, becoming voids in the house that Claire was soon to exit as well. It was as if the books had fled into the pines and reassembled at Tom's place as tapes. She fancied that notion, running her fingers over the plastic boxes. The breadth of his collection astounded her.

Claire glimpsed through the cabin window, seeing orange labels on a stack of old tires and a detached car bumper. A chair with the seat punched through had a label as well. What was Tom's madness with collecting trash? He'd harvested her from the streets too, like an abandoned piece of furniture. She almost expected to find an orange sticker slapped across her forehead. What might he scribble on her?

A black and white photo in a gold frame sat upon the mantelpiece. Claire pulled it down and examined the spry woman in a dress uniform and cap. It was a portrait of a military nurse, a standard headshot given to a new enlistee, Korean War if Claire had to guess. The woman looked vibrant, focused on duties that probably no longer existed. It took Claire awhile to identify the angular lines to her jaw and wide brown eyes. She knew a different version of Tom's mother—heavier, more mature—but recognized her features in Tom's face.

Claire hadn't known Mandy King very well. Like a lot of people, she'd always meant to set aside the time. Mandy worked at the local clinic. She gave Claire a flu shot in the fall, asked about her family, remembered everyone's name. Claire recalled seeing Mandy's job posted on the board outside town hall. Claire had missed the funeral. She hadn't even heard about it. It was one of those times where you felt like you'd done wrong and no one noticed, but not until her own mother passed away, did she sense the whole truth of it.

The table by the window was covered with an absurd amount of food. Claire giggled at the arrangement of fruits, breads, and spreads that filled one end, until she noticed the careful placement of the plate and silverware in front of the chair. Tom had folded a napkin in half. She bet he'd never do that for himself.

Claire rested Mandy's picture back on the mantel. Her sights drifted over the junk boxes and shelves of book cassettes again. A map of New Jersey hung beside a topographic chart of the Wharton Forest. A chessboard waited beside the couch, the pieces askew as a game paused in play.

Thomas King wasn't anyone that she knew. She knew the town flunky, a whipping boy for less interesting men. She had never fully believed the rumors, especially when she crossed his path in the woods and they shared the trail for a time. He was certainly no child molester, no threat of any kind. He was a quiet man, who might offer a comment about the trees or the squirrels nesting above. She found his observations to be detailed and a touch unusual, like he was deep inside a private conversation with himself. His words lingered with the opposite effect of the ugly gossip that she'd heard about him, and so she didn't know how to place the two images of Tom side by side. She had no reason to think him stupid, and she always felt safe around him, unlike the men who crowded her, who spoke to her breasts instead of her face, who had plans for her and didn't necessarily seek her approval. How dumb was she? She hadn't bothered to give Tom a proper chance, just because he didn't force her to see beyond the common perception of a benign fool and the town hermit.

She walked to the table and picked up a spoon and the jar of peanut butter. Even as she prayed others might give her a second chance, she promised to keep her eyes open and really listen to Tom, hopefully half as well as he listened to her.

Chapter Twelve

A Cabin by the Lake

Tom saw Claire seated in the old rocker on the porch. She was wearing his sweater and sipped from a chipped coffee mug, which he'd won at the final annual cranberry festival after landing three softballs atop a milking jug. The sight of her, as comfortable as any woman at home, cooled the anger that had blazed his path from town. He rolled his truck to a halt. The scene looked too good to spoil, but she needed to know about his meeting with Geneva, although she didn't need to hear the details.

The parking brake creaked, as he stuffed it to the floor. He got out and strode to the porch. He assembled his excuses for leaving her alone for half of the morning.

Claire didn't seem annoyed. She was turning the pages of Gray's Anatomy, one of the few books he kept in the house. She looked up toward him. "Did you know how complicated the foot is?"

He stopped short of the porch, unprepared for an anatomy quiz. He was dying to take his feet out of his shoes but worried it was somehow inappropriate, given the question.

She raised her mug. "There's coffee on that pitiful stove."

"It's battery electric. I meant to install propane. I haven't gotten to it yet."

"You could use an update or two around here. At least the shower works." Her hair was damp in places, and his mother's afghan covered her legs. A pair of his socks covered her little feet. The socks collapsed and bunched at her ankles, like rhinoceros skin.

"I redid the plumbing last year."

"I bet you're handy, too."

He stared again, wondering exactly what she meant.

"I guess you know how to do the repair work yourself," she said.

"It's not difficult. You have to be patient, deal with your mistakes and the ones other people left for you."

Claire pursed her lips as if he'd said something prophetic. "Are those all your tapes in there?"

"I didn't find them in the road, if that's what you mean? Well, I found one or two. People throw out good stuff occasionally."

"No, did you listen to them all?"

"Not all at once. It took a few years."

She laughed, although he hadn't meant to be funny. What had happened to her since he left? Last evening, she verged on tears, depressed. He didn't understand women. Each visit with Alicia Hardaway confirmed that point.

"I'm going to get coffee," he said.

She held out her mug. A tinge of blue stained her left cheek, all that remained of the bruise, but there seemed to be fresh marks, like scabs from abrasions on her wrists and arms and another fresh cut by her lip. "Can you fill me too? There should be enough in the pot."

Inside the cabin, he saw that she'd cleared the table. The food was put back, and the plate and flatware sat in the drain board beside the sink.

He returned with the coffee.

"Were you expecting guests for breakfast?" she asked.

"I didn't know what you liked." He felt a glint of embarrassment. Claire was cool and edgy. He should have let her fend for herself in the kitchen.

"You covered the bases." She sipped the black coffee and looked toward the clearing where the ridge dropped down to the lake. A bald eagle swept over the glimmering pockets in the blue water. "I've been watching the view all morning."

He nodded. "Watch as long as you'd like."

"You haven't kidnapped me then?"

Her remark put him on guard again.

"I'm just joking, Tom."

He noticed she didn't call him Tommy. Did she need to be drunk or had he really done something wrong?

"Thanks for last night."

"Okay." He found the horizon and the lake again. The eagle was nowhere in sight.

"You asked me to stop drinking."

"We don't have to discuss it."

"I don't want you to scrape me off the street anymore."

"I couldn't leave you."

"I don't want you to have a reason to do it again." She sipped her coffee with both hands around the mug. The book sank in her lap, forcing the blanket into the depression between her thighs. "What's with the garbage collection?"

"I told you."

"Told me what?"

"They're cases."

"Oh."

Tom saw that she'd forgotten. It was the booze. Stretches of time, their brief encounters on the street, might no longer reside in her brain, at least not the way they did in his. "It's trash people left behind, organized by case."

"What do you do with them?"

"I find the litterer and issue a fine."

"Have you ever found one?"

"All of the time. It's just details."

"Wow. What do they say?"

"They're surprised. A few are annoyed. Trash, I guess, is supposed to be overlooked. It's supposed to be forgotten."

He thought of Geneva again, but Claire was wearing half his clothes and more peaceful than he'd seen her in years. He let it slide and retreated inside the cabin to take off his boots.

Claire followed him. She folded the afghan and draped it over the couch. The big socks flopped off the ends of her feet, and she paused on each foot to tug them up her calves. "I hope you don't mind?"

"Help yourself to anything."

"You're so agreeable, Tom. That's why everyone takes advantage." She looked worried that she'd offended him.

He hung his vest on the peg by the door. "I mean it. Help yourself. I don't offer the same hospitality to everybody."

"Why do people keep cutting me slack?" she mumbled.

That was easy for Tom to answer. She was beautiful and deft at whatever she set her mind to, and for this innate talent, she'd been thrust high above everyone else. She possessed the right elements of guts and glory that kept Cranlakers' hopes alive. People never wanted to see her dragged through the mud, even if she was responsible for it.

"I don't know what you're talking about," Tom replied.

She sat on the couch and pulled off the socks, tucking her bare feet into her dusty white sneakers. Her stockings were balled in the pocket of her work apron. "I need a lift home."

"There's no rush."

"I've wasted enough of your time."

He grasped for the right words. A minute, a day with her was never a waste of time. Why couldn't he just say that? Fresh images appeared in his mind: Claire wandering inside his cabin, Claire relaxing on his porch, Claire comfortable enough to do as she pleased.

She walked to the door, stopping beside the crate with the colonial diary wrapped in plastic. "I was curious about the old book. You don't have many books in the house."

"I find listening to tapes more convenient."

"Oh, well, this one looks very old."

"It is."

"I didn't touch it."

"Go ahead." He watched her open the plastic, before he retrieved a pair of latex gloves from the first-aid kit. "You better use these."

"How old is this?"

"Colonial, I think."

"Did someone throw this away?"

"I found it at Old Forge. It was in the forge."

"Seriously?"

He nodded.

Claire opened the book and ran her latex-covered finger-tips near the large picture of the star. Tom assumed that Michael Nutley had drawn the star to match the buttons or vice versa. He watched her study the text.

The pages crackled as she creased the spine. Some-thing caught her eye, and she read for a minute before lifting a section of prose. "I am low in the shrubs, beyond the peat fires of the Batsto Forge. Today, they burned cured oak from the sheds, because the pine was wet from several days of rain and the pit would not produce iron. Is it their smoke I smell or that of my own forge on my clothes? You used to remind me, David. You washed my hands in the porcelain basin of your house, enclosed them in linen, kissed the groove where the fire scarred my palm."

She looked for Tom, who was only a step away. "Who's David?"

He wasn't paying attention, only riding the motion of her lips and the music leaving her throat. The diary never sounded so much like poetry. "Excuse me?"

"Have you shown this to anyone?"

He shook his head.

"Why not?"

"I'm not ready."

"Do you think it's important?"

"I think it's the diary of a Revolutionary War spy."

"You can't keep this to yourself."

"I won't."

"But you haven't let anyone know?"

"I need to figure out something first." Mostly he needed to know who to trust and how far to trust Claire. He believed in Claire, but her association with Drew Spatt made him nervous. He'd shown her too much already, although he'd squander all of his recovered booty to impress her. Knowing that made him feel somewhat helpless in her presence.

Claire closed the book. Her neck arched like the cranes on the lake before they took flight. "You have a lot going on, don't you?"

He wasn't about to speak and lay waste to the chance illusion. He straightened his back from leaning over the diary.

"Promise to let me know when you figure it out?" she asked.

"You'll be the first."

A puzzled look swept over her face. "You better get me home. I'm sure you have a lot of investigating to do."

He wanted to kiss her for being vulnerable but without having him suffer her trademark wit. He thought of the meadow dragonflies, which danced about his head in summertime. They were exciting to view up close yet sported a nasty bite. Still, he wouldn't mind being stung by her. In all of this, he realized that she no longer intimidated him.

He pulled away from her, figuring that was what she needed most. "I'll get my keys."

They drove the pickup, approaching the intersection of highway 623. The road was empty, too early in the season for the weekend shore hoards to begin ripping through town.

Tom saw a panel truck teetering in the drainage gully. Its rear tires slowly rotated, several inches off the ground. A mass of plump birds wandered in the intersection. They looked like pheasant or wild turkeys, but they circled and fussed without purpose, like any animal bred to be stupid.

"Chickens," Tom announced.

Claire hadn't noticed. Tom had just broached the subject of Geneva Bogdan, divulging his morning encounter. Claire's eyes remained glued to Tom. "What did Geneva say?"

Tom saw chickens escaping the rear of the panel truck. One bird lay beneath the rusty tailpipe. Its blood-smeared feathers were splayed like a crushed Indian headdress. "Chickens everywhere."

"What are you talking about?"

He pointed ahead. "A truck ran off the road."

"Oh my, God."

Tom stopped alongside the poultry truck. He reached behind the seat and yanked the canvas strap of his emergency bag. He rushed outside, slinging the large green sack onto his shoulder.

The smell of antifreeze and burning oil permeated the air. A red sedan was spun around, half into the trees. A tire trail hooked off the blacktop and into the sandy shoal of the road. The car had sideswiped the Pitch Pines, stripping the bark from several trunks. Fragments of glass and colored plastic scattered over the highway.

The truck driver thrust his door open like the hatch to a space capsule. Two flannel-clad arms propped the door ajar, as a bearded man emerged. He was bald and the crown of his skull cupped the sunlight, like a pan sifting water. He scanned the milling fowl and grunted at the disarray.

"Check the car." Claire was steps behind Tom, closing in on the truck. Her feet skipped atop the pavement with a familiar spring.

Tom dropped his emergency bag for Claire and turned for the sedan. He ducked below the tree branches.

A young woman sat behind the wheel, staring at the mat of pine needles that painted the windshield. Her face was flat with a sloping nose that hooked at the end. She wore an ecru dress with an open collar, which nearly matched the off-white airbag deployed on the steering column.

Tom yelled through the window. "Don't move."

The woman's eyes rolled toward him, leading her head with a slight tilt. She blinked softly, barely registering the notion of a voice beyond the glass. A red welt cut across her neck and chest, detailing the path where the seatbelt took hold when she stopped short of the windshield.

Tom yanked the handle, but the door opened just a few inches, before it bit into the collapsed front quarter panel. The hinges groaned and ceased.

"Hello?" He squeezed an arm inside, waving his hand in front of her eyes. He jostled her shoulder. "Are you okay?"

Her sights swung past him, never achieving focus. Her skin was flushed yet fading. She opened her mouth, but no words came.

He watched her lips. *She can't speak.* He noticed the unnatural stillness of her neck and chest. *No, she can't breathe.*

He sprinted for the crowbar beneath his truck seat.

Claire knelt on the pavement, rummaging through the emergency bag. She looked up and read his face. "Tom?"

He retrieved the crowbar, rushed back, and jammed it into the sedan door hinges. The steps for CPR raced through his mind, cartoon diagrams from the American Heart Association manual. He'd taken the course three times. He'd have to do it, here and now.

The woman's head listed. Her eyes crossed.

He leaned into the metal bar. The hook pressured his ribs, before the door popped and swung wide.

Her arm tumbled out the door. Her fingers grasped for open space.

He reached across her lap and released the seatbelt. He knew he wasn't supposed to move the victim but needed to get her flat on the ground. What were the rules for this? His brain gridlocked over the steps in the rescue manual. The words he'd memorized became a jumble of ancillary maneuvers, as if he'd forgotten the most important points.

She started to slide forward and out of the car. He grabbed hold of her body, and her dead weight surprised him. He strapped an arm around her shoulder. Sometimes a heart burst on impact, the arteries tearing away from a jolt that the human body was never built to withstand. He braced for her death, the passage of life slipping through his arms.

He broke into a sweat. His hand clamped against her wrist. A steady pulse pumped beneath her skin, surely slower than his own. She was alive.

The wind blew the pine needles from the windshield. The radiator hissed and gurgled. A crow screamed above the trees. Tom abandoned the logic that confounded his existence, and he took hold of his instincts. He pushed the woman forward and smacked his hand between her shoulders. A fat red candy shot from her mouth and stuck to the plastic air bag.

She inhaled a desperate gasp for air. Her warm breath brushed his forearm. Her eyelids broke open. Her face flushed, her spirit reversing direction.

An uncertain length of time passed before Tom propped her up in the seat. She did it mostly on her own, the power returning to her limbs.

She looked up at him, full of questions.

"You've been in an accident," Tom said.

"I couldn't…" She felt for her throat.

He glanced at the red candy clinging to the airbag.

Claire and the truck driver stood a few paces back, awed by the maneuver. Tom had performed magic, found the switch to restart life and flicked it up. He was certain he'd never repeat such luck.

They stepped closer. The truck driver pressed a disposable diaper to his bloody nose. Tom's emergency bag contained more than the typical road flares and bandages. He packed essentials, like diapers, water bottles, and candy bars. Visitors to his stretch of the woods regularly demonstrated that the need for a clean diaper or a couple of aspirin created the biggest emergencies. He was glad to see Claire put those things to use.

The driver's voice muffled beneath the plastic diaper, as a pastel line of teddy bears ran beneath his eyes. "She didn't stop."

The woman gently massaged her throat.

"Are you okay?" Tom asked.

"Yes," she said, in a raspy voice.

Claire opened a bottle of water from the canvas bag and handed it to the woman. "Try this."

The woman sipped, grateful for the attention.

Tom watched Claire. The accident victims were in surprising shape, but Claire still looked worried. She was hardly speaking, deep in thought. She stood up from the car and glanced down the highway, as if anticipating more trouble.

Her sights turned upon Tom. "What did Geneva say?"

The conversation fell back in line, as if the accident was merely a pause in their dialogue. He understood Claire's hardship with Geneva. He wanted to say so, but it didn't matter. "I don't think she wants to help."

"Of course not." Her tone rebutted his foolishness for approaching Geneva.

"I was only trying to help."

"Oh Tom, what did you do?"

Cackling birds assembled by the roadside, bobbing and strutting in a sort of poultry square dance.

The driver dropped the diaper from his nose. Blood stained his upper lip and beard. "Look at this, will you? I've got birds everywhere."

Tom diverted his attention to the sprawling fowl. He'd rather chase greased pigs than confront Claire's line of questioning. He knew what he'd done, from the moment he stood at the scorched lot of the movie theater on 309 Main

Street. He'd complicated Claire's dilemma by underestimating the depth of Geneva's resentment and her ability to act toward any end. He thought that was the stuff of Shakespeare and Greek tragedies, when in fact real people aimed their worst intentions at misplaced targets. He of all people should have expected that behavior.

"Stay with her." He walked away from the sedan and into the road.

A pair of white fryers pecked at the stones in the road shoulder. Tom grabbed for one, and it landed its pointed beak upon his index finger.

He shook his hand, checking for blood.

"Let me show ya." The truck driver snatched one by the legs, with an impossible move. "There ya go."

The bird wriggled and flapped upside down, until the driver tossed it in an open cage and set the latch. "Look at these birds. I'll never get them back in."

"Tom?" Claire tapped a foot on the ground. "What did Geneva say?"

The driver glanced at Claire and back at Tom. "This ain't about the car accident, is it?"

Tom reached for a speckled hen, and it dodged his grasp, scampering beneath the truck with two others.

"Thomas King." Claire demanded his attention in a way that both enticed and worried him. "You're stubborn, just like the rest of them."

"I was trying to help."

Claire glanced down the highway, rubbing her temples. "What did she say?"

"Nothing." Tom stood on the dotted line, deciding which chicken looked the easiest to trap. The birds watched him out of the corners of their beady little eyes.

"What?"

"She didn't say anything. She took me for stupid."

"We know that isn't the case." Claire left her post by the sedan. "You can't fight her. You shouldn't have tried."

He heard the strain in her voice. He'd wounded her, at the very least wrought disappointment. He didn't want to be like everyone else in her life, but maybe that was the way things went for her. Perhaps it all balanced out in the end. She'd been so blessed early on and lately damned in all quarters.

"Stay out of my concerns, Tom. It'll bring you nothing but trouble."

"Then leave them. Leave those troubles behind."

"What is it with you?" Her violet eyes drew him in. "I used to think you were dumb, but I see that you just won't go down easy."

He received it as a compliment. "Why can't you turn your back on the people that hurt you?"

"It's more complicated than that."

"Why?" He tried to ignore his enemies. He didn't need the people that didn't need him.

"It'd take too long to explain."

He waited for her answer. He'd wait long enough to catch every loose chicken on the highway and then some. He lunged for a fat gray bird but plucked a feather instead. The chicken glanced over its skinny shoulder, squawking objections.

Tom faced Claire again. "What can I do?"

"I wish you'd asked that before talking to Geneva." Claire's focus changed. She glanced down the lonely sun-bleached road that slashed the Wharton forest like a surgeon's mark. She covered her eyes for a moment.

"Geneva can't hurt you," Tom said.

"She can. So can others."

"I don't understand."

"You've got your own problems, if you haven't noticed."

"What are you saying?"

Claire wrought emotions from a place he didn't fully understand. She grew spiteful, peppering him with a harsh tone. It was the thing he liked least about her—how she turned to defend herself even when it wasn't necessary. No, she hadn't always been like that either.

"You know that historic site you're trying to save?" she said.

"What about it?"

"You obviously haven't seen it lately."

"Not in a week or so."

"It isn't going to be around much longer."

"What do you mean?"

"You didn't hear it from me, okay?"

Claire retreated to the sedan. The woman had thrown her legs outside, preparing to rise.

Tom waited for an explanation. A van approached on the horizon, about a half mile off. He glanced at Claire, but she was helping the woman stand, trying to avoid Tom's eyes.

The noise of the van grew. The tires hummed on the pavement. Tom raised his arms and waved for it to stop.

Chapter Thirteen

The Piney vs. Civilization

Tom smelled sawdust and bits of chewed up bark, before he reached the plateau at Old Forge. The scent of pine, oak, and cedar wafted over the ridge, like the pungent draft from a woodshop. His fear quickened his steps, and he sprinted the last few yards, until his eyes met the destruction.

The house sat in the sudden clearing, exposed as never before during its prolonged life. It tilted to the east, or was it the gentle slope that lent this appearance? He hardly recognized the place awash in sunlight. A section of roof was exposed, and a spiteful chainsaw gash opened the southern wall. The remaining windowpanes looked as frail as a spider's web, waiting for the next passerby to knock them into dust and oblivion.

He lost the trail, stumbling on a fresh stump. The geography of Old Forge was amuck. Boards from the outhouse lay tossed in a heap. The campfire ring—ash and stone alike—was smeared in a black stain across the dry pine needles and trodden ferns. Someone had scathed the woods, sparing the bulk of the house out of pity or sheer luck.

Tom stood on the edge of his dream to save Cranfield Lakes. It teetered above the abyss that swallowed up a man's best ideas as if they'd never been conceived. His jaw fell slack, but he didn't speak or stutter. There were no words to assuage the loss. This gross act—clear-cutting a sanctuary to generations of people—was proof again of the insanity that had befallen the region.

Out of the woods, up into commercial suburbia of central New Jersey, Tom merged his truck onto US 1, the mother of paved highways. He felt the life being sucked from the landscape, not unlike the hatchet job at Old Forge. Pollution-strangled trees and mealy patches of grass withered beside the road, amid enough trace garbage to keep him busy for years. Visitors to the Pine Barrens referred to this as "civilization" and called out for it when tired and sweaty or harassed by swamp gnats. But to Tom's thinking, their civilization had no soul. He saw the future of Cranfield Lakes whip past his truck windows in concrete and steel synthesis. He envisioned Old Forge twenty years down the line, when JJ's gift shop turned dingy brown and Drew Spatt's miniature golf course assumed the character of faded indoor-outdoor carpet, haunted by battered replicas of gargoyles and national monuments.

Tom searched along a desperate stretch of commerce—the most oil-soaked blacktop on the highway, littered with shattered glass, crushed cigarette butts, and other human discards. Living in the woods, he felt the temperament of the environment, a tepid balance between man and nature. The landscape on US 1 looked mortified, angry, and the worst of it mirrored his soul.

But it wasn't just the long trip or the crowded highway that unsettled him. Too many things had occurred that day to process all at once. He recalled the girl in the red sedan, Geneva's vicious prank in town, and again, the mess at Old Forge. Everything was seasoned with visions of Claire—her distant stare, her confidence of language, that spunk—as if she'd experienced his entire day beside him and knew how to put it into words. Dozens of times, he'd fantasized about this, but today they had walked together and spoken together, or was that going too far? They'd shared more than just time and space. He amused her. He confused and irritated her too, but Claire in any state of mind made everything more palatable.

In Lawrenceville, he parked his truck outside a strip mall with angular front glass. The sign on the roof read: Princeton Contemporary Electronics. Fluorescent lights shed a beige glow over the rows of budget equipment and hi-tech displays.

In the spirit of Stan Zytko, Tom planned to arm himself with communications equipment to battle for the future. Zytko owned it all: satellite dishes, short wave radios, and beepers. He was "wired," like the teenagers loitering in front of Stower's Grocery often said. If Tom owned a cell phone, he'd call for help, summoning news people or the State EPA. He hadn't worked out the details, hadn't assembled his contact list, but getting the phone was the first step. He needed to reach beyond Cranfield Lakes. It was pretty clear that the town lay vulnerable to its favorite sons, Drew and JJ, neither of whom had cornered the market on inspired concepts. He paused on that thought. People would be surprised to learn that he gathered opinions about them as well.

Inside, Tom studied the cell phones behind the counter. He understood the basics of modern technology. He'd forced himself to be functional with the library computers. He tackled the Internet, too. Wading through a dozen pages of information was no longer a Sisyphean event. He'd learned to work the high-speed tape duplicators in the annex or just about any piece of electronics after toying with it long enough, but as he stared at the cell phone options through the glass, the awesome variety stymied him. Why did anyone need a fire engine red or Bahamas blue phone? He needed the strongest type, with a long range. He hoped it wasn't the action green one with the neon yellow whipcord antenna. That would frighten the deer back at the cabin. The flashing purple keypad alone might petrify several Cranlakers after dark.

"Excuse me." Tom called to the woman behind the counter. The store was busy for late Sunday afternoon, at least more than Tom had anticipated. The only free salesperson fought to ignore him. She slowly stirred her styrofoam coffee cup with a wooden swizzle stick, as if mixing a prescription medication.

He raised his voice, stretching out the word. "Hellooo?"

The woman committed eyesight to his position. She had hips the size of a garbage can, which matched her overall proportions. She wore an ankle length skirt of natural fibers and a plain white cotton shirt with amazingly austere embroidery on the collar. It was clean and somehow meant to be unassuming. Tom would later hear Claire refer to this look as "Princeton dowdy" or "frump" for short, sort of like Amish wear with color, but at the moment, he was distracted by the silk-screened cell phone in the shape of a blonde teen-aged girl pop star's head.

The saleswoman meandered to the counter. "Do you need assistance?"

"I'd like to purchase a cell phone."

"You?" she said, overbite like a pensive beaver.

Tom glanced backward. Was someone else near him? "It's for me."

"You don't look like the cell phone type."

"I'm not that cell phone type," he said, pointing at the phone with the orange polka dots. "At least I hope I don't have to be."

"Those are designer phones. They're very popular."

Tom didn't answer. *Sounds expensive.*

"I sell to celebrities," she said. "I deal with celebrities, you know."

He noticed the word "manager" on her gold nametag. It was the most ornate thing on her body.

"I don't typically work the floor," she admitted.

"Is there someone else that can help me?"

"I suppose I can."

"I want a basic cell phone. Do you have one of those?"

"Basic."

"Nothing fancy. Something that does the job."

"With a cell, you're talking size, plan, and then ultimately..." she lowered her voice. "... cost."

He feared the onset of the car salesman pitch, where she discussed the price he needed to pay rather than the type of purchase he wanted. He'd lived through that experience once and grew so frustrated that he walked out and stuck with the old Ford.

"What about size?" Tom asked. "Does size affect the strength of the phone?" He wondered if color affected it also.

"Even the little phones are full range." She picked up a slim flip phone with her chubby little hand and clipped it open. Her chin lifted in the air. "This one allows you to be discreet. Princetonians prefer discretion. It tucks away and causes only a slight bulge in the pocket."

In Tom's experience, these were the people who had cell phones ringing from difficult places on their bodies or personal baggage, making music that sounded better than the AM radio in his truck dashboard. He'd be giving trail directions to a hiker and notice them frantically digging into pockets or knapsacks, apologizing for the philharmonic interruption. "I want something that clips on my belt."

"As you like," she said dryly.

"Okay."

"Down the street at The Electric Discount Factory, there is a full line of industrial cell phones."

"Industrial?"

"Common cell phones."

"Common?"

"Working class cell phones. Basic. They are used to dealing with those clients."

Tom balked at her suggestion. Normally, he avoided a confrontation and would be on his way, but Geneva Bogdan had crimped his tolerance for snobbery and condescension. Sure, he might struggle to spell those big words, getting the letters jumbled and out of order, but he recognized those attitudes at thirty paces, and this woman was in his face.

"I want the silver and gray Motorola." He'd scanned the store's website before his trip. They seemed a whole lot friendlier online.

"Which Motorola?"

"The one that's on sale."

"The sale?"

"The one on the big poster in the front window."

"Ahh, yes. That one. I'll go look."

She disappeared quickly and returned with the exact phone that Tom requested. It took almost no time for her to set up the new number and complete the purchase, but Tom wasn't finished. He'd bought the right to better treatment. For thirty-two years, he'd paid the price. He suddenly understood the guy who went bonkers at the checkout line in McDonalds because his fries were cold, after years of waiting patiently with never so much as a sigh.

"You know, it says Princeton Electric on your sign."

"Princeton Modern Electronics." She spoke with the patience of teaching a three-year-old how to pronounce words.

"Whatever. You're not even in Princeton."

"Excuse me?" The sales lady to the stars peered over the brim of the cash register.

"You're in a strip mall in Lawrenceville on Route One."

"That is technically true."

"Princeton is miles from here."

"Well…"

"Do celebrities shop here?"

"Certainly they…"

"Just give me the phone, and let me out of here."

She over-bit her lip, chewing on a reply, but Tom shot her a look that told her to save it for the next customer.

A sharp and painful sensation passed through his mind, like a kidney stone in his brain. He snatched up the phone and pocketed his receipt, never bothering to look back.

I love you still.
That longing surrounds me,
and I hate myself for it
and this town for driving you south.
I will forge this hate, like the bog iron,
like your silver teapot gift to me.
It is the metal I smelt above the fire,
the buttons adorning my coat.
I will fashion my hate like their own,
let theirs come to me and work against them.
After the rebellion,
the British will level this town.
They have sworn to burn it,
and I will watch from the hill.
I will dance on the ridge above
and think of you.

Tom sat in his cabin, flipping through the diary. He'd come to know Nutley as a traitor-spy during the American Revolution. Nutley monitored the great stoves, like the foundry in Batso, logging the production of munitions into his diary, creating a ledger, exchanging local facts for British favors or supplies on the third day of the month. Some might think it drastic to become a turncoat, a secret Benedict Arnold, but Thomas King understood Nutley's motivations more than most. Tom had been spurned by the same town, albeit two hundred years later. There is a congenital flaw about a place that rejects what it cannot understand.

When he read the diary, Tom envisioned the jilted lover turned traitor who worked daily over the forge. Nutley smelted iron and silver, face aglow in the firelight, driving the hammer to the anvil, crafting metal into utilitarian form despite his fellowman.

The cell phone sat beside Tom on the couch. For nearly a day, he switched between the diary and the owners manual. The diary was easier to decipher, so he kept with it longer, nearly finishing the old book, taking notes in his own handwritten script. But learning to use the cell phone created another issue. The operating procedures seemed simple enough. He figured how to dial out and receive a call, although programming the speed dial gave him a migraine. He'd constructed a panic list—area newspapers, the park service, the EPA—anyone who might care about illegal tree clearing in the Wharton Forest, but it all seemed for naught if he couldn't plug the damn numbers into the phone. The manual claimed it was "easy" so many times that he considered stuffing it into a rabbit hole.

He plugged in another number and hoped for the best.

The line started ringing, and a woman answered in a metered tone. "Reference desk."

Tom sketched a picture of Alicia Hardaway in his mind. He saw the flat oval spot on the bridge of her nose, a lightning burst of a wrinkle on the left side of her mouth, and blonde hair mauled as if with sheep shears. "Alicia?"

"Yes."

"It's Tom."

"Tom who?"

"I bought a cell phone."

"Tom?" She sounded surprised enough to stumble off her prosthesis. "A cell phone?!"

"Yup."

"Welcome to the twenty-first century."

"I was just testing it out."

"I guess I can call you now."

Strangely enough, he hadn't considered receiving calls. Sure, the phone worked two ways. "It sounds good, don't you think?"

"While I have you on the line, let me ask you something."

"Go ahead."

"Have you thought about our conversation from the other night?"

"I guess."

"Do you want to say something?"

"I'm sorry I didn't get back to you sooner."

"It's no issue."

"I should've called or wrote." He almost said he should have sent a card but was glad he didn't. He never sent cards. How stupid would that be? Was there a section in the card store labeled: Congratulations, I've Knocked You Up?

"There's no rush," she said. "It's not going anywhere."

"I guess not."

"No, there's no guessing about it."

Her use of "it" meant that *it* really existed. *It* was a living thing between Alicia and him. *It* didn't have a sex yet. *It* didn't have a name either. That was another complicated issue. Whose name did *it* get?

"I've been very busy," he said.

"I understand."

"There was a car accident, and…"

"I heard you saved that woman's life."

He wondered what else she knew and who else knew about *it*. There'd be a period of shock and disbelief that he was responsible for *it*, then resignation over *it*, and the eventual malice leveled on him and *it*. He treaded lightly into this territory—the business of *it*. *It* was going to be a problem. *It* was going to require a lot of on the spot decisions. He wasn't good on the spot. Other people seemed to handle life by grace and moments. He didn't even know when or where the spot came up. "So, how's it going?"

"It?" she asked in her definitive way, where it meant only one thing.

"Yes, I suppose, and you. You and it. How are you both doing?"

"It's too early to tell, but I puked up a quart of Haagen Daz this morning."

"Is that normal?"

"I never eat ice cream for breakfast. I'm completely thrown off my routine."

"Should I bring you soup or something?"

"You have no idea what you're doing yet, do you?"

About *it*, he thought, or about everything else? He supposed the answer was the same. "No, I don't."

"Call me back when you get it together."

He sorely wished she'd selected a different word. He listened to her hang up without waiting for a reply. This is the conversation that divorced people had on television sitcoms. He'd run the entire gamut in only a few days: ex-girlfriend, mother of his child, future child support payments with strained discussions about discipline and schools. He'd gone from outcast to cliché in a single weekend. That was his style, skipping the easy parts.

He stared through the window and into the trees. The pine needles wavered in the breeze, gentle, hypnotic. He started thinking about how you could search the rings of a felled pine and see all the droughts and storms—a perfect record of the past. He recalled the stumps at Old Forge and their history cut short. He considered the rings of his own life, where they'd be thick and dark and full of angst, where the rings would be soft and blonde and no trouble at all.

When the cell phone started buzzing, Tom grabbed it expecting Alicia to pick up where she'd left off, but a man's voice came on the line.

"Stan?" Tom finally said. "Zytko?"

"The one and only." Zytko's energy resounded through the receiver.

"Are you with Alicia?"

"With who?"

"How'd you get my number?" Man, Tom thought, this guy really is wired. Tom only owned the phone for one day.

"You were unlisted, and I thought to check the cell directory." Zytko obviously didn't know that Tom never owned a phone before.

"Are you all right?"

"Why wouldn't I... You must be talking about the Atlantic City business."

"The last time I saw you..."

"Maybe the stink bomb was slightly over the top. Forget about that. I was out on the street before sunrise."

"How'd you manage that?"

"I didn't call for idle chit-chat. I had Mary check out your Nutley character. Old Forge's got a neat set of legends. Very sexy for a historian, but nothing verified."

"That's what I said. I mean, nothing verified."

"Unfortunately, Nutley doesn't raise a flag, and Mary's pretty good with research."

"You have to read his diary. It's compelling—Nutley, that is."

"I'd love to get my hands on it," Zytko said. "I've got a gut feeling about your colonial."

"Hey look, things have gotten more serious around here. They're cutting down trees at Old Forge and hauling them off."

"Who's cutting?"

"The locals. I haven't caught them doing it, although I've seen the mess. I'm keeping an eye on the place."

"It must be your amusement park geniuses."

"The state is supposed to send someone down from Trenton to investigate, but it's not a priority."

"Been there. Done that."

"They told me to call the cops, but the local cops are in on it. I'm afraid they're going to tear down the Nutley house next."

"So you're running out of time."

"Yes."

"Get me the diary. I can get a court injunction with the right information."

"What should I do about Old Forge in the meantime?"

"I'm on my way into a meeting. I'll give you the crash course on Zytkology."

"What's that?"

"Stop them before they get started, a preemptive strike."

"Like what?"

"Simple stuff: pour sugar in their chainsaws, flatten their tires. One thing they hate is to lose money on the deal. Oh baby, capitalists hate losing money. Make the deal cost more than it's worth."

Tom's presence outside of the woods drew a great deal of attention. He'd never pull off a clever stunt like that. "I don't know."

"Do you know where the trees went?" Zytko asked. "Do you know the people involved?"

"Not entirely. I guess they sold the trees."

"You guess?"

"I don't know. They're gone."

"Try calling the papers. That's simple enough."

"I'm working on that."

"What have you got?"

"There's a reporter in Voorhees who promised to call me back."

"Is that it?"

"I'm trying the others."

"Tell me. You're new to this game."

"I'm not in your league, Mr. Zytko. I've been a forest ranger my whole life. I do handiwork."

"Well, unless you're going to build a ten-foot barbed-wire fence around Old Forge, I'd start formulating a better plan."

"I need suggestions."

"There must be something you can do? Everyone has a skill."

Tom camped on that notion. The cleverest thing he did was find literers by sifting through their trash. "I investigate trash dumpings."

"That's good! What is that?"

"I can figure out who littered by researching their trash."

"You can do that?"

"I found a lot of people over the years."

"I never heard of that. You can really do that?"

"What do you think?"

"About what?"

174

"My skill."

Zytko paused for a second, a very long time for him. "It's useless. Unless they scattered Polaroids of themselves in the trash, I don't see how you can deploy your talents."

"Oh."

"Don't fold yet, kid. Think about it. An idea will come."

Tom wasn't so sure. He'd never beat the likes of Drew and JJ. They held all the cards—the law, the will of the town. They were going to level Old Forge.

"Make a plan," Zytko said. "And get me that diary, comprende?"

Chapter Fourteen

The Battle Blaster

Claire's possessions sat haphazardly on the sidewalk, unclaimed and unwanted, like the staples and sundries of a bag lady. Bulging cartons and stuffed plastic bags spilled over the curb. Her shirts and pants, most still on the hangers, draped over the couch that Elliot and she purchased on their honeymoon. Faye's stuffed animals mounded on the grass, and Ronald's baseball bat poked from a milk crate of pots and pans.

The sight braced her, although she barely flinched. She was used to holding still and pretending to be numb when she was sober, too. She imagined Geneva leering from an upstairs window, the old queen soaking up the pleasure of a grand misdeed. It probably cost Geneva only the price of a couple of teenagers to rummage through Claire's possessions and toss as much as possible to the curb before Claire returned home from work.

"Damn you!" Claire raised a fist to the silent house. "Go to hell."

The sun rode high in the evening, and a car slowed down, but once Claire turned and glared, it hit the gas and sped off.

She scanned the street, waiting for the next unfortunate passerby. She wanted a fight, a reason to unload her emotions, but no one stared or even paused long enough to notice. If they recognized her stuff piled on the curb, they kept their distance. She turned in tight circles around it, like a wasp buzzing the gutted innards of its nest.

"I can't believe this," she hissed, all but disbelieving the evidence. She kicked a cardboard carton, and a stream of pure white sugar crystals sifted into the dirt. The mess satisfied her initial urge to tear something open, but she still felt like mashing everything to rubble and walking away. Then Geneva might understand that the stuff didn't matter. *It's just metal, cardboard, cloth—plastic for shit's sake.* She was still standing.

The air was humid, and her cleaning uniform clung to her back. On the drive from her job at the Lakeside, she'd planned an evening in the big tub upstairs. She anticipated the soap bubbles touching her skin, both wet and cold, and the steaming water by her feet. She wanted to stick her toes in the running spout, while thumbing through a late edition of Robert Frost or Edna Saint Vincent Millay. Her big decision involved a bottle of Pinot Noir—whether to have a glass or not—but now she needed a place to sleep.

She rescued the kids' books from the damp lawn and laid them inside the Impala's generous trunk. The space was big enough to hide a body, and this notion guided her vitriolic thoughts. More than once she'd told Elliot, "I'm going to kill your mother," but did she really mean it? Murderers didn't make such proclamations ahead of time. It seemed preposterous, funny even, like something out of supermarket tabloid. "I'm going to rub her out," she'd sometimes said as well.

Claire took anew to the idea of Geneva's demise and paired it with her anger. How would she kill the bitch? With her bare hands? Drown her in the big footed tub upstairs? No, Geneva needed to die at the dinner table—that oak monstrosity in her dining room where she presided over the family with fat forkfuls of mashed potatoes and vegetables dripping in cream sauce. For shit's sake, she was clogging their arteries, cutting off their words so only she might speak. It was witches' work, and Claire needed to put an end to it.

Claire felt the tumbling waterfall of her life. Geneva had waited for the right moment to set Claire adrift and over the edge, and Claire's imagination ran the rapids of it. She slowly rounded the pile on the lawn, as if circling Geneva's dining room table. She checked the faces of Elliot and his reticent father. They suspected trouble brewing, wondering if her temper might finally burst, unwilling or unable to stop her. Their apathy was as good as a nod of approval. She caught Geneva from behind, grabbing fistfuls of hair, dunking the Basque queen's fat face into a cherry cheesecake. The woman's arms flailed, until the pulpy filling choked her lungs, and she fell limp, cake-faced and silent. *A perfect finish to a fine meal.* Claire pulled her up, resisting the urge to paint a smile in the goo that stuck to the old crow's face.

The basketball—the prop for Geneva's head—slipped from Claire's hands and bounced on the sidewalk, bringing her back to reality. Lately, she found herself daydreaming and with increasingly violent scenarios. *Shit, I need a drink.*

She started packing for real, piling the kids toys and clothes inside her car. She stuffed her own clothes in the backseat. The couch had to stay and the crappy glassware, too. She'd pawned the good china and flatware months ago at a yard sale in Medford to finish paying off the worthless detective in Philly. It felt liberating to leave things behind; all of the food, too. Cooking wasn't on her near-term agenda. Like a shiftless bum, she stowed only the things needed to bridge the gap to tomorrow.

Slipping behind the wheel, she digested the idea of abandoning the house in which her children were born.

Rooms, little compartments of memories locked up, like the new padlock on the front door, secure for now, to be re-opened one day when fate swung in a completely new direction. Another plan was taking shape. The kids will have to get used to someplace else.

Her goose down coat was balled up high and blocked the sightlines of the rearview mirror. She reached back, unable to pull it clear.

"Damn it, anyway." She wasn't using the rearview mirror. She swore against it. She was hitting the road toward someplace better, and as she tapped the gas pedal, part of the load shifted and dropped to the floor. The old Chevy's transmission rumbled beneath her feet. She felt like Tom Joad in *The Grapes of Wrath*, darn near busted and chasing a promise of who knows what.

"No, no, no." Raffi said. "Up front, or I take from your pay."

Claire stood in the tiny Lakeside front office, wavering on the scuffed linoleum. Raffi roamed behind the counter with the kicked-in front paneling and the sideways hanging calendar, but he was only a warm body to her, the guy who handed out measly paychecks. The smell of curry and a throbbing headache blinded her thinking. She needed a taste of whiskey. Wine no longer cut it, and the relentless desire knocked her from inside, like a carpenter testing the walls to see if they'd collapse. Claire wasn't so sure they'd stand.

"I need a couple of nights," she finally said.

"Credit card is fine. Cash is better."

Claire looked away from Raffi and his encroaching odor —a fog that she tasted, imagined she could see in the air. It caught in the curves of her throat. "I don't have a credit card."

"So, cash."

Claire spotted the girl in the background—a teenager with a thin neck and Raffi's cranberry fungus brown eyes. She looked uncomfortable in crisp bluejeans and a bright red T-shirt, like people did when they donned American clothes for the first time, as if they'd borrowed them from a stranger.

"I..." Claire rubbed her forehead with the butt of her hand, trying to massage away the pain.

"Cash, or I take from your pay."

She returned to Raffi. He guarded the desk, unmovable, challenging, ready to argue a penny into a nickel. What did it matter to her? She was gone after sunrise or perhaps the next. "Just give me the keys."

Raffi slid B-7 across the desk.

The girl fiddled with the stiff loops of her jeans, still not talking. Claire wondered if she really existed. Sometimes Claire talked to imaginary strangers, as she wandered home from the Lazy Eye. She knew they didn't really exist, but this was a night for crossing the line, believing in the unreal.

"Your dad's a prince," Claire said.

The girl stared. Black eyeliner contrasted the whiteness of her eyes in a way that made American girls look sluttish instead of exotic like this girl here.

"Do you speak English?" Claire asked, but it wasn't her real question. She wondered how the girl's life might unfurl in this dying town. Was it better to come here or remain in whatever forsaken and crowded place across the globe? Claire didn't have an answer for that. She was mostly glad she was leaving.

She snatched up the keys. "Take it from my pay. Take it all." She left, doubting she'd be around to collect her last check.

Sleep. Sleep was what she needed—glorious sleep, a self-imposed coma. If she closed her eyes, her pain lessened, suffused with images of happier times. Even a nightmare was better than her conscious state where all she gauged was her distance between drunken highs. She fell toward the mattress, anticipating a soft reception of sheets and pillows, but she bumped her head on something firm beneath the sheets.

She'd forgotten about the dildo. That afternoon, she'd discovered the eighteen-inch-long monstrosity sprawled beside the door. She'd pinched the rubbery skin tone device between her thumb and forefinger and dangled it in the air like recovered evidence from a crime scene. "This must be what killed her," she had announced in an official tone. She read the inscription on the veiny veneer: Flesh-Feel Battle Blaster, Erotix Corp, Illinois.

She'd dropped it in the garbage, but the can tipped over from the weight. The Battle Blaster refused to go down easy. It was two inches thick, forget about the bulbous head. What sort of woman needed a device that big? She probably grew tired of fighting the thing and tossed it aside, or maybe her partner surreptitiously sprung it on her that afternoon. "Hey honey, let's give big boy here a try."

Claire recalled carrying the Blaster from the bathroom and tucking it beneath the sheets, a gift for the next happy-go-lucky Lakeside matinee patron. People never complained at the Lakeside. That's why she re-hung old towels and skipped mopping the bathroom floor. They sheltered their faces from view, and if they crossed her path in the breeze-way, Claire never made eye contact. It was the perfect arrangement, where no person acknowledged the other, but now she wondered who in Cranfield Lakes deployed the Battle Blaster for recreation.

Thank God, Drew never tried that crap on her—or maybe he had and she'd avoided it. Sleeping with him was unmemorable. It wasn't that he was fast or ungenerous. She simply retained no memory of him. She was always drunk. She never kissed him before three cocktails; never allowed his hands on her before six. That's how she paced herself, like a schoolgirl stretching time with a groping boyfriend before curfew. She couldn't say if Drew made love well or what it felt like with his big chest over hers, or if he preferred that position. His weight seemed like too much to bear, yet she got through it. That's not the way you describe a lover, but she held the notion that he wasn't anywhere near Battle Blaster size, and that both surprised and relieved her.

In room B-7, the dildo lay on the carpet where she tossed it. The monstrosity had clicked on by accident, vibrating like an unmanned power tool. She knelt down and checked the tiny refrigerator beneath the bathroom sink. The Lakeside rooms no longer had mini-bars, but she opened the refrigerator just in case. She was supposed to check the contents each time that she cleaned but never did. This one held an expired orange, which resembled the lakeshore beach in color and texture more than it did fruit. She stared into the cold white box, grateful not even an open can of beer remained. She might have gulped it down without thinking. She'd done it before. That was when you knew you'd crossed the line, but she never realized it until she tried to resist it. She kicked her foot and sent the Blaster spiraling into the wall where it stopped humming.

Claire fell back again, this time on the rough carpet. The stucco ceiling swirled in maddening circles above her head, and in the corner of her eye, the dildo aimed at her temple like the needle of a compass.

What are you going to do? Sleep? Was that possible? How many days might she stay in this position, her left foot bent beneath her thigh, eyes wide open in the tepid darkness. She imagined Faye just home from the hospital, the curtains drawn, swaying in the rocker, little arms and legs curled upon her chest. She envisioned Faye's life: first steps, first words, leaving for school. None of this had plotted a course for the Lakeside Motel, not for Faye, not for Ronald, but here she was alone, a ghastly wrong turn determined beyond her control.

The air conditioner ceased, and the change ripped her from her trance. She snapped up to a seated position, as if someone was watching. A car passed in the rear lot and faded away.

Claire walked to her Impala outside the door and rifled through the boxes and scattered clothes for a bottle of whiskey, wine, or schnapps, even though she knew there was nothing. She might've made a mistake, left a bottle beneath the seat. Maybe Geneva's house-clearing crew tucked one in the garbage bags with her underwear. She tossed fistfuls of socks and shirts into the front, until she uncovered the hump in the floor. Her joints felt swollen, and the ache in her head grew sharp. It resonated throughout her body, guilt and shame made tangible, networking through every nerve. She put her hands over her face and buried it in her fluffy down coat.

After awhile, she came up for air. Sweat and hair clung to her temples. She returned to the room and stripped bare, kicking her uniform beneath the bureau. The air conditioner iced the beads of moisture in the well of her back, and she shivered.

She stepped into the shower. Hot water ran over her until the heat soaked through her skin. She fancied the colorful cleaning bottles in the locked maintenance closet at the end of the building. Many contained ethyl alcohol—the cheapest and deadliest of all of the boozer options.

"That's pretty desperate," she said, knowing her proximity to that solution. Was she still sweating or was it the hot water? She'd be far away from this dreadful motel soon. It was good she was doing this here, opening the vein, finally letting it go free.

"You've dug a deep hole for yourself," she said in the way people admit when they're alone, not even sure they want to hear it themselves. She imagined her father knowing. He'd rarely raised his voice with her. He never said a great deal unless he really meant it. That's what she liked about Tom. His words were few. They had impact.

She liked other things about Tom. He was handsome, not stunning but workable cute. There was boyishness in the way he glided around a room and double-backed over things. He was sincere, unlike Drew who flashed that little boy smile whenever he wanted something. She let him get away with it, but enough of Drew. She was thinking of Tom. He distracted her for the moment. She recalled being carried in his arms. "Anytime," he said. Why did it make her feel good? Was she starving for attention?

Before she realized it, she'd dropped the washcloth and was rubbing her chest with the soap. Her nipples were firm and red. She stopped and stared. The water rushed down between her legs and into the drain. The Battle Blaster crossed her mind. "Claire, you're going insane."

The shower turned cold. Claire stepped onto the mat and wrapped herself in the largest towel, the one she knew was clean. Her pores were open, receiving the clammy waft of the air conditioner. She kicked the dildo out of sight beneath the bureau with her uniform.

She lay down on the bed and clicked on the TV, but nothing caught her eye. She followed a report on Amazon natives but refused to stick with it once they began spitting into a homebrewed elixir. She switched over to a report from a New Jersey winery. Was every show about drinking? Was it National Booze Awareness Day?

The porn movie box waited atop the television. It required two quarters for each fifteen-minute interval, which she figured had to be annoying when you were in the middle of things. The dial showed three settings, running the gamut from soft to hardcore.

Claire spun the dial to C. The hardcore setting in room B-7 was always working, quarters or no quarters. It was broken or rigged up by a patron, and Claire discovered this weeks ago and wondered why Raffi hadn't noticed. She sometimes turned on the set as she cleaned, and although she never stopped to watch for long, she knew the players and the plots, if you called them plots, and she recognized the moans and groans, the curse words used as foreplay.

A Brazilian woman with breast implants and bleached blonde hair proceeded to give the waiter a blowjob amid the first course. The waiter, after inadvertently spilling a carafe of water down her dress, was apologetic and well-hung, desperately trying to mop up her dampened chest with a cocktail napkin. Apparently his charm and good nature had won the annoyed diner over, and she, not wearing a bra or underwear, decided to strip off her soaked dress and service the kindly young man. That was pretty much the story, a fair exchange of illicit dinner requests. Claire waited for the next one to cycle through.

She began timing the vignettes. Each one was about fifteen minutes in length, so that answered that question, but you needed to time it just right, or you might be forever pumping in extra quarters to view the climax—no pun intended—of the next skit, which was always the same: a visceral display of body fluids and contrived pleasure. She wanted to see real life: hollow promises, discreet cleaning of private areas, difficult departures. That was the real deal.

With two pillows propped beneath her head, she studied the parade of chance encounters that resulted in penetration. Was there a higher message to be learned? We're always talking about screwing this person or getting screwed by another. If we just screwed everyone else, we'd reduce the shame and turn the tables on the whole anger and disrespect thing. That's what Geneva Bogdan needed for sure—a good fucking. It was only a matter of time before someone gave it to her. Claire was hoping it'd show up on this loop, preferably the next frame, but she could only wish.

And who would be doing it to her? Drew Spatt of course.

Claire felt her head throbbing. Her ankles and wrists ached too. She'd already had way too many aspirins and her stomach gurgled. She loosened the towel above her chest and curled into a ball on the mattress. Her hair hadn't dried, and damp and twisted strands fell across the bridge of her nose. Her breath reflected off the mattress and back at her eyes. She heard her heart beating, as an ill feeling resonated once more in her stillness. If someone drove a nail through the base of her skull, she'd have to be told.

The real estate agent on channel C was closing the deal, writhing on the interior steps to a grand estate. Her dress was hiked up over her breasts, and she clutched the banister in one hand and a good faith contract in the other. "Si-si-sign. He-he-here. P-pleeeeeeeeeeeeeeease."

Claire gasped for air. This was going to kill her. Maybe you weren't supposed to quit all at once. They did that with cigarettes, gave you a patch, told you to cut back one at a time. This cold turkey routine was for sadists.

She squeezed her temples, attempting to force the urge from her head. How did she get through the whole day without a drink? She'd failed her kids. No question about it. She dug deep for her last bit of gumption. She never thought of it before. Playing field hockey in school, giving birth to her kids, she never worried about getting through. Okay, she may have worried about the moments leading up to it but not while she was in it. No end to her reserve existed once she was in the middle of things. She attacked, but now she found nothing to draw upon as she fought this addiction. The attack was coming to her. She never believed what people said about her stamina, until she had nothing left to give. She'd been faking it for so many months that she needed to get out of town before they figured her out.

The air conditioner hummed beneath the window. A truck roared past on the highway. Familiar strangers screwed like dogs on channel C. Claire hugged her legs to her chest, burying her face in the bony knobs of her knees. She was completely jackknifed, as slight as a steel blade.

She started shaking and held on through the wave of pain that detailed her body. Her heart seemed like a fragile organ that might fail her even at this stage in her life. She might outlast the rushes of adrenaline, or not. She couldn't let Raffi's daughter discover her like this.

Chapter Fifteen

Other People's Trash

Tom knocked several times on room B-7. He'd scouted the mess in front of Claire's house, and the rest was easy to surmise. What were her options? He drove by Drew's apartment, not seeing the Impala, afraid she had skipped town. He passed The Lazy Eye and Nat's Café. He spun through the library parking lot. He even headed for the lake, thinking the worst.

Along highway 623, he passed the motel, spotting her car from the highway. *Good, she hadn't left.* The thought of her suddenly leaving crushed him, unseating everything that he believed might be happening.

The room sounded dead quiet from the outside. He knocked a few times. Had she gone for a walk? He scanned the covered porch that shielded the connected series of room entrances. This wasn't the most scenic section of town, although Claire liked to walk. She seemed obsessed with hiking. He often discovered her legs cutting through the trails like a tireless bog thrasher.

Tom pulled back, just as the door went ajar. It was night, and the amber hue of the canopy lights lent a supernatural glow to the one eye peeking through the slot.

"Tom?" Claire's voice was raspy. She cleared her throat, although it didn't seem to help.

"I've got it." Tom had been chewing on a new idea, focusing his energy on tracking her down, but now that he found her, he ramped up his hopes. "I know what I can do."

"What are you taking about?" Claire cracked the door wider. Her hair was pushed to one side, as if waking from a nap. She looked tired and fractured, never at peace.

He'd gotten used to that look—her twisting on an idea, like a tree branch that threatened to snap in the wind but didn't. "Were you sleeping?"

"What are you doing here?"

"I saw the pile at your house."

Her voice wrought a touch of sarcasm. "Geneva's terminated my lease."

"Can she do that?"

"I'm surprised she let me go this long."

"Oh, it's like that."

"So what's the big news? What can you do?"

He'd lost track of the question. Her image captivated him. She stood with a sheet wrapped around her tiny frame. She bunched the linen in her fist and pinned it against her shoulder. He imagined her waiting for him, as if this was the place they met and no one knew.

"Tom, what can you do?"

He reigned in his desire. "I can analyze trash."

"You came here to tell me that?"

"I was thinking of how to help Old Forge."

"Not that place again."

Tom remembered her stuff strewn over the curb. She was having a bad day, a really bad day. "Look," he said, "if you really think Geneva knows something, then it's in her trash."

"What's in her trash?"

"Your answers. I know from experience."

"You think so?"

"You should see what I've done with just a bag of bolts."

"You're crazy," she said.

He admitted to himself that he had it bad for her. Tonight, he saw his chance, as if events had lined up in his favor when she hit bottom or at least came close to it. He was going to make a run right here, do anything possible. What could happen—wind up in his cabin alone like every night?

"Would you do me a favor?" she asked.

"What?"

"Get a clean shirt and shorts from the Impala for me?" She turned from the door, leaving it further ajar. He studied her shape as it disappeared into the bathroom. She was a ghost slipping through walls.

Tom dashed to the car. The interior was strewn with clothes and mashed up boxes, as if Claire literally dumped the contents of her house inside. He pushed aside her lingerie, not daring with that, but then no. He scanned the bras and panties. Some looked worn and frayed. He selected a modest set with pink roses, his boldest move in some time. He almost forgot about the shirt and shorts. How embarrassing would that be? He found an orange T-shirt and cut off jeans. He was dressing her. He was getting hard just thinking about it.

He folded the clothes and set the underwear on top. *Don't speak about it; just hand it over.*

"Here you go!" He entered the room.

She poked her head and arm from the bathroom. Her hair was brushed and tied into a ponytail, and water ran in the sink. "Let me have it."

He handed over the stack.

"You like pink flowers?" she asked in her way that went right to the core of the matter.

He glanced at the underwear in the palm of her hand. He wasn't going to say a word.

"I should've known you were a sensitive type," she said and disappeared through the door.

If he left now, it was a pretty good night. So he formed a plan. They would have a brief discussion, and he would split like he had someplace else to go, like he was a man in demand at places she hadn't known. That was good. That was cool. He didn't know cool, but that had to be it. That was the thing about a woman like Claire. She made you feel cool. He'd watch her do it with other people, unless she didn't like you, then you were on your own, hung out to dry, like a bruised piñata waiting for the final whack to bust open. He wasn't going there. He wasn't giving her the excuse.

Claire came from the bathroom. The lights were low, and she didn't seem to mind. Tom liked it too. It made him comfortable. Damn, she looked great in those shorts and T-shirt, and he knew what was underneath them too.

"So tell me about your plan," she said.

He didn't have a plan. He had an idea. The idea was the plan. "We need to analyze Geneva's trash, every bit of it."

"How do we do that?"

"I guess we have to get it." He pictured himself staking out the curb on garbage day.

"You guess?"

"We have to get it. We just get it." This cavalier attitude fit nicely with the evening. Why not break the law? And was stealing trash really a crime? Everyone wanted to get rid of it. They left it everywhere they went and even places they didn't.

"Do you propose we break into Geneva's house?" She didn't seem alarmed by her own suggestion. "Do you know where to find her trash?"

He didn't know and especially didn't expect to get derailed this fast. He hadn't imagined her embracing his idea so well. He stood exposed like he always did, waiting for a hard rain. *Dumb Tom. Tom the Idiot. What did he know?*

Claire came closer in the bad light. Her mind was moving rapidly, like she hadn't slept in days and every lost hour hung in the dark wells beneath her eyes. "I don't think I ever saw garbage cans at her house."

"No?"

"She used to keep it by the door, one bag at a time like groceries."

Then the heavens graced Tom. That was how he'd referred to it later. He recalled the bag of trash in the front seat of Geneva's Cadillac. She was taking it someplace, but where? People paid for trash pickup in Cranfield Lakes. If she dumped it on the roadside or in the woods to save money, he'd have busted her a long time ago, like he did with Ernie Baker, to whom he gave a stern warning. Where else would Geneva put her garbage? She didn't seem like the type to drive ten miles just to drop it out of sight. The answer was much simpler.

Tom reveled in the gold-strike moment. Who knew that a sack of trash might change everything, but who knew the value of trash better than him? "There's a dumpster behind her apartment building. I guess she uses that."

"How do you know?"

"I saw trash bags in her car, just the other day. We should check out the dumpster."

Claire sat on this revelation. Tom awaited her praise. Communicating with Claire was akin to climbing Mount

Everest. He'd achieved a new summit and wasn't about to give back the real estate.

"Great," Claire said. "Let's do it."

"Do what?"

"Raid the dumpster."

Tom froze. "When?"

"Right now."

"Okay," Tom shot back, without thinking. Being cool had just ratcheted up another level. He needed to climb that mountain even higher.

They drove around to kill time, making small talk but mostly keeping quiet. After ten o'clock, they pulled into the parking lot outside Geneva's apartment complex on Young Street. The building was a brick structure with six apartments, no balconies, and only a single course of white brick detailing the flat roofline. Tom had lived there in his early twenties, until the waiting list grew and rent got too high, but lately, the building remained half empty.

He pulled his truck around back by the blue dumpster. He'd been noticing Claire during the drive. She touched her forehead at times, and at others, she kneaded her fingertips.

"Are you okay?" Tom asked.

"Fine."

"Really?"

"Don't I look fine?"

Her response reminded him of Alicia Hardaway, when she tugged the hem of her skirt over her false leg. "How do I look?" was what she really asked.

He knew the answer. "You look great."

"Thanks."

He left the truck, taking a flashlight and a green garbage bag. He brought the crowbar if needed to split open a box or bag. He slipped on a pair of canvas work gloves.

The dumpster stunk yards short of his approach. Trash in summer created an unpleasant experience, not that trash was ever pleasant, yet organic matter in the heat of summer transmuted into a sinister composition. He raised one side of the split metal lid and was affronted by a medley of festering vegetables and meat, gestating maggots, and unholy chemical cocktails, and those were only the things that he'd venture to say in conversation.

He glanced back. Claire stopped short, her hand over her mouth and nose. She stood in her fraying cutoffs and a T-shirt that exposed her navel. There was little doubt who was going into the dumpster. In a single evening, he'd transitioned from idiot to cool to fool, and that was okay with him. Finally he got to choose.

The stinking, filthy dumpster awaited. Tom climbed over the edge and dropped into the mound of bagged and scattered trash. It felt like a child's moonwalk, spongy and uncertain, until he tripped over a bike frame and fell to his hands and knees.

"You all right?" Claire called in a half-whisper. Her job was to lookout for nosey residents and passersby.

Tom was about to answer, when something hissed. He spun the flashlight on the pair of yellow eyes hovering just inches from his face.

A raccoon was stunned by the recent arrival to the dumpster. It clawed a rotten apple core, scowling and hissing. It opened its snout and bared its jagged teeth.

Tom leapt backward, scraping his leg on a bike pedal and crashing his head into the wall. A dull thud echoed in the metal bin. The raccoon growled, but when the noise settled, it returned to the apple core.

"Are you all right?" Claire asked a little louder.

"Raccoon," Tom whispered, so as not to incense the animal further.

"What's that?"

Tom scanned his companion in the dumpster. It was the size of a small dog, with razor claws and teeth like most raccoons, and if it truly mimicked the species, it didn't mind defending its space. Tom was lucky it hadn't gouged out one of his eyes.

"Raccoon," Tom said.

"Where?"

"In here."

Claire seemed to be thinking. "You better get out."

"Not yet."

"What?"

"Not yet."

"Tommy? Be careful."

"Keep your eyes on the street."

"Are you sure?"

"I know what I'm doing," he declared, when of course, he did not.

The pair cruised opposite sides of the dumpster. Tom alternated his flashlight between the trash and the raccoon, garnering a growl or hiss. The raccoon dug into a plastic snack bag, licking potato chip specks from its claws. Tom saw a stack of birthday cards and checked through the names. The raccoon licked an empty ice cream carton and tore up the box. Tom discovered a paper bag filled with church missals. The raccoon munched on an orange peel.

Tom used the crowbar, stopping at every brown paper bag to wedge inside. He prepared to declare the dumpster idea among the stupidest of all times, when he discovered a paper bag topped off with coffee grinds.

The raccoon hopped twice, drawing near the bike in the center of the dumpster. It was either getting bold or antsy. Neither one was a good scenario.

"Be nice," Tom whispered.

The raccoon glanced sideways, gnawing the spent plastic wrappers of a freezer pop. Bright pink dye dripped from its snout.

Tom swept the coffee grinds aside and searched the bag. He pushed past an empty pasta sleeve and a dirty can of tuna, spotting Geneva Bogdan's name printed in bold typeface letters. It looked like a pre-approved credit card application. It was torn in half, like the other letters.

"Bingo!" He stuffed the contents into the green plastic bag.

"What's that?"

"It's her mail."

"Her what?"

The raccoon tore into the coffee filter and mopped up the grinds. Great, Tom thought, a raccoon on caffeine. *I'm out of here.*

He lifted himself onto the dumpster sidewall, but the green bag felt heavier, stuck almost. He aimed the flashlight downward. The little critter was latched onto the bottom, making quick work with his claws.

"Git!" Tim straddled the dumpster edge. He tugged the plastic, opening a wider slit in the bag.

The animal growled, a fairly nasty sound in raccoon language. He swiped at Tom's foot, strafing the iron toe of his work boot and shredding the leather.

Tom swung the crowbar, banging the dumpster like a gong. "Git!"

"Oh my God!" Claire shrieked.

Apartment windows illuminated above them, and shadows shifted before the glass.

The raccoon sunk its claws into the bag and yanked it into the dumpster, leaving Tom with a fistful of plastic.

"Get out of there!" Claire yelled, from her position as the discreet lookout. "Get out of the dumpster now!"

Tom seethed. He'd just discovered possible evidence to assist Claire, and a greedy animal planned on stealing it? *No way.*

He leapt into the dumpster so fast that it surprised even the raccoon. It reared up on its back legs, threatening to strike, but Tom raised the crowbar above his head and drove straight down like an ax.

The raccoon dodged the blow

A man yelled from the window above. "What's goin' on there?"

Tom wasn't finished. He'd reached that tiny place in a man's mind that spun in a loop, playing the same desperate message over and over. *Kill! Kill! Kill!* He stepped forward and swatted at the animal another time, shattering an old light bulb into whirling fragments.

"What the hell?!" the man on the third floor yelled.

Two more windows slid open, as the residents queued up for the late night show. They leaned over their sills to spy the gray shapes rumbling in the dumpster.

But even a raccoon jacked-up on coffee grinds recognized when to quit. Any animal on earth knew when another had slipped over the edge, although it often seemed that men were the last to notice. The raccoon skittered back and forth. Tom fisted the crowbar and drove for the deathblow, banging a dull note on the metal sidewall.

The animal scampered up a discarded vacuum cleaner, barely escaping over the side. It vanished, as Tom mounted the heap of trash.

"That's right," he said, waving the crowbar. "Get lost."

"Are you guys in trouble?" the man above called again.

"Come on," Claire urged.

Tom stared at her, sweating, stinking from trash. He'd forgotten why they'd come. Ridding the world of raccoons was a perfectly fine agenda.

"Let's go," she said.

The flashlight shone on the tattered plastic garbage bag. Tom saw the dirty letters splayed from the open bag.

He lifted up everything with both hands and tossed it outside the dumpster.

He pulled himself over the edge, scooped up the trash and his tools, and tossed them into the bed of his truck. "I think we've got it." He threw a poly tarp over everything.

All abuzz and anxious, they drove toward his cabin to decipher the trash. When his cell phone rang, Tom wondered what it was.

"Do you want me to get that?" Claire reached for the glove compartment and the intrusive sound.

Tom retrieved the phone and pressed it to his ear. "Hello? Hello?"

"So you're still up," Alicia said.

"Yes?" He glanced at Claire, acting business-like.

"What's that noise?"

"My phone, I guess."

"That noise in the background?"

"I'm driving," Tom said.

"Where?"

"Home."

"Where were you?"

He wondered what concern it was of hers, but then he recalled the child in her belly. Everything he did was now her concern: the places he went, the food he ate, the people he was with too. *Shit.*

"Tom? Are you still there."

He drove beyond the Cranfield Lakes city limits, clear of the fiasco at the dumpster. The poly tarp atop the trash in the truck bed flapped in the breeze. "I'm here."

"I just wanted to know where you were."

"I'm headed for my cabin."

"That's what I hate about those phones. Someone could be either around the corner or in Alaska. I need to picture them when I'm talking."

He imagined Alicia just home from her library shift, her stomach starting to bulge. She sat with a carton of ice cream and her feet up on a couch he'd never seen. In fact, he'd never seen the inside of her home at all. Their relationship took place entirely inside the library, and when he imagined their future child—a boy with crazy blonde hair like Alicia—growing up, it always took place among the dusty stacks of books. Frankly, her phone calls disturbed him. Anything outside the library seemed unnatural for them.

"Tom?"

"Yes."

"I keep losing you."

"It must be the connection."

"I'm sorry about the other night."

"Don't keep apologizing."

"It's the hormones. One minute, I want to strangle you, and the next, I want to wrap my arms and legs around you."

He didn't know how to console her. They'd been fun, a lot of fun, but they'd been transported beyond fun. Where were they now? He spotted Claire in the corner of his eye. He hoped she wasn't listening.

"Alicia, you shouldn't be thinking either of those things." Tom spoke as calmly as someone withdrawing cash from a bank teller window.

"What does that mean?"

"Shouldn't you just be sleeping or something? It's late."

"You're right. I need my rest."

"Do that."

"There's a reason why I called."

"Not tonight."

Her tone abruptly shifted. "You're not alone, are you?"

"Well, no."

"Who's there?"

"Claire."

"Claire?"

"Yes."

"Claire Whethers? Cranberry Claire?"

"Yes."

"I'm not going to ask what you're up to. I called for another reason. You want to go on a date?"

He refused to discuss this now. As far as he was concerned, he was on a date with Claire, even if she might not say so. "Let me think about it."

"What's to think about? I thought we'd go canoeing, or you can show me the lake."

"Sounds good. We'll discuss it in the morning."

"You're being mysterious."

"I'm not. I'm tired." He knew he sounded like he was try-ing to hide something, which he was.

"There's not a situation between you and Claire?"

"A situation?"

"That's a funny response."

"It is? It is." Tom had reached his limit of being low key and nonchalant. He wanted to just hang up.

"I hope you're being honest with me."

That was a rare sentiment coming from Alicia. Every-thing about them was covert and concealed, outside of the sex. He decided to drop the thread of the conversation alto-gether. He knew why she was really calling. In his lifetime, a great many problems saddled him but never in such close connection with another person. He wasn't going to be able to let this problem sit and vanish on its own. He must find a suitable solution to Alicia and the child, whatever that might be, and then offer it to her as a means of reconciliation. This issue went on his to-do list, along with saving Old Forge and getting Claire to love him. *No small list really.* He'd sort out his priorities later.

"We'll work it out," he said, thinking of the larger issues.

"Good, we'll set the time tomorrow, if you want."

"Good."

"Love ya." Alicia disconnected.

Tom took a deep breath, as quiet and unseen as possi-ble.

Claire was all over it. "What was that about?"

"Just a friend."

"A friend? Are you seeing Alicia?"

"Did I mention Alicia?" Tom wanted to put the brakes on her interrogation. He should've let the voice mail take the call, yet he'd struggled to set it up and retrieve messages, so the phone just kept on ringing in the glove box. Anyway, he knew Alicia. She'd just call over and over, even if she got his voice mail. She'd act as if he had an overdue book and demand satisfaction.

"I heard you use Alicia's name. I only know Alicia Hardaway from the library. Was that her?"

"She's looking something up for me."

"It sounded really important to be calling this late."

"You think?"

"Are you seeing each other?"

"Not exactly." *How the hell did Claire make that leap of thought?*

"That's a strange answer," she said.

"It's complicated."

"Are you dating or not?"

"Not exactly."

She turned away, shaking her head. "Sounds like a typical man's answer."

He didn't mind the wisecrack. He was glad to be lumped in with the boys, for better or worse. "Neither of us call it anything, so it doesn't have a name."

"Oh brother."

"I'm not trying to cover anything up." He double-clutched on his words. Had he just said he wasn't trying to cover anything up?

"Do you go to dinner? Do you talk on the phone?"

"It's only the first time she's called." He failed to admit that he'd had the phone for only two days, and he'd called her once already.

"Is it a relationship or not?"

Tom liked that she was curious. It fed his ego a dozen different ways to see both women interested on some level, but it was Claire's direct questions that put it into perspective. No, screwing the Cranfield Lakes librarian on chance occasions was not a relationship. It was exciting, outrageous even, but he didn't know Alicia much better than the woman who sliced his lunchmeat at the deli in Middleton. In fact, the deli woman was a little more stable and reliable.

The truck turned onto the rocky path leading to his cabin. The trees comforted him, affording him a little relief. He saw the ways of love. Sometimes it was as simple as telling the other person what they needed to hear. Anyway, he and Claire weren't dating either. That was the truth. "Alicia and I don't go out. We don't really talk."

"What do you do?"

"We meet in the library."

"Oh." Claire sounded half sure of his answer. "I always thought she was pretty."

Tom knew better than to touch that one. He saw Claire across the seat. The most beautiful woman that he knew sat in his truck beside him. "I'm not partial to blondes."

With that, he was finished with Alicia. He'd been crunching his brain for weeks, working out scenarios where he and Alicia created a family. He'd do his best to care for the child, but in the end, Alicia was just too bossy. Claire was spunky and downright acidic at times, yet she never forced it on him. It was a more tolerable flavor of independence.

Claire looked down the lane of trees. Tom imagined that she thought as he did whenever he toured the forest, absorbed in the wonderment and constant fluctuation of nature. He saw possibilities, rebirth, a chance to redeem himself, while Alicia probably saw sawdust and pulp—the pages of next year's *Encyclopedia Britannica*.

"I wonder who cuts Alicia's hair," Claire said out of the blue.

"She cuts it herself." Tom guided the wheel, eyes on the darkness splayed by headlights.

"She told you that?"

"It looks like it, doesn't it?"

Tom needed a shower but fired up the generator outside his cabin and started up with the trash. He draped a plastic sheet over the dinner table and spread out the dumpster booty.

"Start organizing any paper that looks similar." Tom connected a halogen desk lamp to an extension cord and set it upon the table. He placed his analysis toolkit—a recovered fishing tackle box—on a stool to his left. "Put the parts to things into the bucket, like the glass from the light bulb."

"What can you do with that?" she asked.

"You never know."

Claire crinkled her nose, looking as if she might gag. The trash cooked beneath the light, a meal fit for varmints and maggots. "What about the food stuff?"

"Sorry, I'm used to it." He motioned his head toward the first-aid kit by the couch. "Get yourself latex gloves and a mask too."

"Good idea."

"I'll get the food out of the way." He snapped open a paper bag, tossed in a banana peel, and scraped the remainder of the coffee grinds in as well. The more he looked at the pile, the more he noticed the torn pieces of mail. He squinted his eyes. Similar colors merged, fragment by fragment. He sought to reconstruct the mangled trash, like the broken pieces of a glass. He'd match them end to end.

He plucked out glossy coupons from the pile with a pair of tweezers. "I hate these things."

"You hate what?"

"Bulk mailers. You can't always tell where the pieces are from. They could be a part of a letter, magazine, or almost anything—but mostly a waste of trees. Everyone gets them, and few people want them."

Claire came beside him in the mask and gloves. Her hairline was moist, and her eyes looked bloodshot. She collected the shredded coupons into a pile.

"You should go sit down," Tom said.

"I have to do this."

"I'll get it."

"Let me get the coupons out of the way."

In a half hour, Tom patched together a two-page letter with numbers and graphs. The graphs were easy, but the numbers gave him trouble. He realized that he was looking at Geneva's electric bill. "She used over 1000 kilowatts last month."

"How's that?" She shouldered him, scanning the bill.

"It's her electric bill." He felt her arm against his. She was warm. The desk lamp threw heat, too. He knew it was bothering her.

"Can that help us?"

"If this was a regular littering case, it'd be all over."

"That's amazing."

"But we already figured this was Geneva's garbage."

"I can't believe you got that much even."

"People think trash is safe, but you can learn a lot from it: what people do, where they go. The list goes on. A person's habits tell their story."

"That's scary."

"If you're not careful."

"Do you worry about trash?"

"Let's just say that since I started doing this, I burn old documents in the fireplace."

"Wow." Claire wiped her forehead with the back of her hand.

"Please, take a break."

"I want to help you."

"Are you coming down with something?"

Claire balanced a look in her eye, like she knew exactly what ailed her. "I can't let you do this alone."

He eyed her for a time, wondering whether he should suggest what he was thinking. "There's a bottle underneath the sink. Somebody gave me a fifth of sherry for shoveling his driveway two winters back. I never opened it."

"What are you saying?"

"It's all I have. Maybe you should take a little. Maybe you want to ease down from it." He thought about that phone call with Alicia. He could use the word *it* a lot of different ways to avoid saying things. It was a great word to throw around in the right places.

"Fine." She pulled off her mask and gloves and went to the kitchen. Tom heard the cabinets opening and the sherry bottle uncork.

He started assembling another section of paper with lists of numbers. He took the tweezers and fitted the pieces together. It looked like a credit card bill, stained from coffee grinds and orange marmalade. He could bleach it later, but he pulled the hot desk lamp closer, waiting to see how it dried up. Sometimes writing appeared beneath the lamp.

Claire padded about his place in bare feet. She plopped on the couch with a coffee mug full of sherry and placed the colonial diary across her lap. Tom heard her turning the pages, and he looked. The color was already rising in her face.

"This guy has beautiful handwriting," she said.

"Yes."

"But he's so sad."

"He's lost his lover."

"Do you know why?"

"Something happened before the war. Something awful." Tom dropped another ragged swatch of paper in place.

"What happened?"

"A scandal in town, I think. I'm not sure. He never uses her name. I assume she was married."

"Then who's Nutley?" she asked.

"That's what I'm trying to find out."

"Is that his lover? I've heard you talk about Nutley. I thought it was a guy."

"It is."

"He's not mentioned anywhere."

"It's the guy who wrote the diary. It's in there."

"Where?"

"Up front."

"I read the front section. I didn't see that name."

"On the first page," he said. "It's Michael Nutley—in the same handwriting." He listened to her flip the pages backward, waiting for her to agree.

"It's Turnley, Michael Turnley."

He wondered if Claire had an odd sense of humor. He put down the tweezers. "It says Nutley."

"Take a look for yourself."

Tom came and sat beside her. Her index finger pointed at the passage he'd transposed to his notes at the very beginning when he'd first found the diary.

"Turnley," she said.

He read the entire page, letter by letter, and flipped it over. He moved his finger slowly beneath each letter, whispering them. He checked his notebook on the end table. He'd written Nutley, but it clearly said Turnley. "I've been searching for the wrong guy."

"I'll say." Her violet eyes probed him.

He was embarrassed, another legendary screw-up for the Thomas King journals, another classic Tom tale. "I swear it said Nutley."

"I believe you."

"It says Turnley, but it looked like Nutley."

"It's no big deal."

"How could I miss that? It looked like Nutley."

"I believe you."

"Don't keep saying that."

"I'm sorry."

"I know what everyone thinks."

She forced him to acknowledge her. "Do you make this mistake a lot?"

He felt the warmth of her nearby, but he never felt further away. He'd never have her. He was a mistake waiting to happen. "Ever since I was kid. I'm famous for it."

"What do you do?"

"I mess up words. I can't get numbers in the right order either. It's hard for me. That's why I listen to books on tape."

"Is that why you left high school?"

"It got too difficult, no, embarrassing for my mother, for me mostly." His sight fell to the tips of his socks. "That's not fair. She wanted me to stay in school."

"Did you ever tell anyone?"

"This is who I am." He'd been exposed in front of Claire, the idiot concretely verified, succinctly seated in his place in the world.

"Tommy." She gripped his wrist, her hand steadier now. "How many years have you been doing this to yourself?"

"Doing what?"

"I thought I had problems," she said. "My problems are all my own."

"What are you talking about?" He didn't like the discussion turning morose. He didn't want to have that effect on her, but he smelled the sherry on her breath. The booze cut two ways: eased her pain but sapped her enthusiasm. "Claire, you're not responsible for your kids being gone."

"We're talking about you now. You only think of other people. You're a freaking saint."

He'd never been described in those terms, not even by his mother. "You say crazy things sometimes."

She set the mug on the table. "Alicia Hardaway should do whatever she needs to hold onto you."

"Don't even go there."

"Why?"

He almost mentioned the baby, but he stopped short, certain he'd never reveal it if he didn't have to. It was weird how he reached the point of confession and then saw it fall deeper inside. "Never mind."

"So why have you been keeping this problem of yours such a secret?"

What did she think she knew about him? And how had her opinion of him just changed?

Claire snatched her purse from the floor and pulled out her driver's license. She held it up in front of Tom. "What does this say?"

"It's your license. Nice picture."

"I'm not joking. Read the numbers."

"Do you know what you're asking me to do?"

"Read it?"

"K534... 53... 72..."

"Stop." She tucked it in her palm, so only she could see. "Read those numbers back to me."

"K534... 7."

"Want to try it again?"

"I don't have the knack."

"Why not?"

"If you just read them to me aloud, I can remember and read it back."

"Why?"

"I hear your voice saying it." He imagined painting them on a wall or carving them into a tree. He saw the double curve of the number three and slanted arrow form of the number seven and the number four.

She glanced at the bookshelf of cassettes. "What are the seven deadly sins?"

"Envy, sloth, gluttony, wrath, pride, lust, and greed."

"Not bad for someone who's not supposed to know anything."

"That doesn't prove anything."

"I'm not sure if I can name them, but they sound right."

"They are." He started to defend himself, until he saw her expression. If she was layering false praise on him, it was the cruelest of jokes.

"The things you used to say to me when we happened to see each other in the Wharton," she said. "I used to think they were strange, but I couldn't stop thinking about your observations of the forest. They made a lot of sense."

"I just see things differently."

"That's my point. You see things like other people don't."

"I don't know what you're driving at."

"You know what your problem is?"

Tom knew his problems. He had a town ready to lynch him, at least the police chief wanted as much. He was nine months away from fatherhood and a lifetime from Claire. These were problems not so easily solved.

"You have that condition," Claire said. "What's it called—dyslexia."

"I'm not that. That's serious."

"You listen to Homer and Dante on tape, but you can't balance your checkbook. You decipher people's trash, but you can't read a driver's license. You're like one of those freaky smart people that I read about in *Reader's Digest*."

"Freaky maybe."

"I bet someone can help you. I bet there's a way."

He let her words sink in. He'd been suspicious that he might have some condition, but he didn't have the time or money to figure it out. Anyway, he assumed there was nothing to do about it except learn to cope, which he did okay if people weren't so impatient with him. He wasn't going to take drugs or submit himself to brain surgery, if that's what they did to cure it. He was who he was, yet seeing Claire so intense, feeling her breath on his face, he became more than he was. "You're helping me already."

"Things are going to be different for both of us." An involuntary shiver swept over her, before she reached for the mug on the table.

"Are you okay?"

"We're talking about you," she said.

She sipped the mug slowly. Tom recalled a novel about a man in detox—the shakes, the painful hours, until all the parts of the body got used to not being poisoned. Claire needed the elixir in that mug. He didn't need to fight through an encyclopedia volume on it. It was obvious. It was making her better, not perfect, but better.

"I think I smell something burning," she said.

He sniffed the air. "Did you start a pot of coffee?"

"No."

"I know what it is." He went to the table. The fragments that he'd set on clean paper puckered beneath the heat, and the slight grains of coffee residue had started to cook. Tom pushed aside the lamp and smoothed out the fragments with a roller. "It's her credit card bill."

"Those are phone numbers," Claire said. "It's her phone bill!"

"Let's check out the area codes first."

"It's all 609 and 856. There's nothing here but local calls and a few 215 numbers in Philly."

"Do you recognize the numbers? Do you think Elliot would keep the kids so close? Philadelphia even?"

"Everyone I spoke to said no, but I spent my last penny searching."

"And nothing?"

"No sign of them."

"Here's 207, and here it is again." Tom's voice grew excited. Sometimes you knew before you knew.

Claire picked up on this. "Where's that area code from?"

"Get the phonebook from the end table."

She dashed back with it and leaned over Tom's arm as he worked. "Where's that area code again?"

"Right there."

"207?"

"Yes."

"Just checking."

"Go ahead. Double-check me."

She fumbled through the guide pages.

"Here it is again." Tom dropped another torn hunk of paper in place. The coffee stained puzzle was starting to look like a Renaissance painting, chipped and brown, cracked in places. "Geneva's calling the same number about twice a week."

"207 is in lower Maine," Claire said.

"Who's in Maine?"

"I don't know. No relatives I know of."

"They grow blueberries in Maine, Claire."

"Elliot can do that. He's done that here."

"It makes perfect sense, doesn't it?"

"You're a genius." Claire said. "Give me your cell phone."

"Why?"

"Why not?" She spotted it on the table by the door and went for it. "Just let me listen."

"Don't."

"I won't say a word. I promise."

Tom followed her. He watched her punch in the first numbers and grabbed her arm, trying not to be forceful about it. "Don't."

She yanked free, clutching the cell phone into her fist. "They're my babies. I have to hear them."

"What if it's Elliot?"

"So what."

"What if the kids are there?"

"Oh God, I hope so."

"They can check the caller ID. What if they realize it's my phone?"

"So it's you." Another involuntarily shudder whipped through her.

"Think it over, Claire." He knew she wanted to dial. He sensed her fingertips moving even before they budged. "Isn't it unusual that I'd be calling?"

"I have to chance it."

"No, you don't. Not like this."

When he reached for the phone, she folded it into her chest. "I have to."

He watched her go for the doorknob and wrapped his long arms around her. He didn't know what else to do. He hugged her tight. Her fists balled against his stomach. He hated himself. He knew that Drew manhandled her, and now he was doing it.

"Cut it out!" She kicked his shin.

He latched onto her tighter, lifting her until only the tips of her bare feet touched the floor. She thrashed some more, smashing her toes into his legs, but if he could squeeze out all the bad feelings—the hurt, the fear, the elements that made her hate herself—he'd hold until his arms broke.

"Let me go!"

"No." His voice was a whisper against her screams. "If you spook Elliot, he could disappear again."

She writhed for a minute more, kicking him again and again, bruising his shin through his jeans, and suddenly she stopped, and the cell phone hit the floor.

Her hair formed a mass of tangles against his chest. He heard her sobbing. Potent tears rolled down her cheeks, like a little girl beset with the impossible.

Her legs fell limp, her body releasing in anguish. He held her slight weight above the floor, and when she shook one more time, he nearly began crying, too.

"It's okay," he whispered, unable to know if she heard.

She threw her arms around him and burrowed in his shirt.

He stroked the mess of hair. "Maybe it's a friend's house or a payphone, then we're close, closer than you've been in a long time."

She looked up at him, gaining her feet, eyes damp and blinking. "I know but…"

"We have this information, " Tom said. "I promise you, if it's him, we'll find him."

"I should trust you. I do trust you."

"We can't blow it. Not like this."

She wiped her eyes and made a motion to pull away, and he let go.

"How do you do it?" she asked. "How do you stay strong?"

"You caught me on a good day."

"Can I have one of your good days?"

"You've had a lot of good days, Claire."

"I'm being selfish, I know. But can I have one of your good days?"

"You're having it."

She stepped back into him and grabbed him by the shoulders.

He'd be hard-pressed to describe the look on her face. "What are you doing?"

"I can't reach you." She put both hands around his neck and tugged down.

The breeze tousled the pines outside, and the halogen lamp set the room aglow. Tom kissed her. It was real, not a midnight dream or a rich afternoon fantasy or something she did when she was drunk and didn't remember, but two people sorting it out for themselves, discovering they were better off merging paths.

Her kiss ran longer than he'd imagined, so he found himself pulling away first, wondering if he should go back and let her finish.

Tom set up his bed for Claire and started the shower. As he peeled off his clothes in the bathroom, he caught the stink of festering garbage on his skin, but it was a wonder he even noticed. Claire's kiss lingered on his mouth and tongue. He practically walked into walls.

The steam rose up and fogged the off-white tiles. He saw her leg enter the stall first, followed by the rest of her divine body. She'd grown thin. Her hipbones showed as much as the ends of her collar bones, although her breasts looked perfect.

She cupped a handful of spray, wiped it across her forehead and onto the back of her neck, matting her hair to one side. Her expression read hesitant determination. "I've changed my mind."

"About what?"

"Alicia Hardaway can't have you."

He thought to say, "no contest" or "sounds like a good idea" or just plain "great," but thought better of using words, so he said nothing at all.

She looked him over before stepping closer. "You're long all over, aren't you?"

He was embarrassed by his erection, the way she hot-wired his arousal, but he forgot this as she kissed him, deeper this time. She lathered her hands with soap and turned her body against his, so that her back was against him.

She lathered his hands and maneuvered them along her body, prompting him to soap her breast and nipples. Once Tom got the idea, she shifted sideways and handled his erection, stroking it slowly, making him very firm. "I think I met you earlier today."

He kissed her ear, smelling her sweet skin and hair. Their pores opened, drinking each other in.

"Have you ever heard of the Battle Blaster?" she asked.

"What's that?"

"I'll tell you later."

They showered until the water ran cold and they were more than clean. Claire toweled him off. She refused to let him do it. She mopped her hair with the same towel and wrapped it around herself.

"First things first." She walked across the cabin.

He followed. He'd always loved her, even though on most days she barely recognized him from the trees, but when he looked back at their blossoming friendship, it made sense.

In the bedroom, he reached for the towel before she took it off. She let him do it, and when it hit the floor, it was like seeing her for the first time.

She took a sip from the mug that sat beside the bed, still leaning on her crutch of booze for the time being. "I haven't been with another man since Elliot."

"What about Drew?"

"He was never really my boyfriend. I can't explain it."

He accepted this excuse and brought her close, feeling his desire surge. He handled her a little rough, as a man does when barely able to contain himself.

She glanced down. "Go easy on me with that thing."

"I'm sorry."

"I'm just kidding. I think I can handle it."

She pulled him down on the bed, rolling on top. He massaged her chest, already defining what she liked, the way new lovers do. She liked her ears kissed. She wanted his hands low on her waist. His thumbs caressed her skin.

The ceiling fan buzzed overhead. She began rocking, taking much of him inside, riding his hard shaft. He'd never seen a woman appreciate his length as much, but it was more than that. She was working it, perspiring along the sides of her neck. She made love and screwed him in tandem, without words or sure direction, just guttural signals and the palm of her hands moving along his ribs.

She paused to look Tom in the eyes and form a connection, and she disappeared again. It had to do with quitting the booze, he assumed, or perhaps she really enjoyed screwing him that much. He put his hands behind his head and watched the show. If this was his last day on Earth, it had arrived at the precise moment.

"Tommy," she fell on his chest. He'd climaxed a long time earlier, but she kept going until she was satisfied. "I did the right thing?"

"You want to do the right thing again?" He expected her to say no.

"Keep it going."

He assumed the top, controlling the tempo. He didn't have full strength, but nothing was going to deter him. He worked into her, watching her spirit fly anew.

She called beneath him, words he didn't quite understand. Her eyes rolled to a distant focus. No surprise Claire boiled beneath the sheets. He teased her by slowing down, which only made her hotter, bringing her back to him. She hit the notes of a dozen fantasies spawned in his mind on nights so lonely they were grafted to his soul. Elliot Bogdan and Drew Spatt, he thought near breathlessness, were the dumbest men alive.

"You know how to do this." Claire flicked her head, swinging the hair away from her nose and mouth.

"All my life."

"You say the funniest things."

"I had a good teacher." He worried he'd said something stupid, but there was no denying it. Alicia knew everything from her seat in the reference alcove. She'd read all the sex manuals, showing Tom a diagram or two. It was one big research project to her.

Claire pushed at him harder. "You're so fresh."

He reached down by instinct, expecting to find Alicia's stump but fumbled on Claire's calf.

"What are you doing?" Claire slid her hands up his rib cage.

He grabbed her by the ankle and pulled her leg up straight. He finished, holding on barely long enough for her to climax again.

But she wasn't finished. Tom fell back on the sheets exhausted. His veins pulsed in his head, and he felt light-headed. He soaked up the oscillating breeze of the ceiling fan.

Claire drained her mug and climbed atop him, her chest pressed against his, an ear monitoring his heart. "Are you dead, soldier?"

"Taking a rest."

She wore a hungry look, as if it possessed her, made her hair stand on edge and her eyes electric. "How'd I do?"

"You did great."

"I mean with that magic wand of yours."

"Is that what they call it?"

"That's what I call it, and you know what else I can do?"

He watched her crawl down his body with kisses. She aimed to demonstrate her intentions, and he owned all the time in the world to watch.

Chapter Sixteen
Red Devil

They made love twice in the morning. Tom didn't expect Claire to continue like this forever, although each time, he felt her draw nearer, more connected to her passion. She started speaking, telling secrets, revealing her desires beyond the parts of their bodies that touched. She wanted to be normal, not average but normal. She wanted to tuck Faye and Ronald in their bed at night. She longed to close her eyes and sleep for days beside someone who desired the same, and she didn't want to be afraid anymore.

It didn't sound like a lot to ask, and she made him believe that he could deliver her wishes, without ever asking him to do as much.

Tom left her sleeping in bed, a rare stretch when she dozed off. He set the breakfast table and organized another overkill arrangement of food. It was funny that he'd done it the first time and downright absurd that he repeated it, but he couldn't help himself. He wanted to assemble a stretch of time where she wasn't left wanting, had more possibilities than she needed.

He checked the refrigerator for milk and decided to go out for a fresh quart, and perhaps swing by Old Forge to check it out.

At the table beside the door, Tom ripped off a piece of scratch paper for a note. What do you say to a woman like Claire? He might try to be sophisticated, recalling a favorite line of poetry or stealing a grandiose phrase from Homer, but she'd see through his jigsaw use of language.

Tom excelled with pictures as opposed to words, and if he had time, he would draw her silhouette in his notebooks. Instead, he sketched an image of the meadow where they shared time talking and hiking, and by using the side of the pencil, he captured the dense overgrowth where she harvested wildflowers. He wrote "for Claire" near the jagged edge.

He drove straight to Old Forge, leaving his truck on the roadside. He sprinted up the short trail. Drew and his logging buddies had widened it for vehicles, and even though large tire ruts bit into the incline, Tom refused to drive up and violate the site any further. He stretched his legs, sore from his marathon night with Claire. He pictured her sleeping in his bed. He'd been lying next to her, smelling her hair, touching the smoothness of her skin. She was passing away an addiction, as he acquired one of his own. He refused to guess how long he might be under her spell.

Reaching the clear-cut summit, he saw the Cranfield Lakes police car parked near the stumps. Drew walked along the edge of the standing trees, pouring something from a big red canister.

Tom smelled gasoline and stopped short.

Drew glanced over his shoulder, as if anticipating Tom's arrival. He returned to pouring gasoline in a line, marking the edge of the forest.

Tom paced closer. "Don't do this."

Drew kept at it.

Tom grabbed Drew's chunky shoulder and spun the chief around. He wasn't angry with Drew any longer, but he needed to stop him. Even if by fate or ignorance Old Forge must be demolished, setting the Pine Barrens on fire during a dry spell constituted sheer insanity.

Drew bared his teeth, not unlike the agitated raccoon in the trash dumpster last night. The similarity took Tom aback.

"Watch your step." Drew swished the gas can so that it washed Tom's boot with fuel.

Tom withdrew. "We can save Old Forge."

"Save it? I don't want to save it."

"It'll be better than an amusement park. It'll be a monument that we can be proud of, a different kind of business."

"I've heard this talk before."

"We can do it."

"Here's the plan, genius." Drew's eyes grew small, like the screens of his soul closing shut. "I'm going to save this town, right here and now. I'm tired of waiting for miracles. We're all tired. Ask anyone around these parts."

"I can do it. I can make Old Forge work."

"You can do more than I thought. I'll give you that, but I never took you for such a snake in the grass."

"I don't understand."

"Don't start. You're not smart enough to lie about it."

"What are you saying?"

The empty gas can thunked the ground, as Drew punched his fat index finger into Tom's chest. "She's toying with you. She toys with men. She's a drunk. That's what they do."

Tom didn't deny it. Claire was an unusual woman. Unpredictability was only one of her facets, but she had been marginalized by her faults, like he had been for being born seeing the world through a different lens. What did it matter? She was his at the moment. She'd grown up on the top and he on the bottom, but their lives had managed to intersect.

"She does what drunks do," Drew said, almost spitting the words. "You can't count on drunks."

Tom saw the bitterness in Drew's expression. Many times, Tom had been that man, the one who had to deal with defeat, but suddenly he viewed the disparity on another's face. He tried to soften it. *Crazy*. He was about to comfort Drew Spatt. "I don't know what..."

"I went to the motel. They told me you left with her. The trouble is that I don't know where. I couldn't find either one of you last night."

He and Claire had been driving around for hours, waiting for night to fall before raiding Geneva's dumpster. They had created the perfect escape, although they never planned one.

"I don't know what you think you're doing with her, but I'll deal with that later. First, I'm getting rid of this place, and next I'm getting rid of you." Drew resumed with the gasoline, spattering the leaves and dry pine needles. Two empty five-gallon containers lay on their sides by the squad car trunk. The vapors prompted Tom's eyes to water.

"No woods. No idiot ranger." Drew splashed the tree trunks. "I owned this town before they thought of you, and it'll be mine when you're gone and forgotten. And they'll forget you. I guarantee that."

Drew's broad back hovered over the gas can. A billy club hung from his side and a fat pistol from the other. What was Tom's best move? If he ran to alert the others, Drew would destroy Old Forge with a flick of a match and then it wouldn't matter beyond the threat of a forest fire in summer. Once the ashes settled, an amusement park on the ravaged property became easier to envision. It might even seem like a good idea.

Tom began pacing. His brain spliced ideas in a familiar way, myriad splintering veins of thought, never reaching a firm conclusion. He glanced at the house, wondering which parts to rescue, but everything looked too big and bulky to carry. How can you move a house? And not one piece alone created a significant historical fact. He needed the whole thing. He wished Stan Zytko were here. Stan might have a plan or stink bomb or stun gun—some gizmo to save the day.

Tom yanked the cell phone from his pocket. He waited for a signal. As Drew started with his fourth and final can of gas, Tom sprinted for his truck.

The cell phone signal didn't pick up at the road either. Of all the stupid things, he'd never tested it at Old Forge, and why would there be a signal out here? Who needed one?

He hurled the phone in the truck and reached behind the seat. He found his emergency bag and ran up the trail. The contents of the bag beat against his shoulder. Was he going to lure Drew away with Gatorade and Hershey bars? Subdue him with a bag of sterile cotton balls and gauze tape? He didn't think so.

Drew was just finishing up, loading the gas cans into his trunk. "You're back?!" he said sarcastically.

"I'm giving you one more chance," Tom said.

Drew shook his undersized head. "You're giving *me* one more chance? I didn't know you had a sense of humor."

"I know we don't get along."

"You really are stupid. I don't know what Claire sees in you, or maybe that's it."

"Please don't do this. There are other ways to get what you want."

"This one will work."

Tom dug into his emergency bag for a miracle. He felt the long shaft of the crowbar, as if handling it for the first time. It was a curved and hooked length of unforgiving iron. He looked at Drew

Drew watched from across the property. "What are you thinking about?"

"I can't let you burn the place."

"You gonna stop me?" Drew unsheathed his billy club.

Tom watched Drew approach, imagining the old football hero crushing the opposition. Tom dropped the crowbar and the bag.

Drew faced him, propping a foot on a tree stump a few yards shy of Tom's position. Drew slapped the club in his other hand. "You're not stupid. You're nuts."

"I can't let you burn the place."

"Do you want me to call your bluff?"

Tom studied Drew's eyes, searching for a hint of the cop's next move, but Drew didn't flinch. Tom wasn't sure if Drew even breathed.

"It's no longer about you and me," Tom said, "when you're going to set the forest on fire."

"Oh, it's about you and me." Drew put away his billy club and lit up a smoke. He double-checked the flip-top box, crushed the lid with his thumb, and tossed the empty aside. "If you don't want to see this place burn, then leave."

Tom recognized the Newport carton. *Case number #477, the smoker.* Sometimes the hardest details to spot were the ones right under your nose.

"Thinking things over," Drew said, "it's better this way—you being here and all."

"How's that?" Tom asked.

"Who are people gonna believe lit the fire—me or you?"

Tom remembered something he saw in Cranlaker's eyes that night by the bogs when the lynch mob came and Claire broke it up. Some of the men were still pissed with Tom, but others were suspicious of Drew. They didn't say it out loud, but Tom saw by the way they had retreated that night. They were angry with Tom, mostly because he'd witnessed their embarrassment. Pride was a powerful emotion, and right here, Tom faced down the worst of it.

Drew retreated toward the trailhead, puffing his cigarette, looking up at the trees. His voice was shadowy from a distance, swallowed up in the open space created by hours of chainsaw demolition. "There's an order to things. You can't fight that."

Tom still hoped Drew might come to his senses, might remember the common thread that held them together. Despite the dead bogs and decaying town, the pines had been the reason why the first settlers put down roots in this place. It wasn't something you could explain. You felt it.

"You tried to change that order," Drew said. "Don't you see your mistake? Do I have to explain everything to you?"

Tom wasn't listening, just watching and hoping.

"You just didn't stay where you belonged." Drew held the cigarette out from his side. "Out of everyone's way. Get it?"

Tom prepared to let it all go—the forge, Drew. He wanted Drew out of his sight. Whatever happened from this point onward, nothing was going to be the same. In his strange bullying way, that was what Drew was telling him.

"It's been nice knowing you." Drew paused. "Actually, it's been a giant pain in the ass."

Drew flicked the cigarette butt toward the edge of the woods and dropped into the squad car. Tom didn't believe it until he actually saw the flames. A piney couldn't imagine a more flagrant act.

The dry underbrush across the property took quickly to its destruction. Tom watched a line of flames build a random course, as the squad car rumbled down the path and quieted on the highway blacktop.

Tom's mind worked a new puzzle. Should he run back to town and try to convince the others that the forest was burning? Had Drew already set some sort of trap for him there? Either way, the fire would be well under way by the time people wrapped their heads around it.

He retrieved the folding shovel from his emergency bag and attacked the flames. The fire began cutting a ring around the property, following the course Drew had plotted. Tom broke the main line in two spots, making progress by keeping the fire in compartments. He dashed between several more spots, digging and stamping, splattering the smoldering peat soil, spitting the tar smoke from his mouth. But he kept at it. Sooner or later, the smoke would signal others.

Chapter Seventeen
Old Wounds

Claire awoke alone and sat up in Tom's bed. She was soothed by the stillness of the woods. The taller trees guarded the cabin like fortress walls, and the birds and squirrels wove through the pine branches, stirring the pillows of needles. The forest didn't mind you like the people in Cranfield Lakes. The forest was busy. It never studied your moves. It didn't judge your deftness or beauty or hawk each slip into mediocrity. The forest took you in and let you fend for yourself. Whenever Claire walked along Main Street, she stiffened up, a complete contrast to her hikes within the solemnity of the woods. Up on Tom's hill overlooking the lake, the discrimination of the town released its grip, and the heat of that escape created warmth in her body like a chemical reaction. In this special place, she'd never want another drink. No, she didn't need John Barleycorn's remedy for peace of mind.

Through the window, she noticed a gray mist skim the treetops. She went to the porch and saw smoke on the horizon. When pineys sensed fire, they dropped everything and moved toward it, just as anxiously as wildlife was repelled by it. The fear had been ingrained in her since childhood. A kitchen grease fire might burn down a house and spread to the dry pine needle floor. A single blaze might erase one hundred acres of forest before man or nature took control of it. She needed to get into the clear and lend a hand.

She hiked a mile along highway 623, looking for the first signs of men and women with buckets and shovels, and for a brief stretch, she stopped wondering where Tom had gone.

Drew brought the squad car beside her and tracked her steps. She did a double-take at his arrival.

He barked through the open window. "You fucking cunt. Get in the car."

Claire saw the smallness of his face. His lips puckered and eyes scrunched tight—the expression that preceded his swarming fists.

"What did you do?" she asked.

"What'd I do?"

"Yes."

"Got a lot a nerve asking that. You're not much different than your boyfriend."

She kicked the sand at her feet. "You're such a moron."

"Yeah, we'll see who's stupid."

"What did you do?"

"Get in the fucking car."

Claire felt she had to talk with him. Otherwise he'd curse her out by the roadside for an hour or do even worse. She didn't have that kind of time. The pines were burning, and he had something to do with it. She knew it by his rotten tone of voice and the way he burrowed his tongue in his cheek. People wondered why she hung out with a brute like him. The answer was simple. He was predictable. She saw his steps with her eyes sealed shut. It made everything easier, including the rough parts, even the nights when she was bombed into oblivion. Both of them possessed skills that didn't always work in their favor.

She saw an olive green fire engine appear over the hump in the road. "What's burning?"

"How would I know?"

"It looks like the ridge near Old Forge."

"That's right. It's the fucking forge. Get in the car."

"Why are you so angry?"

Drew left the squad car. The lights on the roof revolved in silence, reflecting off the shiny brim of his cap. He moved deliberately, unconcerned with passing traffic and the burgeoning fire down the road.

"Are you going to make this difficult?" he asked.

Claire heard herself grunt. It was deep down, involuntary, like a laugh struggling to break free. She recalled when Elliot served the divorce papers. He'd accused her of souring the marriage, and he was partly right. She turned life into a pissing match. Even her drinking was part of a sacred endurance test, in which she neither knew the rules or limitations. How did she expect other people to understand this?

"I'm going to keep walking," she said, "and when I turn around, I hope I never see you again."

"You switch horses pretty fast, lady."

"What are you talking about?" she asked with the indigination of a woman who already knew the answer.

"I know you're shacking up with King, and who knows who else."

"So what if I am?"

He reached for her elbow, but she withdrew faster than his grasp. A good part of her time with Drew involved watching the quickness of his hands and feet. It was exhausting.

The fire truck sped past, tailed by two other emergency vehicles. The breeze tousled her hair. She imagined herself pushing Drew beneath the wheels. It was a shot of pure adrenaline. It charged her soul.

Drew seemed to sense her temper and gave her space. "Your boyfriend started the fire."

"No one's going to believe that."

"They will."

She stepped into him, not caring if he smacked her this time. "What did you do? I know you're involved in this somehow."

"You think you know."

"Where's Tom?"

"That's hard to say."

She grabbed his big stupid arms—arms that might club her into tomorrow if she provoked him. "What did you do to him? You didn't...?"

"He's all right."

"What do you mean?"

"For now."

"Tell me."

"If he's smart, he'll leave town. I can live with that."

"He's not going anywhere."

"Leaving is a smart move for him, being an arsonist and all. He should stay clear of the woods and children."

"He didn't start any fire." Her fingernails dug at his shirtsleeves. "Where is he?"

"Can't you keep track of him?"

"Tell me. You son of a..."

He pushed her to the ground, and the sand and gravel scraped her knees.

Drew reeled back his boot to kick her in the stomach. Claire sucked in her middle and covered up, but he didn't strike. The target had become too easy.

"If you find your lover boy, you better tell him to start running." He turned away from her, mumbling. "That settles things."

She got to her feet, moving like one of the squirrels atop the railing on Tom's porch. She scampered to the squad car and blocked the door before he could get inside. "Tell me."

"Tell you what?" Finally, he knew more than her. "You..."

"I what?"

"You really have a thing for that dummy."

"You don't understand anything. Where is he?'

"How should I know? Go find him yourself."

She threw an arm across the door and clutched the handle with the other hand, but Drew grabbed hold of her shoulder like a coat on a rack and ripped it free.

When she hit the ground a second time, she felt the scrapes on her hands and elbows burning. Her mind raced past all the things she'd done wrong, leading her toward this errant moment.

"You made me do that." He sounded partly ashamed, when typically he only flashed his red-hot temper.

Claire shuddered. Drunk, she realized, this sometimes turned her on, to be flogged about like she believed she deserved, but sober, it frightened her for a variety of reasons, most of which didn't involve Drew. She knelt in the road and looked up at the rough man that had wedged into her life in many ways yet none of true worth. She watched him sink into the squad car and shut the door. If she held her tongue for once—*oh God, just once*—he might vanish.

He stuck his head out the window. "You gonna be okay?"

She didn't answer. *Fuck you.* She stared down at the dirt, certain her eyes said "fuck you" as well.

"I'm leaving now," he said. "You can see I got things to do."

The car pulled away, kicking up a cloud of dust. It covered her in the bright morning light. She tasted it, too.

Chapter Eighteen

The Law of Forest Fires

Tom breathed the smoke, working the line until his eyes teared against the worst of it. Already some of the trees were burning. Flames scaled the trunks, like candlewicks lit at the base. Wet sap and green needles popped and crackled, drowning out the quiet. It overtook him so fast. Only minutes earlier, he had believed that he'd sectioned the fire. He hunched over, aware that the smoke choked his lungs, even filtered the light of the sun.

An oak stood several yards ahead, and he crawled toward it. Shinnying up a tree was easy for Tom, but with the flames rising faster than he imagined, he clung to the trunk and fought for air.

The trees to the north burned like kindling. Black Pitch Pine smoke choked the mouth of the trail. A ring of fire built three quarters around him, boiling and hissing like dozens of busted steam pipes. He turned from the sweltering heat. How long before this tree took flame?

He forced himself to rise, catching another lungful of the black smoke. He coughed and spit it out, only to take in more. His throat burned, and he fought back the nausea. Was Drew going after Claire next? He imagined it, and this fear urged Tom onward.

A burning pine snapped and fell toward the center, setting off the dry needles upon the floor. Flames crept forward like fingers, joining in a suffocating web, threatening to close the ring of fire. Tom reeled back and tripped over boulders.

He smacked the ground hard. He heard all the old voices taunting him. He owned no instinct for fighting, but where was his instinct to survive or his common sense at least?

A deadly haze shifted over the property and fogged his view. The heat raged against his face, like an oven from which he couldn't withdraw. He stifled the urge to crawl away from the head fires. No, he needed to exit here.

With his bearings diminished in the smoke, he lost his place on the property. He searched for the forge and house, seeing the jagged tear in the colonial wall. He spun his head for the stone forge, making out the cracked mortar and a section of wood from the old Holub grain still.

Tom called upon his memory of the layout he'd penciled in his notes, time and time again: a house, outhouse to the south, stone forge, a stand of birch trees to the north. *Fire burns uphill. It'll go north.*

Last night, as Claire worked her wonders above him in bed, he'd kidded himself about dying. Had he summoned it? Do people get to choose?

He crawled, gagging, spitting up tar. The three-dimensional image of Old Forge reappeared in his mind. He knew all the vectors in every direction: the field of stones to the west, the eastern gulley that confounded inexperienced hikers. He'd have only one shot at escaping, but he knew what to do. *Head fires are short. Get onto burned ground.* Any piney knew this. It took courage and the knowledge that the laws of nature were consistent, unlike the acts of men.

More trees fell to the center, glittering torches, exploding on impact. He was spent and dizzy but refused to submit the end of his story, even though his final legend seemed to gather by the second—Tom King, the man who lit himself on fire at the forge, perhaps by mistake. The dummy who burned himself to death. He was certain that Drew already sowed the seeds of this tale.

Staggering to the southern edge, he grabbed some air and raised his head into the cloud of drifting smoke. His pants hung loosely around his waist. He was exhausted, a scrap intent to ignite beside the flame.

He built a running start and leapt through the blaze. He clamped his eyes tight, covering his face in his hands. Generations of pineys had done this, many living to tell others. He felt the weight of them on him, as the smoke and heat passed through him. They spurred him on, pushed him along, called for him to perform the ancient dance of the flame, and he ran, scraping his elbows on tree trunks. Sticker bushes ripped across his pant legs. He fumbled on stones, teetering yet keeping his feet, zigzagging down the slope. He ran faster, lost a boot but kept going, dropping his hands by his sides to propel forward. He ran as if on fire, but he was not. His clothes were singed and steaming, smoldering in places, but not burning. He smelled the horrific residue of mass incineration all around him.

When he stopped and opened his eyes, he stood five hundred yards or more downhill from it. His chest stretched in pain, his pulse raced through his head, and he recognized his awesome luck. The toasted ground appeared to have the reticence of water, but the flames rose thin and spotty to the south. If he'd waited another minute, the fire would have won the gamble. He watched the flames grow head high, igniting the dry huckleberry, creating a formidable backfire for the inferno. He was in good company. Even the smoke jumpers, the professionals, got themselves trapped from time to time and didn't make it clear.

But he had.

He stumbled about the woods, gathering air and his wits, searching for a glimpse of open road, and when his soles touched the pavement, he collapsed on the shoulder and kicked his remaining, melted boot free. The other foot was burnt so that he felt unable to walk further.

In the distance, fire trucks and cars for the bucket brigade assembled. Sirens wailed on the approach. Cranlakers were yelling orders, armed for a common purpose. He pictured them with shovels and pails, eager to fight for their lives and landscape—the last barrier that kept the inevitable progress of the world at bay. No monster real or imagined frightened men more than fire in the pines, and nothing brought them together faster.

His forehead touched the hot, sandy pavement. *Someone will find me.*

Smoke stained the morning sky, as a line of Canadian geese passed overhead, unconcerned. Tom lay on the roadside, forming a message in his mind. He sealed it up and sent it out for Claire.

Chapter Nineteen

Self-Portrait

Claire determined to get back to town. If she couldn't find Tom there, she'd seek help locating him. She kept thinking about her kids and those phone numbers in Maine. She hadn't seen them lying around in the cabin. She'd even rooted through a couple of drawers, but now she had a more immediate problem with Tom missing and Drew on the loose. He had a strange look in his eye, crazier than usual.

The sirens raced past on the highway. Smoked nestled the treetops. Claire kept walking, her legs scuffed and bleeding. She recalled that Chinese proverb about the yin and yang. Her entire existence had been one sided, and lately, she paid for it with the other. She blamed herself for getting too close to Tom, showering her bad luck upon him. What was that story about the man who discovered his poisonous effect on people and determined to drink himself to death? Suddenly, that decision appeared noble. Her life wasn't all that important if it laid others to waste.

She hitched a ride from a Medford volunteer who was running back for supplies. He'd nearly passed her on the roadside yet stopped to ask about her bloodied hands and knee.

"I fell jogging." She climbed into his tall truck with fat oversized tires.

"Jogging?"

"I tripped and skidded on the blacktop." The lie rolled right off her lips. Covering up the bruises from Drew was second nature. The volunteer didn't seem to buy her story. No one ever did, but they always let it slide. People were funny like that.

At the Lakeside Motel, she phoned the Wharton ranger station, inquiring about Tom. She called the emergency dispatcher too, and nothing came of that either. Distracted by the fire, people were short in conversation. No one owned a personal stake in Tom, and the general lack of concern felt casually cruel to Claire.

By the time she got Nat from the Lazy Eye on the line, she was panicked. Nat was closing down the café to deliver meals for the fire crews, and the mention of the burning woods at Old Forge fortified her resolve to find Tom.

"Are you sure you haven't seen him?" she asked.

"What's the problem?" Nat said.

"No one's seen him at the fire either."

"That's strange, but that boy's strange anyway."

"What's that supposed to mean?"

"When did you get so sensitive?"

"No one's seen him?"

"Why do you care about that stray dog anyway?"

She hung up and took a shower. She pieced together bits of conversation with Tom about Old Forge and the phone numbers from Maine, forcing together the sketchy facts. She tried to rinse away her worst thoughts—maybe it wasn't for real, maybe it all meant nothing. The water ran cold before she realized that she'd been running down dead-end scenarios for almost an hour.

A towel strapped her torso as she moved about the room. Fresh blood dotted the worn white cotton, and she sat on the corner of the bed and dabbed her wounds with tissues until they clotted. She recalled the brush burns she used to get cheerleading at Cranfield High. The scabs caked and itched all season long.

Claire bandaged the final wound as best she could, wondering where she'd be when it healed. Her time was running short at the Lakeside and scabs took time to mend. First they dried and flaked, leaving little bits here and there. Next came fresh pink tissue from underneath, like baby's skin starting anew, but there'd always be a scar, and she wondered what shape these scars might assume.

She stood and let the towel fall from her waist, glimpsing her bony frame in the mirror. She saw a much older woman, a body withering. She turned her eyes away. What did Tom see in her? Did he really feel for her? Or was she the best that he could get? She had never asked him important questions. Had she asked him any questions at all? Or was it only about her and her crippling inability to get on with life?

The local cable access station played 50's oldies, as it scrolled community information on the screen in flickering white letters: Thursday's Town Meeting—discussion of plans for the ridge property along highway 623. ...

It was ironic that that swatch of land burned at this very moment. Then Claire remembered Mayor Jameson. JJ was involved in the property debacle, too. Tom had told her so.

Claire dressed in long pants and sleeves and tracked JJ down at the firehouse. A dozen volunteers moved about the main garage. The mayor and his wife Junior prepared dinner for the next shift of firefighters. They draped checkered plastic over folding tables, as Nat unloaded aluminum trays from his van.

JJ noticed Claire approach. "Just in time. We could use another pair of hands."

Claire came to him, feeling a bit of her old self again. Her passion ran hot and cold. The parameters of her life felt perpetually in flux. "We have to talk."

Junior peered over stacking cups by a ten-gallon jerry jug of iced bug juice. Nat paused with a steaming tray of beans and franks.

"What's it about?" JJ asked.

"What happened to Tom?" She noticed Nat look in another direction. She hadn't thought Nat lied on the phone, but she figured he knew something now.

"If you want to add anything to the investigation..." JJ started.

"Investigation?"

"The arson at the ridge property."

"What's that got to do with Tom?" she asked.

"You haven't heard?"

"Tell me."

"We found the gas cans in back of his truck."

"Gas cans? You're saying Tom set Old Forge on fire?"

"It appears he may have had something..."

"Don't give me that bullshit."

Nat and Junior busied themselves again. The other volunteers were only now catching the tone of the conversation. They puttered in the background, like people pretending they weren't listening.

"He wouldn't set Old Forge on fire," Claire said. "He loved that place."

"Maybe that's why. There's no logic in arson cases. That's what they tell me."

"Has everyone in this town gone mad?"

"I know you kind of looked after the poor bastard."

"He wasn't a poor bastard until this happened."

"I understand. You're upset."

"What has Drew gotten you into?"

Everyone in the station stopped moving. They looked over, waiting.

"Let's be reasonable, Claire."

"Arson is not reasonable. Something tells me that you better have a conversation with the Chief of Police."

"Hey, it looks like the fire is under control. No one is hurt. There's no property damage, but torching the woods carries penalties. It's out of my hands."

"Where is Tom?"

"You know, if he didn't come back to town..."

"God, you sound just like Drew."

JJ didn't appreciate her last remark. Claire read it directly on his face.

"Is Tom all right?" Claire asked.

"He got trapped in the fire, I think."

The image of Tom injured or worse crossed her mind, and she wavered, as if unable to continue standing. If she ever needed a stiff belt of whiskey, it was right here and now. Weren't there times when she could cheat—take a little nip to get through? She shutdown those thoughts as best she could. Tom needed her. She wrung her hands to conceal the fact that they were shaking. "I thought you said no one got hurt."

"You know what I meant. I was talking about..."

"Yeah, I know what you meant. You were talking about important people—everyone else but him. Where is he?"

"I hear they found him on the road and took him to Middleton."

"Why didn't you say so in the first place?" She began to choke up. "Is he alive?"

"Yes."

Claire pulled away. She saw the open sky ahead but stopped beneath the huge overhead doors. She pivoted to take in everyone milling about the room. She saw Kevin Stower and a dozen others she recognized—people who probably expected more out of her than she was capable of giving. They were watching her, not knowing whether the town's favored daughter was going to burst into tears or another rage.

"This whole situation is despicable," she said. "I imagine some of you know that but are too scared to speak."

Nat called over from the van. "You need to calm down, honey. Think this through."

"What arsonist gets caught in their own fire?"

"It was probably an accident. You heard JJ."

The scrapes on her arms and legs burned from the salt in her perspiration. "It's no accident. I think some of you know that, too. Talk to Drew."

"Come on, now."

"Don't forget I was there when you boys wanted to lynch Tom for no reason. I was a witness at the bogs that night, too."

She scanned their faces, registering their disbelief. It came toward her like a wave, a reflective sheen of ignorance. This was the greeting that Tom received every day from his fellow Cranlakers.

"You people have a lot to learn," she said and stormed off on the head wind that drove her there in the first place.

Chapter Twenty
Being Invisible

om hitched a ride back from the Medford Hospital with a nurse going off duty and reached his truck on the roadside after dark. Her car stopped several yards from the cross street. His feet ached, as did his legs and arms, from the burns, but it was nothing he couldn't manage with patience.

The nurse had freckles and peach lipstick. "You should have stayed a night in the hospital."

"I don't see much use in it." He got out and stood to watch her car taillights disappear south along highway 623. He wondered if he should follow that same path away from town.

The woods looked like burnt matchsticks stuck in rows, and daylight seeped through the scorched and twisted columns. The air smelled of ash, and the latent heat of the fire resonated from the dead forest. Blackened stubs of huckleberry poked up from the ground, and no birds flew overhead. Nothing survived a blaze like this. The colonial house was gone for certain, and the old stone forge had probably split and collapsed. Nighttime served him well to blind his view from the devastation.

He thought of Claire—her hands upon his ribs, the spare words she whispered in his ear. He remembered her losing her temper not far from here when they'd come across the wreck of a chicken truck. Which version of her was he supposed to keep in mind? Perhaps a little of both.

At the cross street, fire crews searched the remains for smoldering pots in the sandy soil. They prodded the dirt with rods and shovels, exposing burning coals that might ignite into flames later. In the past, Tom had joined crews like this. The woods were his responsibility, but today, he boarded his truck and turned over the ignition. There was nothing left to salvage.

At the cabin, Tom gathered the diary and his notes on Old Forge. He swept Geneva's garbage into a trash bag and double checked that the recovered phone numbers for Claire were still in his wallet. He packed a bag for a few days, convincing himself he could return anytime. He wasn't sure what he stuffed into the sack: underwear, socks, a handful of cash. What did he need for dodging the inevitable?

Claire's hair-tie sat on the end table. He picked it up and looked at the twists of black hair caught in the elastic. He slipped it in his pocket. He noticed she'd taken the note he'd drawn for her. Big dreams, he had. *Big dreams.*

Tom drove twenty miles or more to the north, still unsure of his destination. He could sleep in his truck and grab cheap meals on the road. He needed to make phone calls and connect with Zytko. He needed to stay out of sight while he was under suspicion for starting the fire. Once again, he had to deal with the immeasurable weight of public scorn. There was a lot of benefit to disappearing for a week or longer.

He stopped at an all-night diner for coffee and a plate of scrambled eggs and toast. He watched the traffic leading onto the Garden State Parkway. The waitress filled his cup and delivered his check. The table beside him filled and cleared twice. The world moved in sped up motion, unconcerned with his problems. His skill at vanishing into a crowd was stronger than ever.

When Tom had pulled away from his cabin that night, he feared that leaving formed the hardest part of his journey. He half-expected Drew to tail him for a few miles, corral him into a remote spot, and try to finish what he'd started on the ridge by the forge. At the very least, Tom feared that he'd never shake the accusations, that he would be on the run for a long time. But disappearing turned out to be the easiest part. He had spent a lifetime trying to lay low.

Tom sat hovering over a mug of lukewarm coffee, keeping one eye on the road outside the diner. Was anyone coming after him? Time would tell.

This moment, when Tom was alone and no one minded his business, generally came as a relief, but today he felt the loss, the absence of purpose. He'd never had much to gain at any particular time in his life. He supposed there were issues of pride and honor, but those seemed to belong to other men. He never possessed much money, so he didn't lay awake at night, like wealthy men were said to do, fretting over theft and the accumulation of further wealth. He owned a cherished cabin in the woods and the attention of a woman whom he adored, yet he couldn't entirely save her from herself. Perhaps that was the favor she really asked of him, to show her how to swim in the mess of her life. His willingness to run and hide probably confused her. Women were complicated animals. They asked for things other than they desired. Alicia Hardaway had taught him that.

Chapter Twenty-One

Penance

When Claire reached Middleton, Tom had already checked out of the hospital. She left the lobby only minutes after her arrival. Where would he go in his condition? The nurse said that he would heal fine, but what was with his personal drive? Had it only been the night before they'd spent lying together? In the morning, he'd barely escaped a raging forest fire, but he refused to rest in the hospital. Even the idea of that seemed exhausting.

She headed for Tom's place in the woods. It felt as if more than one day had elapsed. Her mind changed rapidly, and back again, and then set upon another course of action. Her resolve appeared firm at times and dissipated with the next thought. She gripped the Impala's steering wheel, as if to attach herself to the rotating earth.

Claire felt Tom's strength like never before and was jealous of it in her tenuous condition. Tom drew from a place that eluded her and most others. Elliot would be cursing, blaming everyone for his lousy lot in life. His mother had taught him to be bitter. Lately, Claire felt as if her nerve endings had pushed to the surface. She was sensitive to the touch, but Tom wasn't like that, probably not ever. He kept his dignity in any circumstance, and people called it stupid. When she used to think of him, she held a healthy amount of curiosity for a man who'd been knocked down so often but never stayed down. She feared Drew might decide to kill him to finally defeat him, and this thought made her shiver. Tom took the shots and kept moving. That was why Cranlakers called him an idiot, mocking what they failed to fathom, rejecting the very spirit they lacked.

At the cabin, the taste of smoke still flavored the forest air. Claire gave the drawers another good turn and scanned the kitchen cabinets. She looked behind the books and checked a number of the countless trash bins in and outside of his cabin. The garbage from Geneva's was cleaned up. *Tom was here and left.* She searched for Geneva's trash bunched up in a fresh garbage bag. It was dawn before she was finished finding nothing at all—not Tom, not the phone numbers, no trace of where they'd gone either.

The bottle of sherry remained on the kitchen counter beside the stove. She knew exactly where it stood, which way the label faced, how high the level stood behind the green glass, but she couldn't bring herself to either take a sip or pour it down the drain. A year of heavy drinking, building up from a few nightly rounds into all day benders, brought her to this—a liter of sherry calling her from the kitchen counter. That bottle seemed to have more personality than half the people she knew in town.

She dropped into bed to sleep while she awaited Tom's return. She tossed most of the night, her nightmares not leaving her even with her eyes open. It seemed like the longest night of her life. And still no Tom.

In the morning, Claire pinned a note to the front door, along with her hopes. She got into her car and hunched over the steering wheel. *God, all that time wasted with Drew when he promised, no, pledged to help locate Elliot and the kids.* Had she lost her chance with Tom? Where had he gone? He was so good for her. She knew it just by the way he looked after her, offered her space and time to reach the place she needed to be. She recalled lying in his arms, hearing his plans for a historic park at Old Forge. The details amazed her, and she found herself plummeting into the depths of his vision. It was like swimming in the warm August waters off Breezy Point, immersed in a perfect notion of how life might be. She had slept in that feeling until daylight. She loved the woods by his cabin. Quitting the bottle was a lot about putting yourself in the right place at the right time. But now Tom was gone along with his dreams.

The image of Drew's nasty expression punched through her thoughts. Claire located the feeling she needed to survive, the emotion that carried her when all else failed. She locked onto the rage that quieted her nerves and made her hands go steady.

She spun her car wheels in the soft dirt outside the cabin and headed for JJ's place.

Town hall looked like the only building along Main Street not up for sale, and it probably wouldn't be long for that one either. She pulled up to the curb and left the Impala with all her stuff jammed in the trunk and seats. In a sense, she was a one-woman traveling show. She might set up shop in front of anyone's house, do whatever pleased her, seek only her own satisfaction.

Through the glass breakfront to the mayor's office, Claire spotted JJ leaning over a set of color drawings and plans for the Old Forge property. He was talking to himself, perhaps practicing his speech for Thursday night's town meeting. Oil paintings of his father and grandfather hung on the wall behind his desk, flanking the current mayor like the turkey vultures flanking the clock tower outside.

Claire thought of Tom and hardened her resolve to settle the score for the injustice—not just for him but for herself as well. She walked past the secretary, barged into JJ's office, and closed the door.

"Claire?" JJ looked alarmed by her presence or perhaps it was the obvious beat of her heart and the breathlessness she'd summoned from her flight up the front steps.

"I've got bad news," she said.

JJ drew a sustained breath. "What is it?"

"I can't find Tom King anywhere."

"What's so bad about that?"

When she heard his question, she immediately knew why she'd been searching for Tom. It was more than getting the phone numbers for Maine and finding her kids. She wanted that more than anything, but another part of her wanted to hear Tom say that he cared for her, confirm that he'd risk everything for her, that she was still worth it. So she was being selfish after all. She needed to hear that he wasn't fooling. This was her way of proving that both she and he mattered.

"Drew has chased him off," she said. "I know it."

"Tom will show up."

"I know more than you think about the situation, and I don't care what it costs me to speak up."

JJ pushed away from his desk. He seemed to be taking her in—her haggard look, her dicey composure. "You look like hell. Why don't you get some rest?"

"Don't patronize me. You and Drew were behind the Old Forge disaster."

"What are you…"

"I saw Drew and his buddies cutting the trees. I saw them. And Tom witnessed the rest, heard you plotting along with Drew."

JJ held his tongue.

"That's right." She wore her bruises like strange tattoos, even if most of them were covered up beneath her clothing. "Both you and I know Drew pushes too far."

"What are you saying?"

"I want Drew gone, and I'll stop at nothing to make that happen."

JJ's high-pitched voice broke over his plea. "Let's be reasonable here."

"Reasonable?"

"You know I'd never harm the woods."

"I don't' care much about you at the moment."

"I wouldn't burn the woods. I'll swear to that on my father's grave."

"I've made my own pledges lately. Either you deal with Drew or I'm going to dig up all the graves around here."

"That's a brave assertion, don't you think?

"Brave?" She shook her head. If she had been this brave sooner, she might not be in this all-around mess.

"Let me think about this."

She heard his tone. He was trying to handle her like a woman. For her whole life, she'd watched men do this, either with words or physical force, but she took them on, surprised them by holding her ground. She out drank half the men and took as many punches too. She wasn't particularly proud of this, although it just occurred to her that even Drew felt bad about beating her that last time. He kept throwing her down rather than raise his fists, but she didn't give in, kept coming back up. There was a whole world about herself she didn't understand, but now she had to acknowledge the flaws because they weren't working for her any longer.

Claire eyed JJ like she did when she was drunk and donned her worst of moods. "I'm not walking out of here until something happens."

"Okay, lets..."

"I've got nothing against you, but I know enough to ruin your day and a whole bunch of other days."

"What, are you on some kind of vendetta?"

"Call it what you want."

"Hell, Claire."

"I'm sure you don't know anything about hell." Right there, she started rolling up her sleeves and showing JJ the spots where Drew manhandled her and downright punched her silly. JJ looked away, but she would take off her shirt in order to seize his attention, show him all the places where she'd let Drew knock her around. For the first time, she admitted that she was one of those women, one of those stupid girls that got suckered into a relationship where a man offered sexy promises and then beat you up just to feel better about himself.

She didn't have to impart much of a confession, before JJ sank in his big mayor's chair.

"Christ, Claire, what do you want me to do?"

Chapter Twenty-Two
Alicia's Gift

By late morning, Tom eased toward the medical reference archive in the Cranfield Lakes Library. Still without a firm plan, beyond common sense even, he'd followed his heart and driven back into the center of town. Claire cast a hard spell over him. How far did he think he was going without her?

Alicia Hardaway sat behind her desk, unwrapping a new shipment of books. Her blonde hair was gelled and combed to one side, tucked behind her ear like a drape. "Look what just fell out of the trees."

"So you heard that I'm an arson suspect."

"Are you all right?"

"Yeah, if I don't run into Officer Spatt."

"Come on, Tom, everyone knows you didn't start that fire."

"Not the people that matter."

"There's more than one person defending your name."

"What do you mean?"

"Claire's been tearing up the floorboards looking for you. I don't know what's gotten into her, but she's more riled up than usual."

"Looking for me?"

"Yeah, you."

He just stared at her. If he told Alicia everything, she'd let him know if he was right or wrong, but he also understood that Claire's emotions spun in different directions at once. She could be tracking him down to pick a fight. Either way, Alicia might be the last person on the planet to whom he should profess his love for Claire.

"Are you going to speak?" Alicia asked, "or is this going to be like your voice mail—no response at all."

"I need your help." Tom placed the Turnley Diary in front of her and waited for her reaction.

"What is it?"

"This is what I found at Old Forge."

"I thought it was a really big horseshoe."

"You know that wasn't true."

"I couldn't figure out why you lied, but you don't give a person a lot of information."

"It's Michael Turnley's diary. He's the builder of the old forge."

"Turnley? I thought you said it was Nutley."

"It's a long story. I got it wrong."

"Are you sure this time?"

"Yes."

"Let me check this Turnley guy out." Alicia left the diary and disappeared into the stacks. She returned with a fresh photocopied sheet of paper. "Yup, he's on the town record in 1774. Michael Turnley, blacksmith and candle maker. Not quite the lost diary of George Washington."

"He was a silversmith, too. I have a few items." Tom spilled the silver buttons on the table.

She picked up one and held it beneath the lamplight. "Cute. I'm sure somebody would be interested in these knickknacks."

253

"I was hoping it'd be more than that. Take a look at his diary."

Tom left Alicia at her desk and got a drink of water, walking lightly upon his sore feet. Alicia knew the town history, top to bottom, and it always bugged him that she never recognized the Nutley name. On the other hand, Turnley didn't seem to electrify her interest either. Tom wondered exactly what he had found at the forge.

From a distance, he saw her flipping the pages with a rubber thumb. Sometimes, she hobbled off to consult another book. The activity went on like this for a while, until he approached her desk again. Alicia never lifted her eyes from her work.

"What do you think?" he asked.

"Why didn't you say his name was Turnley? It would've saved me a lot of trouble."

"Like I said, it's a long story."

"His writing style is wonderful. You could publish this."

"Do you think?"

"Look at all these facts about the town."

"Want to hear the best one?"

"What is it?"

"He was a spy for the British during the Revolution."

She looked up. "Why do you say that?"

"It's in the diary. That's why he made all those lists about the town. He spied on the furnaces in Batso and other towns. He tracked their production for the king's army."

"Tallied the ammunitions?"

"And other things."

"That's an interesting story."

"He had a scandalous love affair, and the town turned against him. This was how he reacted. He wanted to get even."

Her eyes went wide, not unlike when they had sex in the archive. He never fully understood that expression. She was a puzzle to him, like a column of numbers to add, utter randomness, no structure to form a picture in his mind. This was what most attracted him to Alicia. She was one of life's puzzles he could get close to and it wouldn't necessarily sting him.

"I'm not making it up," Tom said.

"Did you say a scandalous love affair?"

"He had an affair and…"

"Do you know what you're saying?"

"It's all in the diary."

"You're talking about the Bachelor of the Barrens."

"Yes, I'm familiar with the name."

"How about the legend?"

"I've heard stories."

"I can't believe you." She pointed toward the local reference section and then dropped her hand. "Are you only familiar with books on tape?"

"You know I prefer them."

"You're pathetic. Okay, I'll tell you then. The Bachelor supposedly bedded the doctor's wife, and because of it, the doctor and his wife left town in disgrace. The Bachelor lived alone in the woods from then on, thus the name."

"That's sort of what the diary says."

"That's why they called him The Bachelor of the Barrens. My mother used to joke about it whenever my father stole dessert before dinner. 'It must be the Bachelor,' she said. That was the legend. Whenever you lost something, you blamed the Bachelor. He snuck out of the woods and took it."

"It's better than the Jersey Devil."

"It was just another Pines legend until now," Alicia said. "Or am I wrong? Does the diary actually tell that story?"

"Sort of. Turnley had an affair but not with the doctor's wife."

"Who then?"

"It was the doctor."

"Get out of here." Her hair seemed to bristle.

"That's how I read it."

"Now that's a scandal worthy of the twenty-first century." Alicia stood up on her slipper leg and shook his hand. "Bravo, Tom. You found him. Wait till Stan Zytko sees this."

"I already called him."

"He probably loved it."

"I couldn't tell, but he's coming to meet me."

"Believe me, he loves it if he's coming out to see you." Alicia pivoted on her stump leg. "This is sure going to change the complexion of Thursday's meeting."

"The town meeting?"

"JJ's introducing his proposal for the property at Old Forge."

"Oh, the miniature golf course or whatever."

She picked up the diary. "But you have this. It might be worth something."

"I was hoping you'd see it like that."

"No kidding." She shook her head. "You're going to pull this off after all."

Tom accepted the book from her hands and felt its old cover. It was something powerful, more powerful than he'd ever hoped. He tried not to get ahead of himself. Small steps, like reading his mail. If he broke it down into small steps, he'd conquer each one.

"Are you all right?" Alicia asked.

"It's been a rough couple of days."

She pointed toward the chair. "Have a seat. We need to talk."

"Is this about..." He glanced at her midsection. "You know."

"I've got news, not that you bothered to ask."

"Sorry." He sat down. He wasn't trying to avoid talk of the baby, but he'd simply put it out of his mind. The baby would come, no matter what he did or said. He needed to work out the details, from whatever distance he found himself from town.

"Don't you answer your messages?" Alicia asked.

"I didn't know you called."

"If you have voicemail, you're supposed to check it. That's how it works."

"I didn't check."

"Apparently not. I want to talk about things."

"It sounds important."

She lowered her voice. "There's no baby."

"What?"

"I've been to the doctor."

"Where did it go?"

"They're not sure. I may not have been pregnant, or it didn't take."

"I don't understand."

"It's a woman's problem," she whispered. "I'll be okay."

"I'm sorry."

"I thought you'd be relieved."

He wasn't sure what to make of his feelings. He felt strangely sad about the loss. "I was getting used to the idea."

"You were?"

"I think so."

"You can tell me the truth. It's okay."

"Is it?"

"Don't say anything."

He saw the librarian straddling several emotions.

"Do you know how I know when you're nervous?" she asked. "Because you start repeating me."

"I do?"

"I'm okay with this. I've been through worse."

"You have?"

"You're just going to keep repeating me, aren't you?"

"Yes."

He smiled. "Maybe the Bachelor stole the baby."

"Tom, that's not funny."

He felt the sheer weight of Alicia's child being gone from his worries. He knew she really wanted a child, and that loss kept him from outwardly expressing his relief. He decided to shift to an earlier topic. "You know, I couldn't have found The Bachelor of the Barrens without you."

"I know."

"I mean, it's a great story."

"It reminds me of you."

"How's that?"

"You're always going to be a bachelor in the woods. I wish I knew what went on in that head of yours."

He touched her cheek, no fear of who might see. Two women by the new fiction shelf stopped talking and gawked. Tom found her eyes beneath a chop of blonde hair.

"What is it, Tom?"

"You're one of the few people who ever bothered to ask."

He left Alicia standing at her desk but turned to find her still watching him. He recalled the crazy sex they had in the library annex and the inverted relationship that accompanied it. Part of him disliked giving that up.

"Hey," Alicia said. "Don't forget to use your library card once in awhile."

Chapter Twenty-Three
Making Even

Claire felt this day was a long time coming. Her old plan was to have her kids back in the house and let Drew fade away from her attention, but her kids and house were gone, as well as the majority of her self-respect. A new plan had to be pushed through, and even though she shivered at times and felt as skittish as an alley cat on ice, she was clear about her intentions. It was about getting back her own.

JJ walked with Claire to the police station next to the town hall. "You don't have to come in. I promise I'll see to finishing this like I said."

"No way." Claire needed to see it go down, no matter how much it scared her.

They walked past the dispatcher and into the office where Drew kept his football trophies and black and white photos from his days playing for Cranfield Lakes High. Claire realized that she'd never once come to visit him, didn't know what the inside of Drew's world looked like, couldn't pick the details of his life out of a lineup.

Drew had his feet up on his desk, reading a copy of *Sports Illustrated*. "What's she doing here?"

"We have to talk." JJ took the wooden chair from the wall and dragged it in front of Drew's desk. He motioned for

Claire to sit on the couch behind him. "This isn't going to be a long conversation."

Drew dropped his feet on the floor. "You look serious."

"I need to speak with you about Old Forge."

"You think that's smart? You know, with her around."

"She's here for her own reasons."

Claire clasped her hands together to quiet the tremors. They weren't as bad as the night before, although their intensity rose and fell. She focused on Drew and the nuance of his expression, waiting her turn to speak. She hoped to see him squirm, but she expected that he would never offer apologies.

"Have it your way." Drew put his chunky hands on his desk.

"Who really set Old Forge on fire?"

"You don't have to ask questions like that. You know Tom King…"

"Tom would never burn that place," Claire said.

JJ didn't look back, only raised a hand for her to be quiet.

"Geezuz," Drew said. "Has *she* gotten to you?"

JJ kept his cool. "She saw you and some men clear-cutting at Old Forge before the fire."

"Prove it," Drew replied. "The place is entirely burnt to the ground."

"The fire is another point of concern. All those gas cans in the back of Tom's truck had to be filled somewhere and by someone."

"So?"

"Tom didn't even own gas cans, did he?"

"You want answers from me? I don't even like your questions."

Claire heard Deputy Richie arrive in the police station, just as JJ had instructed him to do by phone before they left the mayor's office. She felt safer with another police officer nearby. She moved to the end of the couch. "I saw you cutting the trees. I'm the proof JJ needs. I saw you driving away from the fire that day. I'll tell everything I know. I'll tell it all."

Drew scrunched his face. "What are you going to do, believe me or some drunk-ass bitch?"

"This drunk-ass bitch," Claire said, "can see clearly, and she's tired of all the lies."

"Shut up."

"Lies about what you've been doing, lies about helping to find my kids. Did you ever once make those calls to the state missing persons unit?"

"Is this what this is about?"

"That and more."

"It's easy to see why Elliot skipped town."

"You good-for-nothing bastard."

JJ raised his hand for her again to be silent. He breathed slowly, digging for words. "It's like Claire said a few moments ago in my office, you go too far."

Drew stood up. "Geezuz..."

"Sit down." JJ waited for Drew to regain control, which took almost a minute of pacing and cussing to himself until he took his seat again.

"I was with you on the Old Forge plans," JJ continued. "But at the moment, I have so many reasons to put you under suspicion that I don't know where to begin. I'm not even sure I want to fill out the stack of paperwork involved."

"Aren't you putting the finger on yourself too?"

"Not for any fire, not for beating the stuffing out of your girlfriend and God knows who else." He glanced back. "No offense, Claire."

JJ squared off with Drew again. "When you set the pines on fire, you crossed a line in these parts that you can't ever cross back over again."

Drew stared at Claire like he did when he was about to crack her across the mouth. His hands clutched his gun belt. "You stupid bitch. Nobody's going to believe you."

"It's over," JJ said. "I suspect you should be making alternate plans."

"Like what?"

"You can begin by turning in your gun and badge."

"You're not doing this."

"I have to."

"You're not cutting me out of Old Forge. They were my plans too."

"The moment you started playing with matches, you cut yourself out."

"What do you want me to do?"

"I want your resignation immediately after you hand over your gun."

"Geezuz, JJ, consider what you're saying. Think about our plans."

By now, Richey had come to the doorway, watching the scene in disbelief.

JJ noticed this. "Richie is replacing you."

"Richie," Drew scoffed.

"It could be a lot worse," JJ said. "Arson, knocking around a lady, both carry stiff penalties. But if Claire will allow it..."

"If Claire will allow what?"

"Let me finish. If Claire doesn't want to press charges, I think you should make yourself scarce in these parts and let this town return to the business of putting itself back together."

In all of Claire's experience, she'd never seen JJ act or even speak with such assuredness and the confidence of his legendary forefathers. Here in the Drew's office, the mayor's screechy voice mustered enough conviction to impress anyone within earshot. But it was the irony in JJ's decision that struck her the hardest. That night out by the bogs, when the men seemed prepared to pin Tom as their scapegoat for a string of rotten luck, Drew had offered Tom the same miserable terms: to get out of town with the next breeze. This time the charges weren't trumped up.

JJ turned back to Claire. "What do you think, Claire?"

"It sounds right to me." She looked Drew in the eye. She was a little shaky. Only with a belly full of booze had she been able to face Drew down with requisite spite, but she didn't need a shot of whiskey to articulate her feelings. In longer than she cared to remember, she hadn't felt in control of her destiny.

"I'm going to tell you this once." She got up and stood beside JJ's chair to face Drew directly. "Isn't that one of your favorite sayings?"

"Spit it out," Drew said.

"I won't press charges if you leave."

"Right." He scoffed but not enough to force the issue.

Claire clutched for her future now. "Get lost, sweetheart."

Chapter Twenty-Four

The History of Garbage

T om sat in his pickup truck outside the wreck of Old Forge. It rained throughout the afternoon. The fire crews were gone, and steam rose from the warmest parts of the scorched forest. Heavy drops of water pummeled the windshield, and the flashers to Stan Zytko's van reflected in the rearview mirror.

Zytko sat beside Tom, flipping through the colonial diary and notes. "Alicia's right. You've got enough here to freeze construction on the site."

"I always sketched the forge, but I didn't know why. I never figured it'd be under assault like this."

"You've made it easy to rebuild."

"Do you think it'll work? Will the diary convince people?"

"It'll stop your amusement park buddies dead in their tracks."

"Really?"

"I wish I had something like this to slap in front of the Terrapin Brothers."

"What can we do?"

"I know people at the State House. This will probably be simple, just the usual government red tape." Zytko looked up from the diary. "What took you so long to get this to me?"

Tom considered the question. "There's a woman. I kind of lost track of time."

"Is she a worthy distraction?"

"There's more than one thing that needs saving around here."

"What does this woman say about that?"

"I don't know."

"It sounds like you're deep into something. What's her name?"

"Claire." Tom pictured her back in town. He hadn't been able to reach her by cell phone, but he pictured her thrashing, fighting the dying status quo of Cranfield Lakes. At moments, she seemed to be making progress, and at others, she appeared trapped like any other Cranlaker.

"Let me offer you a piece of advice," Zytko said. "I don't know where I'd be today without Mary. If it doesn't kill you, keep sinking into whatever Claire has going for you."

"Then I need your help. I hesitate to ask, but I don't know where else to turn. I don't trust anyone else at the moment."

"What is it?"

"I have some phone numbers. I need to know where they lead." Tom explained the situation with Claire, her kids, and Elliot Bogdon.

"Your phone numbers are an easy problem."

"I figured you knew how." Tom handed Zytko the phone bill from Geneva's garbage. "I don't know if this is legal."

"Don't lose sleep over it. Legal is a relative question in this day and age, which is ironic because there's never been more laws at any time in history. You can't break wind without violating a law somewhere."

"I guess so, but I stole the phone numbers."

"You? From where?"

"The garbage." He made Zytko laugh over the whole raccoon and dumpster story.

"So you're the garbage maven."

"There's a lot of stuff in people's trashcans."

"You keep saying. You are perhaps the most unique individual I've ever met."

Tom accepted it as a compliment, for Zytko was truly a unique man. "When can you get back to me about the numbers?"

"Give me a couple of days."

"You understand the delicate nature. Her ex-husband can't suspect."

"Have some faith, Tom. If this pans out, there's a guy up in Maine I can call."

"You know people everywhere, don't you?"

"I suppose now I have a guy in Cranfield Lakes, too."

Tom shook his hand. "Yes, you do."

Zytko had a tight grip that meant business. "For starters, you've got to teach my guys how to do this garbage research thing. It's going to add a whole new meaning to the term *junk science*."

"Actually it's called garbology."

"Really."

"I'll get your guys up to speed, but I need one last favor."

"Shoot."

"I need to lay low for a couple of days. Can I crash at your place until this business with Old Forge shakes out?"

"No problem. You can have the couch. Mary's one hell of a cook."

"I appreciate it."

Zytko had a faraway look now. "I wonder what kind of gems are in the Terrapin Brothers' trash dumpster."

"I'll help you take a look."

"I'm starting to believe in trash."

"Trash doesn't lie."

"Apparently not."

"I borrowed the whole idea from a picture in *National Geographic*—some researchers digging through Mayan ruins. I thought, why couldn't I do that at Old Forge?"

"Trash archeology," Zytko said. "I like it."

"After all the stories, your trash says what you're really up to. It's like those guys in *National Geographic*. That's what they're looking at most of the time, people's garbage, the stuff they left behind, the things they couldn't use, even the bones of their dead. It's like a footprint. You can't avoid leaving footprints wherever you go."

"Tom, that's damned poetic."

Chapter Twenty-Five

Michael Turnley,
Blacksmith, Candle Maker
Province New Jersey
February 12, 1778

For three long years,
I've suffered your absence.
Why are we put to this earth as we are,
if we are not to live the life which we most desire?

You are gone,
and I am ridiculed along the south lake.
Yet the forest quiets the noise,
and I can reflect.
I hear our talks by the forge,
and the moments in the soft pine needle beds
by the eastern shores.

For a time, you opened your heart,
and I am thankful,
as sure as I forge these buttons
that will never don your coat.
You have taught me much,
and I am thankful.
We are as courageous as we intend to be.

Chapter Twenty-Six
The Legend of Tom King

F our days. Four mornings Claire walked the fields at sunrise, parting the humid mist that rose from the extinguished bogs. Four afternoons she sat on Tom's front porch rocker, breathing in the scent of the mature pines, searching for a holistic cure or just a single thought to carry her through the hours. Four nights she lay in Tom's bed, smelling the sheets where they'd made love. A few times she'd heard the sound of a passing truck and snapped up from bed. She emptied her bank account and, at moments, the contents of her stomach. Four days without a drink, and during parts of those days, she thought differently about whiskey burning her lips and throat. Four days was a long time. She felt cold in the peat stink of summer. She stared at the ceiling as if she were walking the face of the moon. She sat in the sun, feeling like she was bleaching her features away. Her soul felt fragile and thin, like a burnt sheet of paper rising from the ashes of her life. On the fourth day, her hands felt steady enough to pour Tom's sherry down the sink. She was preparing to leave Cranfield Lakes for good.

She missed Tom and the feeling of him inside her. Did she love him, or was it the belief that he was no longer possible? His absence confirmed that her decision to leave was correct, even though she felt abandoned by him.

Peeling herself away from another was an imprecise task, but she'd had practice.

Tom had promised to research the phone numbers, but her hopes faded. She tortured herself with impossibilities: hope for the bogs to bear fruit again, hope for her co-op job to return, hope for Tom strolling among the pines, hope for her children and their voices at play in the next room. God, she'd held on for so long. It was what everyone did in this town as the shops closed and the youngest generation drifted away. With a sober mind, she abandoned hope. It had served nothing but the passage of time. She was leaving Cranfield Lakes without Faye and Ronald, without anything but fewer days in her life. This reality crept into the small places that the booze used to numb. A year of poison brought her back to the afternoon when Elliot stole the kids. She'd reached for the bottle then, and this backward path guided her to the same crossroad. She must choose another direction. She decided to renew her search for Faye and Ronald from a new address, be smarter about it this time, work the clues Tom had unearthed, not rely on other people to help. But Tom had helped her and asked for nothing in return. Then he disappeared.

On Thursday evening, Claire prepared for the town meeting. She didn't plan to say goodbye or hint at her departure. She rescued a skirt and blouse from her Impala and hung them in the shower until they unwrinkled enough to wear. She bought a box of chocolate donuts for the snack table. She wanted to shake hands and kiss the cheeks of the people who had helped and lauded her throughout the years, and the next morning, she'd vanish. No one would learn that she went to be with her father two states away. Like the bogs that disappeared with each passing day, she'd recede into talk of the good old days in Cranfield Lakes. She was queen of the dead cranberry bogs and required a graceful exit, a touch of honor to close a year of shame.

She reached the public theater beneath the library annex before 7:00 P.M. The parking lot overflowed with cars and Cranlakers pressing for a seat inside. A truck from the local cable network sat outside, and video cables twisted down the steps toward the theater. The fire had heightened anticipation for the next phase of Cranfield Lakes. The *Courier Dispatch* ran a series throughout the week, revealing parts of the mayor's plan to revive the former jewel of the county.

JJ and Junior met Claire by the stairwell. Junior carried a platter of gourmet cookies wrapped in clear cellophane like a holiday gift. She wore a blue dress and the exaggerated smile that she reserved for public greetings.

"Hello, Junior." Claire thought to speak first, especially after the business at the police station, but she saw JJ was pretending like it never happened, or at least like it happened but was never to be mentioned again. Maybe it had to do with JJ's part in the destruction at Old Forge, or maybe it was her erratic behavior. She never noticed the tornado of her personality so much as she did that afternoon in the firehouse garage, staring down half the town.

"That's a lovely outfit," Junior said.

"It's something I had laying around." She examined her short black skirt. Her legs were pale and thin. She had to gather and pin the skirt at the waist to keep it from sliding down. Her blouse hid the safety pin in the back.

"I wish I could keep the pounds off like you," Junior said. "You must tell me how you do it."

Claire considered the Whiskey Sours and the lack of sleep and meager sustenance that kept her gaunt. It wasn't a program she'd recommend. She wondered what she had done to her body, but no one noticed her starving. People only chastised you when you gained a couple of pounds. No one ever said, "Hey girl, you look emaciated." She pledged to start writing down daily menus of food and sticking to them. How dumb was her life when she needed to remind herself to eat? In many respects, she felt profoundly stupid.

"I exercise," Claire said, not knowing what else to offer.

"That's it. I'm starting my own regimen tomorrow."

Claire spotted Alicia Hardaway walking past the cable network van and decided to wait. "I'll see you inside." She let Junior and JJ disappear down the stairwell ahead of her.

Alicia approached the stairs. She seemed prepared to pass without speaking.

"Alicia?" Claire called.

Alicia planted her fake leg, balancing her weight atop the steps.

"Have you seen Tom?" Claire moved across the mouth of the stairs.

"Tom?"

Her coy response only increased Claire's curiosity about his relationship with Alicia. "Thomas King," Claire said.

"Oh that Tom."

"Has he called?"

"He hasn't called *you*?"

Why am I jealous of the librarian? Claire had only just hooked up with Tom, but he had cut a long groove in her in only a short time. "I know he talks to you," Claire said.

"I saw him Monday after you came looking for him."

"And..."

"He didn't leave a message for you, if that's what you're after. I told him you'd been around."

"Is he well?"

"He looked tired and a little sore."

"Did he say where he was going?"

"That's odd, Claire."

"Why so?"

"I had a feeling *you* would know. I guess I was wrong."

"Do you know?"

"He had questions about the forge. That's it."

"He didn't mention anything else?"

"Like what?" Alicia asked.

"I don't know. Phone numbers. Something like that. Did he ask you about long distance phone numbers?"

"I don't know what you're talking about."

"Did he say if he had a place to go?"

"Boy, you're really curious about him, aren't you? Did you try his cabin?"

"He's not there," Claire said.

"Where did he go?"

"That's what I'm asking you."

"Did you try his cell phone?"

"I don't know the number."

"He didn't give it to you?"

"I thought since you were his friend."

"Claire, aren't *you* his friend?"

They studied each other across the entranceway, two women trying to force together mismatching information. People passed between them, ignorant of the standoff. Claire heard the excitement in the Cranlakers' voices. She might be the only person who didn't care what JJ had to say.

"I'll give you his cell number." Alicia opened her purse and scribbled it on the back of her business card.

Claire closed the card in her fist. "I appreciate it."

"What's going on with you two?"

"I don't think…"

"I heard it in his voice." Alicia cast one of her patented stares into Claire's eyes. This was the look that froze unruly kids and noisy adults beside the book stacks. "I've known him for a long time. You'd better be someone who wants to take care of him."

"I am."

"You'd better be."

"I understand." Claire didn't pull away. Alicia's look explained everything. Tom's relationship with Alicia went deeper than overdue books, but she had no right to judge. She'd always been loose and foolish with how she treated people. She'd assumed everyone loved her regardless.

"Thomas is my friend," Alicia said, "as much as he has one."

"I promise."

"I'm going to hold you to it." Alicia took to the steps.

Claire waited, before descending.

In the theater, most Cranlakers were finding seats, and the room smelled of cigarettes, coffee, and too many sugary desserts. Metal chairs slid on the linoleum floor.

She came alongside Nat from the Lazy Eye and poured a cup of black coffee.

"Hey, Claire." Nat held the sugar jar upside down, streaming crystals into his cup. He appeared tentative, wondering whether to start a conversation. "Haven't seen you in a couple days."

"I'm taking a break."

"I can afford to lose a customer now and then, just not the pretty ones."

"I'll stop in for dinner." She wished she hadn't said that, because she knew she'd be gone at sunrise. She hoped he didn't take it personally. She wondered how many things she'd said and done while drunk and didn't remember. She bet they were worse than the lies she told now. She'd have to live with that as part of her record.

"It would be nice to talk." He retrieved a thick slice of chocolate cake and a plastic fork. "How about a piece of my triple layer delight?"

"Thanks." Claire dug the fork into the cake and let the cocoa and sugar melt on her tongue. "Not sour enough."

"What's that?"

"I'm just kidding."

"Oh, I get it." He flipped open his blazer. "No Whiskey Sours on me."

"That's okay. I'm going to stick with coffee for now."

Claire wandered to the back of the room near the exit and the man behind the video camera tripod. The event was going live on Cable 8. She hoped JJ's plan offered solace for Cranlakers. What other options did they have?

Her appetite was sated after only a few bites of cake, but she forced down about half of it and drank the coffee.

JJ stood at the podium. Three easels showed architectural layouts for the property at Old Forge: a series of outlet shops, an amusement park with kiddy rides, and something he described as a "wave pool." It was a funnel for time and money, as Tom had explained, enriching no one except the wealthy investors. It was the Atlantic City model for success. When they had grown cranberries and blueberries for a living, they produced something people really needed. But if the forge property went up in flames a second time, JJ's version of Cranfield Lakes wouldn't be missed outside of a single week.

Claire wondered how Tom had gathered such a poignant vision of the future. She listened to JJ's promises of jobs and the general influx of much needed cash. She thought of being in Tom's bed: the sweat running from her neck and down between her breasts, her skin sticking to his, his smell. Tom had predicted JJ's speech, almost word for word. He whispered the lies and promises that the mayor now broadcast across the theater and into the cable network that served the Pine Barrens. Tom said that Cranlakers would believe JJ until it was too late to turn back. He was a freakin' savant.

Something crashed on stage, and feedback shot over the PA system. One of the easels had fallen and the presentation cards slid on the floor like an unfurling deck of cards. A bald-headed man seemed to materialize from behind the tripod and march across the stage, dressed in black jeans and a black T-shirt. He toppled the second easel with his camouflage boot, followed by the third. His round face looked familiar to Claire.

Tom let Stan Zytko go ahead. He was reluctant to enter the theater, but the desire to see his ideas reaching the ears of Cranlakers overwhelmed him. He took the steps behind Zytko and spotted Claire in the back of the room.

Zytko started tossing over the presentation easels, even though he'd promised Tom to make a smooth entrance. Tom imagined that Stan couldn't do anything else but stir the pot. And why not? Cranfield Lakes begged for Zytko's guerrilla-style assault. He might jolt them out of their funk. Tom admired Stan's zeal and his instinct for drama. All Cranlakers directed their attention to the man hijacking the platform.

"This is an embarrassment," Zytko announced.

Noise riffled through the crowd. JJ stood speechless, gripping the podium.

Zytko nudged JJ from the microphone, and a twist of white noise passed over the audience. "Most of you know my record. I fought to keep the bogs alive. I tried to block the state from burning the fields. I've protected the Pines for most of my life."

The crowd searched each other's faces. Several people shrugged. Tom saw an old lady thump her cane on the edge of the stage, and the talking subsided into sporadic hushes. JJ took two steps backward, stabbing his hands in his pockets.

Tom saw Claire staring in his direction. He found himself drawn to her violet eyes. He felt hopelessly vulnerable to her trust.

A few Cranlakers noticed Tom, seeing Claire coming to his side. She held onto his waist, whispering in his ear. Tom sensed that this was very confusing to a town that defined roles for everyone. Being away for a few days made this clearer. Being in Trenton, where people only judged him for what he brought to the table, gave him the confidence to hold his ground.

"Where were you?" Claire asked. "I couldn't locate you."

"I'm sorry. You haven't been easy to find either." Tom wanted to explain the business with the phone numbers from Maine. He wanted to break the news slowly, but he needed one more phone call from the authorities up north to be sure. The last thing he wanted was to get Claire excited and then break her heart. It required all of his will not to speak about it too soon.

"You have to keep in touch with a girl, you know."

Her response took him aback. Did she almost say *his girl*? "I haven't stopped thinking about you."

"I lost faith that you'd come back."

On the road, working feverishly to solve the many puzzles on his plate, he had often paused to think of Claire. He had phoned the motel and Nat's Café, only to learn she'd vacated those gloomy haunts. He was happy not to find her in either place, but he wondered if he'd ever see her again and, if he did, how she might welcome him with a sober eye. But seeing her in the flesh erased a number of his doubts. He studied the lay of the room instead, keeping a watch for officer Spatt.

She got close to his ear. "Drew's gone."

He saw that she was serious.

"Haven't you heard the news?" she asked. "JJ fired him."

"When did this happen?"

"You should learn to check in once in awhile."

"Okay." He was stunned. He spoke apart from his thoughts. "It's a deal."

Zytko folded his arms over his chest. JJ held his spot to the stage side, as if he'd approved the disturbance as some kind of publicity stunt.

"Those of you who know me realize that I never speak without the facts," Zytko said. "I can't believe one of you set Old Forge to flame. What were you people thinking?"

Kevin Stower rose from his seat. "The ridge has been burnt to a crisp. We can't bring it back. And that's not why we're here."

"You've got to start thinking bigger than that."

"I think I speak for most of us. Old Forge was a tremendous loss, but we also have to move on."

"That's my point exactly. It's what happens next that matters."

"With all due respect, what do you have to add to this meeting?"

"I'm getting to that. Have you actually considered what these plans will do to this town?"

"We were trying to," Kevin replied. The audience grumbled behind him.

"Look, I've seen some dumb plans before." Zytko picked up the layout for the arcade. It showed a thirty foot cranberry beast hovering over a cartoon-like entrance. "If they ever build a museum to hideous concepts, this one will be in the front hall."

A portion of the audience applauded, while another griped about the economy and lack of jobs. These were practical concerns, but in Tom's mind, it was JJ's response that dictated the meeting. Even if Drew was gone—a fact that Tom was still trying to accept—Tom needed to win over the mayor to carry sway with the crowd. If Tom's ideas for the ridge property convinced JJ, the rest would follow.

"What's Zytko doing?" Claire asked.

Tom felt her come close, smelled her too, the wonderful sensations that fueled his return to town. Larry Mullins still glanced to the back, but Claire sneered at him, and he whipped his head around front.

"I missed you." Her lush voice curled in his ear.

He nodded in response to her remark, while at the same time trying to keep a bead on the stage. He harbored serious doubts about his plans, how the town might receive his logic. The town wasn't entirely ready. They appeared to be placated by the prospect of fast food chains and ice cream stands. He imagined that they already saw their coffers replenished.

Zytko leaned into the microphone. "This was once a proud working town. Productive too."

Kevin Stower yelled. "Pride doesn't fill your dinner plate, Stanley."

Many agreed with Kevin, groaning and stamping their feet.

"I understand," Zytko said, "but you've got someone to help you right in town. He has a vision for all, not a get rich quick scheme for a handful of people."

People looked about the room. Tom felt the moment sinking. *This was an utter mistake.*

"I suppose it's not the plan you came to hear tonight," Zytko continued.

JJ stepped forward, kicking aside a scattered display poster near his feet. He seemed comfortable with Zytko on stage, at least for the time being. He was the consummate politician taking a straw poll of the crowd reaction. "We're all curious, Stan. You are the last person I expected to see tonight."

"I know a face that might surprise you more. He's been living in the woods, and while most of you were folding up shop, he's been searching for Cranfield Lakes' future."

"The woods?" Kevin said.

"Right outside town, you know who he is. He's one of your own."

"Maybe he means Tom King," Kevin joked.

The audience laughed as one. Punch lines to familiar Tom tales bounced about the room. It was the funniest line they'd heard in awhile. Perhaps the town hadn't laughed this hard since the years before they shut down the annual cranberry festival.

Tom felt Claire squeezing his arm. He didn't look at her. He knew what Cranlakers thought. *Maybe the town deserves to go under.* If Claire offered to leave with him now, he'd let Cranfield Lakes became a shopping mall.

"Exactly," Zytko said. "Tom King."

"Get off it," Kevin said.

"You have no idea what he's done," Zytko said. "He's a clever man."

The crowd stalled, except for one woman who gasped. Tom swore it was Geneva Bogdan.

Zytko eyeballed Tom in the back of the room. "Come on up here."

Tom froze, as everyone looked back.

Claire nudged his arm slightly. Tom felt some relief at that, but he didn't need to go onstage. Cranlakers had been astonished enough for one evening.

"Come up here." Zytko said.

Tom waved off Stan.

"You know this best," Zytko insisted. "Tell it like you did to the Governor this morning."

Claire pulled back to see Tom's face. "You've been talking to the Governor?"

"Yes."

"Well then go up there, Tommy. You tell them."

Tom didn't want to disappoint her. He walked to the podium, praying he didn't trip over a chair leg and create another classic moment to go with his others in the past. The room was so quiet that a man coughing came as a relief. He recognized everyone in profile, because he'd studied them all for years, wanting to be more like them, but Claire had said a funny thing when she was lying in his arms. She confessed that she wanted to be "normal," as if who she already was wasn't good enough.

He ascended the stage, all eyes upon him. This was not what he wanted. His dream of saving the town was private, not a public spectacle. He only wanted people to stop fingering him in the street with disparaging remarks. Like

Claire, he wanted to be treated as a regular person, but it was just like Stan Zytko had told him, "For better or worse, kiddo, being a regular guy is no longer in the cards for you."

He hunched to use the microphone and then adjusted it so he might stand straight. His fingers felt clumsy, but he managed to get the microphone aimed at his mouth. He swallowed against the dryness in his throat.

"The Governor has agreed to set up a n-new cooperative. I, I mean, I should back up. There's a, a f-forge in the woods." He saw Claire in the back. She gave him two thumbs up, and he stopped talking.

"Go on, Tom," Kevin called. "Let's hear it."

A handful of Cranlakers repeated the sentiment. They weren't mocking, just curious. They actually wanted to hear him. Most of the men who'd almost lynched him out by the bogs that night were present in the room, but if he didn't know better, he might say they wanted him to have a solution. So many different emotions flowed through him that they numbed his fears.

"I found a diary at the forge," he said. "It belonged to the blacksmith who lived there. He was a spy during the Revolution, and according to Alicia Hardaway, he's the answer to an old legend. It's a bona fide piece of American history and folklore rolled into one."

Tom waited for a response other than dumb looks. He glanced at Claire who motioned for him to continue.

He dove into the story of Old Forge and the Bachelor of the Barrens, recalling bits from his notes and sketches of the property. He didn't hear himself speak or fumble over words, even though his talk didn't go like it had in the Governor's office. His thoughts just poured out, like he had practiced thousands of times hiking through the woods alone. He took them through his meetings with historians and state officials.

"I have to thank Stan Zytko. He introduced me to the right people. He's the best."

"What does this mean for us?" Kevin asked.

"We can do JJ's amusement park," Tom said, "but it'd be much more educational. It'd be a cooperative for the entire town. We'd own it and run it. We'd leave it to our children. Not like the other plan where parcels of land are sold and lost to the town forever. Oh yes, and the library too. We don't use more than a third of it, and I was talking to the Governor about a research center, like a satellite to one of the state colleges. They do it at other places. He was thrilled with the idea. We'd become kind of a small college town."

"The Governor agreed to help us with this?" Kevin's question seemed to echo the minds of Cranlakers in general.

Zytko leaned into the microphone. "You're damn right he did. He promised to put it in the budget."

"Was he serious?" Kevin asked.

Zytko withdrew a piece of paper with the official seal of the State of New Jersey and held it aloft. "Here's his letter of intent."

There was a moment when Tom wasn't exactly sure, even after spilling his story. Like never before, he felt undressed by his own honesty. No one spoke or even breathed in the Cranfield Lakes public theater. Like a man awaiting a jury verdict, he passed into a quandary, suspended in time, uncertain if he might land safely. Then as the silence broke and applause enveloped the room, he bridged that uncertain gap, and he found his break from the past.

Alone on stage, the questions rained on Tom for nearly an hour. Claire brought him a tall glass of water. He thought she was beaming, and it charged his soul to deliver his best responses. He understood the highlights and pitfalls of altering the town's future and crafting a new existence. It was an optimistic version they'd never conceive on their own, but he was a man of vision and hope. This complete vision— Zytko had admitted on the trip back from Trenton—had influenced the Governor to pledge his full support. It sounded like magic, but standing before his townsfolk, Tom suddenly believed in it.

"We need a development plan." Tom searched the crowd. "The state requested that, and I was hoping one of you might help me."

"No problem." JJ came to Tom's side. "I think we learned many things about our future tonight. Thank you, Tom."

Tom listened to another round of applause. Most Cranlakers were standing. Tom felt like he might float away, but JJ's proximity kept him grounded.

"Thank you again," JJ said. "I anticipate more questions and meetings like this as the plan develops with the state, but right now, we have to let Tom take a rest. If you hadn't heard, he was knocked around pretty good after trying to put down the fire on Sunday."

As Tom left the stage, he endured the handshaking and pats on the back that at times sent shards of pain across his mending wounds, but he was most interested in the faces of Cranlakers who had barely ever glanced his way. They peered at him like a foreigner who'd just drifted into town but they somehow recognized him. Some were surprised when Tom knew their names and the names of their children. The joke was on them. They would have to spend time getting to know him.

Tom pushed for the door. He needed open space. He came upon Claire with Zytko talking in the stairwell. Claire was animated, shifting her feet quickly in the small space.

"I can see why he feels the way he does about you," Zytko said, turning toward Tom.

"Did you tell her?" Tom asked.

"Sort of. I figured you knew the details best."

"Is it true?" Claire looked at him, her lip quivering, her eyes verging on tears. "Have you found them?"

This image burned into his memory. He'd pitch aside everything that recently transpired on the stage, just for her expression. This was the diamond that he had mined for ages, from the myriad offerings of the forest, even from the multitude of trash. Tonight, he held it with both hands and brought it to light.

His cell phone started ringing, but he stared into Claire's eyes. There were important messages waiting that had built up when he'd switched off his phone during the meeting. He needed to share them with Claire but failed to grasp the necessary words. The picture of perfection spun in his head, and he'd never have the words to express it, even if one day he learned to speak like Winston Churchill. He wondered if it might be easier for Claire to read his mind and see what he was thinking.

"It's your phone," Zytko said, after the third ring.

Tom fumbled through his pocket and pressed the cell phone to his ear. He caught Claire's eye, grateful that he no longer had to deliver the news in his own labored words. The days ahead looked more certain than ever, lots of questions but more certain. He envisioned a steady course, where people who belonged at home were home and he was made an intricate part of it.

"I understand," Tom said. "When? … Right now?"

He handed his phone to Claire, whose hands were trembling.

"Who is it?" Her voice broke over the question.

"It's your daughter. Ronald is there too."